A PERFECT AMBITION

A NOVEL

DR. KEVIN LEMAN
AND JEFF NESBIT

Revell

a division of Baker Publishing Group
Grand Rapids, Michigan

© 2015 by Dr. Kevin Leman and Jeff Nesbit

Published by Revell
a division of Baker Publishing Group
P.O. Box 6287, Grand Rapids, MI 49516-6287
www.revellbooks.com

Printed in the United States of America

Library of Congress Cataloging-in-Publication Data
Leman, Kevin.
    A perfect ambition : a novel / Dr. Kevin Leman and Jeff Nesbit.
        pages cm — (The Worthington destiny ; bk. 1)
    Summary: "The firstborn son of the powerful Worthington family has been groomed for political power since his first breath. Will family secrets keep him from getting there?"— Provided by publisher.
        ISBN 978-0-8007-2332-3 (pbk.)
        1. First-born children—Fiction. 2. Ambition—Fiction. 3. Choice (Psychology)—Fiction. I. Nesbit, Jeffrey Asher. II. Title.
PS3612.E4455P47 2015
813'.6—dc23   2015001797

This book is a work of fiction. Names, characters, places, and incidents are the product of the author's imagination or are used fictitiously. Any resemblance to actual events, locales, or persons, living or dead, is coincidental.

"To those who are given much, much is required" is a paraphrase of Luke 12:48.

Edited by Ramona Cramer Tucker

15 16 17 18 19 20 21   7 6 5 4 3 2 1

///

To all those curious enough
to seek, question, and forge their own path in life.

And to those who choose to do the right thing,
no matter the consequences.

///

Glossary of Acronyms

AF: American Frontier
AIA: Aleut International Association
AP: Associated Press
API: American Petroleum Institute
ATF: Alcohol, Tobacco, and Firearms
BP: British Petroleum
CEQ: Council on Environmental Quality
COEB: Center for Ecological Biodiversity
CryoSat: Cryogenic Satellite
DA: District Attorney
DHS: Department of Homeland Security
DNC: Democratic National Committee
DOE: Department of Energy
DOI: Department of the Interior
DOJ: Department of Justice

DSCC: Democratic Senatorial Campaign Committee
EPA: Environmental Protection Agency
FBI: Federal Bureau of Investigation
FCC: Federal Communications Commission
GOP: Grand Old Party (Republican Party)
INS: Immigration and Naturalization Service
IPO: Initial Public Offering
NASA: National Aeronautic and Space Administration
NCAR: National Center for Atmospheric Research
NGO: Nongovernmental Organization
NOAA: National Oceanographic and Atmospheric Administration
NSA: National Security Agency
NSF: National Science Foundation
NYPD: New York Police Department
ODNI: Office of the Director of National Intelligence
SEC: Securities and Exchange Commission

1

The sun didn't have a chance to set on the lake by the Worthington family's summer home before Will's father put him on the hot seat.

"Why haven't you seized control of American Frontier yet?" William Jennings Worthington V demanded. "That CEO position has your name on it." His dark eyes burned into Will's as he gripped the arms of the patio chair.

Will sighed. His mother, Ava, simply exchanged a glance with him at the well-worn topic, then got up from her seat where all three were supposed to be enjoying the beginnings of a radiant Chautauqua sunset.

"Think I'll go check on dinner," she announced. Pausing midstep, she placed her hands on slim hips and shot a look toward her husband. "Bill, William hasn't even been here an hour. Give him a chance to breathe before you hit him with the grand inquisition, will you? This is supposed to be a break . . . a family time."

He waved her off. "I know, I know. But the boy's got to think about his future."

And upholding the Worthington family name, Will told himself. Like he didn't feel that every day of his life. Not to mention he was now 39 and the successful head of Worthington Shares Equity, far from a "boy." But that was just the way his father talked to his firstborn son.

To avoid his father's eyes, Will scanned the meticulously manicured wood-framed and stone home with the large front porch. The structure went back generations and carried lots of fond memories.

But the old house also harbored secrets—secrets of a blue blood family that stretched back six generations of unimaginable wealth, with its roots even farther back to the era of monarchs and royalty in Ireland, Scotland, and parts of Europe. Their family crest, Royal Blue, included a picture of the Tara Stone, the Lia Fáil—once known as the Stone of Destiny, which was thought to have been the inauguration stone for Irish kings and later for Scottish kings, and ultimately became the coronation stone in Westminster Abbey.

The Worthington family had vacationed in Chautauqua every summer while Will was growing up. They'd spent other holidays and weekends here as well whenever the family could get away.

But Will's father, a financial tycoon who had built an even greater dynasty of wealth on the foundation of the previous Worthingtons, was rarely ever home. Vacationing in Chautauqua with his family meant he was there for a dinner or two before he received an urgent phone call and had to head back to New York City or somewhere else to defuse a crisis.

That he was semiretired now merely made his laser-like focus on Will even more intense.

Will leaned forward. "The current CEO is pretty well entrenched and comfortable."

"But it's the next step for you," his dad argued. "The Worthingtons have always won in the financial world, and you're no exception."

So there it was again. His father was never satisfied with enough. There always had to be more. Will had to admit, though, that most of the time he was the same way—a cookie cutter of his father regarding the Worthington drive to make his own mark on the world in the largest way possible. But lately he had started wondering when enough was enough.

Will clasped his hands in front of him. "Dad, you know it would take a financial meltdown, a huge drop in stock, or some other kind of disaster to threaten the CEO's position and open the door for me to enter. And until or unless that happens—"

"It will—destiny works that way," his father interrupted. "And when it does, you need to be there, ready to take control." When Will didn't respond, his father said more softly, "Son, I only want the best for you."

"I know."

Bill Worthington loved his kids, even though his public image of "family first" didn't always play out in his private life. But he had made sure Will, his brother, Sean, and his sister, Sarah, had never lacked for anything. And he had gone out of his way to provide adventures and opportunities for each of the kids, to encourage them to follow their natural talents. But it had been Ava O'Hara Worthington who kept them all connected. That was why Will's memories of the family home in Chautauqua were so warm. His Irish-heritage mom, with her light auburn hair and vibrant sea-green eyes, made their summers fun and lively, not to mention educational. She'd insisted on no kitchen help or maids when they came to Chautauqua, claiming that the kids needed a taste of "normal life" and that she liked to cook but rarely got an opportunity to do it at their home in New York City. A debutante well sought after by admirers and schooled at Harvard, where she fell in love with Bill, Ava seemed happiest in the kitchen with a smudge of flour on her cheek.

She poked her head out of the kitchen door now. "Okay, you two," she said, "it's time to come inside for dinner. And your brother and sister better not be late. They promised."

Will rolled his eyes. "You know they won't be on time, Mom. They never are."

She laughed. "I keep hoping."

At that moment, a rapid clicking of heels resounded behind his mom, and an enthusiastic voice called through the door, "So, what's for dinner?"

A second later Sarah Katherine Worthington, dark curls bouncing, exploded onto the scene. She hugged her mother profusely, then stepped through the patio door with a dramatic flourish. "Ta-da! I'm here." She checked the time on her watch, and then, green eyes sparkling as she looked directly at Will, she teased, "And exactly 10 seconds early too, big brother."

"Wonders never cease," their mother proclaimed.

"And Daddy, don't you look comfortable!" Sarah hurried over to envelop him in an embrace. "All you need is one of your infamous cigars, and . . ."

Will had never been so glad for the interruption. His

bouncy sister always shaved the edge off their father's driven nature. And now was no exception. She'd had him wound around her little finger since the day she was born.

The Worthingtons were already past the soup and salad and on to the delicious main course when Sean Thomas Worthington arrived. Dressed in khakis, hiking boots, and a "Save the Polar Bears" T-shirt, he kissed his mother on the cheek, then slid into the one remaining empty seat next to Sarah at the expansive oak table.

"Nice of you to join us," Bill noted wryly.

Sean stuck a fork in the seafood pasta and took a bite. "I was packing up. I'm heading out right after this."

"Where to this time?" Bill asked.

"The Arctic Ocean." Sean grinned at his sister. "I'll get to check out the beluga whales firsthand."

"Cool," Sarah replied. "I read that—"

Their father cut them both off. "Glad you're able to have some fun on Worthington money. But someday you're going to need to focus, decide what you want to be all about . . . and get a haircut and shave." He swept a hand toward Sean's slightly awry reddish locks and stubbled chin. "Now your brother here"—he swiveled toward Will—"has got some big decisions to make while you play around in the Arctic."

"Bill," their mother chided, "you know what Sean does for the company and how important it is." With her eyes she aimed an apology in Sean's direction, but he only shrugged.

It was like every family discussion where their dad was involved. Bypass Sean and Sarah and zero back in on Will. Like what he did in this family was the only thing that mattered.

13

In his best moments, Will was flattered by his dad's attention. He wanted to please his dad, make him proud. But the majority of the time, Will felt the pressure, as he did now—it ricocheted off every wall in the room, and each family member's head pivoted toward him.

"Oh, you mean he doesn't make any big decisions every single day as the head of Worthington Shares? Come on, Dad." Sarah speared a shrimp with her fork and waved it around. "We all do. It's in our DNA. Worthington stock 100 percent." She elbowed Sean. "And this handsome one does a pretty good job as the public face of Worthington that everybody loves to love, don't you, bro? Even if you're looking a little scruffy right now, I doubt the whales will care."

Leave it to his baby sister to try to lighten the dinner conversation. She had a way of bringing everybody together. Not that she was any slouch herself, working long hours as the deputy assistant attorney general in the Department of Justice's Criminal Division. But it still grated on their father that she'd removed all her legal obligations to Worthington Shares Equity Fund when she took her job. Now she was like any career person in the trenches, he said—only with a lot more money in her trust fund and bank account.

Their father had assumed all three kids would fall in line like ducks and be a part of Worthington Shares. Without even blinking an eye, Will had. As the sixth-generation Worthington male heir, he'd literally been born to it. From the time Will was able to talk, Bill and their good friend and financial advisor, Drew Simons, had groomed Will to take the helm of Worthington Shares when his father announced his retirement. Will had looked in the mirror that day of the transition and had seen a reflection of his father, only younger. Dark, curly hair, intense dark eyes, and a six-foot-one build. The realization had both excited and scared him.

From that moment on, Will had commanded the ebb and flow of the family effortlessly—except when his dad stepped back into the picture.

"So, son," his father continued, eagle-eyeing Will, "the CEO position at American Frontier may not be yours yet. Then what's your next step? No Worthington has made a run for president for six generations. It's about time."

Will held a hand up. "I'm not sure a White House run is right for me—"

"Well, somebody in this family's got to take control of the broken political system and fix it. And it's sure not going to be your brother or your sister. Now you—you've got the skills, the natural talent to turn this country around."

"Like he's not busy enough anyway." Sarah laughed, but there was a brittle edge to it.

Will knew that tone of his sister's and that a steely determination lay behind her bouncy exterior. Like the time when she was eight and she'd caught the neighbor boy swinging a cat by its tail and had given him a sound scolding. That day had sparked her interest in going to law school. Sarah was a fighter, always championing the underdog, whether it was one of her brothers, herself, or anyone else. It was why the job she was doing now made sense to Will, even if it didn't to their father.

"But hey," she told Will, "if you ever decide to do it, you can count on me for support. I might even have a few ideas of my own." She caught her dad's eye and said pointedly, "Since I'm not like the scarecrow in *The Wizard of Oz*, and I do have a brain."

"Why don't we sit outside for dessert?" their mom cut in quickly.

Dear Mom, Will thought. She just wanted them all to get along. Wanted the waters of life to be smooth. *Good luck with that in this clan.*

Sean sat silent, pushing the remaining food around on his plate as their father got up and stepped out the patio door.

Will could feel the tension and aggravation radiating from his younger, middleborn brother. They didn't always see eye to eye, but he loved his brother with all his heart. From the instant four-year-old Will had held Sean and touched the red curls on his tiny head, he knew he would do anything to protect his brother. Anything.

Yet even after 35 years, Will couldn't stop the barbs their dad threw Sean's way. He also couldn't miss the sadness on his mom's face every time that happened. Will wished he could fix it, like he fixed things in the financial world, but he couldn't. No wonder Sean went out of his way to avoid family dinners or to shorten his time at them. Who could blame him?

Sean had always walked to the beat of a different drummer, and it drove their dad crazy. Sean found uses for the Worthington money, mainly in start-ups and in ecological and conservation causes, but he didn't feel the same drive to grow their wealth that Will and their father did.

Sean also thought and acted differently from the rest of the Worthington clan. He had a touch of the fiery Irish spirit their mom had, but hers had mellowed over the years, except for when she felt the need to defend Sean. It was no wonder Sean didn't even bother answering their father when he got in moods like this. He simply rode out the waves of conversation until he could head out the door.

The sooner, the better.

Like now.

Sean pushed back his chair. "If you don't mind, Mom, I'm going to skip dessert. I really have to get going." With a nod at Will and a hug to Sarah and their mom, Sean strode out the front door.

Their mom got up quickly and started to follow him.

Sarah turned to Will. "Well, bro, if you're going to make a bid for president, you're really going to be in the eye of the media hurricane. And they're going to dig deep. Hope you don't have any skeletons in your closet that none of us know about." She laughed as she moved toward the patio. "Because somebody is going to find them and announce them to the world."

Will heard a slight intake of breath behind him and glanced back. "Mom, you okay?"

She had stopped, frozen, several steps from the table. "Uh, yes," she murmured, but her fingers played with the scarf at her neck, the gesture she used when she was nervous. When she looked up, he saw a flicker of fear in her sea-green eyes before she forced a smile. "Go ahead, dear. I need a few minutes in the kitchen to finish up the dessert."

"I can help if you want," Will offered.

But she shooed him out the patio door.

Will stepped over the threshold, then swiveled back toward his mom. She still hadn't taken a step toward the kitchen. Instead, she was positioned stiffly toward the front door and the driveway, where Sean's Jeep was revving up.

As the sound of the Jeep receded down the long cobblestone driveway, he heard another slight gasp and saw her body tremble.

"Mom?" he called softly.

She paused, then turned toward him. Tears glimmered. "I just wish . . ."

"I know, Mom." He stepped toward her and embraced her.

"Your father doesn't see in Sean what we see," she whispered. "What an amazing man he is . . . and can become."

Nor will he ever, Will wanted to say realistically, but he couldn't hurt his mother that way.

She pulled back and gazed into Will's eyes. "Are you considering making a run for president? I mean, seriously thinking about it?"

He hedged. "I don't know."

"Promise me you'll put this family first," she said, lips trembling. "Promise me you'll put Laura and the kids first. They can't grow up like . . ."

She left the rest unspoken, but Will understood. He'd decided long ago that when he and Laura had kids, they would have an actively involved father who was home for them. His own father's absence had left a hollow, disconcerted feeling. He never wanted his kids to feel like he had—that his life was like the 2,500-piece puzzle he'd put together one summer, only to discover a single piece in the middle was missing and not to be found.

He also didn't want his kids to have to live every day in the spotlight of the media, as he had growing up. But living out those vows day to day, in the midst of the blue-blood business world, was often tough.

As Bill Worthington always said, "To those who are given much, much is required." Will was just starting to figure out what the "much is required" part of it meant.

"I promise," he told her. "Family first . . . always."

She nodded, but there was still a hint of fear and sadness in her eyes. "And you'll always be in your brother's court? Look after him?" she pressed. "Even in places where I can't?"

He frowned. "Of course. But why would you ask that? You know I will."

Her expression grew determined. "Promise me you will watch over your brother, no matter what. Because I know if you do, you will never break that promise."

He felt a stirring of unrest inside, as if there were more to the promise than she was letting on. But he said, "I promise."

And he meant it. Will had been the safe hub for his mother and siblings as long as he could remember, with his dad away so much. He wasn't about to let any of them down . . . ever.

2

THE ARCTIC OCEAN

Sean stood with Dr. Elizabeth Shapiro by the railing of the ice cutter USS *Cantor*, watching the pod of beluga whales move through the cold waters as one. Attuned to each other, the whales reacted to threats and opportunities almost as a single entity. They fed together and, when necessary, took on predators together. The simple beauty in that unity had always amazed him. Why couldn't that work with families too?

He exhaled, recalling the last Worthington family dinner and hightailing it out of there. If it wasn't for his mom and his love for his siblings—even his perfect brother—he wouldn't even have tried. Sean respected and loved his dad, but he'd never felt like he was on a level playing field with him.

"I can't remember a time when I didn't feel at home among the creatures of the sea," Elizabeth murmured to Sean. "Now, among people? Normal people? That's a different matter."

Sean chuckled. "I'm glad to know I'm not a normal person then."

At that, Elizabeth laughed out loud.

Sean, Elizabeth, and Jon Gillibrand, a reporter for the *New York Times*, had all run into each other some years back at an environmental symposium. The lean, leggy blonde had been stating her opinion vociferously at a lunch table, arguing down the best naysayers with carefully reasoned research until, one by one, they skulked away. All except Sean and Jon, that is, who were intrigued. They liked that kind of dialogue in anyone and were challenged and motivated by it, but they'd rarely seen it in a woman. Over some bland cafeteria food, the three had bonded and had kept in contact regularly since then, even as all of them traversed the globe. To Sean, his expansive network of friends was his family, and it was with them that he could relax and enjoy life.

With Sean's wealth, connections, rakish red-haired good looks, swaggering confidence, and amiable disposition, he gathered Facebook and Twitter friends like his brother collected ties. That was something he and SB, his social butterfly sister, shared in common. He couldn't remember a time when he'd had to work hard to get a date. But to him, all the beautiful models on his arm at black-tie social affairs were just that—beautiful models with nothing beyond the skin-deep looks.

Elizabeth, on the other hand, had a natural, simple beauty he appreciated. He'd never seen her wear a stitch of makeup even when she stood at podiums to give scientific presentations. She was also wonderfully quirky and brilliant. The only child of a world-renowned scientist, Elizabeth had grown up surrounded with oddball dinner guests who talked as easily about coastal biodiversity, environmental data gathering, and the mating patterns of harp seals as most families talked about soccer practice and the weather.

Sean had always been intrigued by ecology and climate change. He and Elizabeth shared fascinating dialogue—often in the form of short texts zipped across the globe—and every once in a while, like now, the experience of a lifetime.

They shared something else too. Both felt abandoned by a parent. Though Sean's father was present, he'd never really been a part of Sean's "important people" circle, and Sean had given up on that idea a long time ago. When Elizabeth was 11, her mother had decided she'd had enough of science and her husband trotting around the planet, as well as the rest of the Shapiro family.

So Elizabeth had gotten her wish—to travel with her father. Since then, Elizabeth and Dr. Leopold Shapiro had been a team. Everyone knew the eccentric scientist went nowhere without his daughter. Now she was a scientist in her own right, having just finished her PhD in ecology and biology at UCLA. It had taken her longer than the average graduate to finish her degree, with accompanying her father on his missions, but she'd had the rare opportunity to work directly in the field along the way.

Elizabeth had guts and spunk, and she loved plunging in to do the kind of work that others merely dreamed of and had to apply for all sorts of grants to do. Sean could have helped her financially—had even offered to—but she'd refused. Somehow that made him respect her even more. He had to admit, growing up as a Worthington made life fairly easy, at least in the financial realm. He never had to think about what he spent.

Elizabeth lived on a shoestring, but she held to her ideals

and views. That was what Sean admired the most. Maybe when he was ready to settle down, he'd . . .

He shook himself free of that crazy thought. At 35, he still had a lot he wanted to do before he was tied down. That was Will's deal, not his. Somehow Sean couldn't see himself in a New York penthouse apartment, changing baby diapers and going to kids' soccer games.

He drew the hood of his parka closer as the Arctic air crept in, and peered back toward the water. There weren't many predators of beluga whales this far north in the deep waters of the Arctic Ocean. It was difficult for even the hardiest Inuit village to make camp close enough to these waters to send out boats to find them, and the polar bears hadn't arrived here with the coming ice yet. That left only the orcas.

But today the pod had company. A lone ice cutter followed slowly after them, marking its passage through ice-free waters. There should have been a cover of ice this late in the summer. But there wasn't. In fact, that was why the ice cutter was trailing behind the pod of beluga whales.

Two dozen scientists, including the two Dr. Shapiros, were on a scientific mission of a lifetime—the first effort to study and document Arctic Ocean conditions tied into a global monitoring system. The USS *Cantor*, the brand-new Navy ice cutter and the first in a generation that Congress had commissioned, had left port at the start of summer, right after Elizabeth finished her degree. As the ship worked its way around the perimeter of the Arctic, the science team dropped buoys to extend Argo—a system of thousands of scientific buoys that had been used to study the amount of warming in oceans in various parts of the world. This was the first effort to study the Arctic.

The plan had been to start along the coastlines that surrounded the Arctic Ocean and then work slowly toward the center as the summer deepened and the ice melted. They'd get as close to the center as they could, cutting ice as necessary. That way, they could put as many buoys in place as the ice melted, and then even more buoys as the ice started to refreeze.

They'd even planned to encircle the series of deep-drilling wells that American Frontier, the world's largest and most adventuresome oil company, had been granted permission to build. It had been an extraordinarily controversial decision, but after two years of near disasters, American Frontier had managed to finish several wells without incident. The Navy ship had planned its mission around a few of the wells that had been operational now for more than a year, even when the ice returned.

But a strange thing had happened that put all the scientists on alert. As the USS *Cantor* completed its trip around the perimeter and then inched its way toward the center of the ocean, the ice had kept melting . . . and melting . . . and melting.

At first none of the scientists on board, cautious by trade and skeptical by nature, had said much to the Navy crew about the situation. But their speculations popped up in their blog posts accessed by a selective audience—including Sean and Jon—that perhaps they were witnessing the first ice-free Arctic summer in thousands of years. When the ice continued to melt more each day, the situation in the Arctic became too obvious to ignore any longer. There'd been a fierce battle between the Coast Guard and the Navy over rights to the ship. The Navy had won.

To the average person, melting ice in the Arctic wouldn't mean much of anything. But the Shapiros were convinced by the data that the melting was only the beginning of what could become a very big deal for the entire planet. Elizabeth had even emailed some of the data to Sean and Jon, two of the few people outside of her dad and their close colleagues whom she trusted to be objective and honest with any facts and evidence they were given. Stunned by the data, Sean had used many connections to wangle himself on board the USS *Cantor*. Not only did he crave being on the cutting edge of major changes happening in the world, but Will was on the board of American Frontier, so their family had a vested interest.

"Extraordinary, isn't it?" Elizabeth gestured toward the Arctic Ocean.

"You mean the belugas?" Sean studied the glow on her face. Power and position were important to a lot of people. Not to Elizabeth. She merely wanted the time and tools to gain the knowledge to make the world a better place for all—people and animals.

"No, not the belugas," Elizabeth said, startling Sean out of his reverie. "I mean the ease at which we've been cutting through the ice. It's not thick at all. Some days just a thin sheet. Other days the chunks are easily broken up. And the volume isn't near what anyone had expected. The Arctic Institute at the U of Washington has been predicting that the ice has been melting for years to maybe a quarter of what it was 20 years ago . . ."

". . . but no one believed them," he finished.

"Yeah, even when the CryoSat system in Europe recently confirmed it." She shook her head. "I wonder how much it'll take for people to become aware of just how much has been lost at the top of the world."

Sean had no answer to that. People in general believed what they wanted to and ignored what they didn't want to know about.

The beluga whales had been with them for the past few days. As the ship broke up ice and generally scared the fish in the environment, it was easy for the whales to follow behind and eat the swarms of fish scattering in the ship's wake. It was a nice, symbiotic relationship.

Suddenly there was a commotion behind them, near one of the American Frontier platforms they'd reached in the past hour or so. A deep, muffled explosion that sounded like it had come from the depths of the ocean.

Sean and Elizabeth jerked their heads, almost as one. Disturbances of any kind were news out here in the stillness of the Arctic.

"What in the world . . . ?" Elizabeth asked.

They waited several minutes, eyes focused on the spot where the pod of whales had been. At that instant, several surfaced and churned madly. Ice and water spouted and roiled.

Then, as if by magic, the water started to change color. Sean stared in growing fascination, which soon morphed to horror, as first one beluga whale and then another thrashed wildly near the surface.

"It's black!" Sean called as one of the belugas flailed close enough to the cutter for them to get a good look. Some of the whales had come in contact with black, sludge-like oil in the water. Many were now coated with the stuff.

The cutter erupted with activity. Elizabeth's father scurried toward them, coat half on and the tail of his rumpled shirt hanging out the back of his trousers. Gripping the rail of the ship, he focused on the spot where Elizabeth pointed.

Almost every sailor on board was on deck within minutes. Elizabeth's eyes met Sean's, then both of them stared back at the slowly spreading oil slick now becoming evident on the surface.

In that instant Sean realized the oil was coming up from the bottom of the ocean floor. Like the BP oil disaster in the Gulf of Mexico, American Frontier's grand adventure in the Arctic Ocean was about to take center stage—in the worst possible way.

And he was right in the middle of it.

NEW YORK CITY

He'd always been odd. At least that was what everyone but his mother said.

They never said it to her face. They didn't dare. But he felt it in every stare of the other school children so intently that at last she removed him from public school and put him in a special school.

"A place for gifted kids," she told him.

He believed her, even though he continued to feel as if he were the pendulum of a clock, swinging between the highest of highs and the lowest of lows.

There at the new school, he found acceptance and other kids like him. And he discovered his love for theater. At the age of twelve, he announced that he was going to be an actor. "Someday you're going to see me in the spotlight, and my name in the headlines," he told his mother.

"I have no doubt," she told him proudly.

Her belief in him is what had made him hang on for years, believing in his dream of becoming a famous Broadway actor. He'd been to quite a few workshops and more than his fair share of auditions. But he'd never gotten a decent callback— either because he was actually a bad actor or because the whiff of desperation clung to him like a damp cloth.

"That's okay, son," his mother would say, patting his arm. "You're just down on your luck right now. Things will turn around. Wait and see."

Then came the day where he'd come home and found his mama slumped in her favorite chair. She'd gone on to her eternal reward.

After that, the darkness that had always fuzzed the edges of his brain started to descend more often, followed by periods of frantic job hunting. Within the year, he'd arrived home to a locked door and a foreclosure sign on his home.

Yet each time he passed through the theater district, close to Times Square, he vowed he'd do right by his mama.

Somehow he would make the world pay attention.

He merely needed the right opportunity.

3

///

It had been only yesterday that William Jennings Worthington VI's life was a little simpler, when he was at the summer home in Chautauqua. *If you could ever call a Worthington's life simple.* Will shook his head.

Early this morning, shocking news had come in the form of an understated phone call from the Arctic Circle. News that would not only sweep across the world once the networks got ahold of it but was likely to swiftly change Will's own destiny. He'd been at home, the sole place he could truly relax and not worry about what the rest of the world thought of him. There it was his wife who kept all the family plates happily spinning. Not that he didn't contribute heavily as a father, but Laura was a master organizer as well as a wise encourager for their three kids, who were so incredibly different from each other.

His firstborn, Andrew, was 12, with Laura's dark brown hair and lean frame. He had Will's serious nature and drive to make a difference in the world, but Laura's inventiveness. Someday, given the right tools, the kid would go far.

Patricia was 10 and had her maternal grandmother's auburn hair, freckles, and startling green eyes. When she wasn't with her friends, she was texting them.

David had just turned 8 and was a real charmer who made friends with everybody he met, including their mailman. Davy was constantly up to something and kept both Laura and Will on their toes.

Together, the three kids and Laura kept their home buzzing with activity.

But now it was empty, and Will couldn't wait for it to be filled again. *Tomorrow night. They'll be home tomorrow night.*

Each year Laura took the kids for two months of their summer vacation to Malawi to build wells and clinics and help the villagers with medical needs. Will met them there for three weeks, the largest chunk he could carve out of his business schedule. It had been their agreement ever since Laura had felt the first flicker of life in her womb.

"I want our kids to experience what life is like for those who are poor," she'd said, her hand caressing her belly, "and to grow passionate about finding ways to help people in need."

Will had wholeheartedly agreed. He'd spent far too much time in prep school with rich, spoiled kids who thought only of themselves and the moment.

So he and Laura had researched places that could use their help even before Andrew was born. And when Andrew was a toddler, they'd launched off on their first trip to Africa. Since then the family had passionately done anything they could for the people of Malawi. Laura, an amazing linguist, could even speak much of the local language now, and the kids had picked up enough words to be passable.

Their trips to Malawi had become fun, poignant memories for them all. Times to set aside the normal world of school and Worthington expectations to experience a simpler, streamlined life. Some of Will's favorite pictures in the family album were taken in Malawi.

He smiled now as he flipped the album open on the table.

Andrew, usually so serious, caught with mouth open wide, laughing hysterically as he played soccer with the locals.

Patricia, so fair and Irish-looking, with her arms slung around a group of Malawian friends.

And baby Davy, his diaper mud-streaked and sagging as he dug in the dirt with a stick while Laura directed the digging of a well nearby.

Will sighed. Those were the moments that truly mattered in the long run. Companies would come and go, but family . . .

The absence of noise hung heavily in the room. It felt good to lounge for a few minutes in his favorite old T-shirt—the one Laura had vowed to throw out many times—and a pair of running shorts.

Will checked his texts, hoping for one from her or the kids. He grinned when he saw his buddy Paul Harrington's message.

Fam still gone? Fishing in B?

He shook his head. Talk about timing. Normally he'd jump at the chance to go fishing in Branson, Missouri, with Paul, a longtime friend he'd met at prep school. Wealthy but centered, Paul was the guy who'd talked Will through all his late-night woes about being a Worthington and always in the limelight.

"So you're a Worthington," Paul had said to him once in their junior year. "You mess up and it's public. You do good and it's public. But that's the public. Nobody knows what's going on in there"—he'd smacked Will in the chest, near his heart—"except you. And man, that's what's most important."

Will had never forgotten that discussion. And somehow, in the midst of demanding jobs and life's craziness, the two friends had managed a fishing trip every year to some remote location. Last year it had been four glorious days of camping beside a prized trout stream in Montana. They'd headed for the airport grubby, grizzled, and nearly unrecognizable, but it was one of the best times Will could remember.

There was something about fishing that relaxed Will's very soul. Maybe it was the quietness of the water, the warmth of the sun on his face, and the fact that fishermen, by nature, didn't feel like they had to talk. They didn't have to solve the world's problems. They didn't have to be anyone. They could just be.

Like during the summers he'd had growing up in Chautauqua, when he and his brother would take their sister trolling for muskies. Life was simple. They only needed snacks and fishing gear. Will always had to make his own bucktails, because the store-bought lures were too flawed—their hooks slightly off center or a bubble or two in the paint. Sean would roll his eyes at Will's painstaking efforts and then be the first to catch a fish with his cheap lures. Sarah would squeal with delight when she got a strike, and her brothers would quickly come to help her land the big fish.

When they got better at their fishing skills, and their dad had some time off, he took them to one of the local trout streams for which western New York was famous. After catching their fill of fish for dinner, the boys and their dad would clean the fish. Sarah would wrinkle her nose in disgust and scamper off, saying she had something important to do. Their mom would fry up the fish with some potatoes, and they'd have a simple dinner. Afterward, they'd make s'mores around the fire.

Even now, so many years later, Will's mouth salivated. He could still taste those graham crackers—the only part of the s'mores he ate, because he hated the mess they created. Sean would eat three s'mores, then reach for another one before his mom called a halt to his sugar intake. And his sister? Sarah ate the gooey marshmallows right off the stick until her face was streaked with the sticky white stuff. Then she'd sing her favorite campfire songs at the top of her lungs, and they'd all end the evening with "Kumbaya."

Will chuckled at the memories. He loved his siblings. He'd do anything for them. But in normal life, they could also drive him a bit crazy. They were unpredictable and didn't think through the consequences of their actions like he did. And that had created some tricky situations over their growing-up years . . . more than he wanted to recall.

But during the summers at Chautauqua, that didn't matter. They all relaxed together and had fun. They were a normal family, not the Worthingtons in the limelight. It had been far too long since the three of them had set aside their adult lives and gathered at the family cottage. Too bad it had ended so fast this time when Sean had to leave.

It was in the midst of Will's early morning reflections that his cell phone had rung. It was Sean's ringtone, and Will knew Sean never called when he was trotting around the globe unless it was really important.

And he was right.

"You might get what Dad wanted faster than you can imagine," Sean said.

"What do you mean?" Will asked.

"That shot at CEO of AF." The line crackled with static.

Will waited. His brother was always short on words but loved to add a touch of drama.

"A massive oil fiasco, right here in the Arctic Ocean," Sean said. "Worse than BP. All AF. That venture you voted down— you were right. It was too risky. Now oil's gushing up from the bottom of the ocean like a backwards Niagara Falls."

Will sat up straight, his reflective mood gone.

"Just thought you should know . . . before it's plastered all over the news." Then Sean hung up abruptly, as was his habit.

Will, stunned, still held the phone. After a minute, he sighed and texted Paul back. *Maybe not. Big oil leak in Arctic Ocean.*

American Frontier's rig? Paul replied.

Yup. And Sean's right there in the middle of it.

Whoa, dude.

Will laughed out loud. He didn't even have to explain with Paul. Paul just knew. He understood how complicated life could be for Will with heading the Worthington empire and simultaneously trying to keep his wild-card siblings out of danger's way.

When Will didn't respond immediately, a second later Paul texted again. *Got it. But those fish are still callin'.*

The fish would have to wait. It was back to business.

After that, Will's relaxing day had taken off like a rocket ship. He'd skipped his usual morning run and instead had taken a shower in record time so he could surf the already breaking internet stories before Drew arrived. Drew Simons had served the Worthington family for over three decades. Will had been eight when Drew was hired in the role of company financial advisor. But over the years he'd become a trusted, beloved uncle as well. He truly loved and understood each of the Worthington children and wanted the best for them. Sean would have called Drew too, and a minute into the phone conversation Drew would have headed Will's way.

At that moment a knock sounded on the door. It was good some things in life were predictable.

The rest of the day passed with lightning speed as Will and Drew strategized and watched news bulletins about the leak. After receiving notice of American Frontier's emergency board meeting the next day, they put in a call to Will's father, who wanted to stay informed even if he was inching toward retirement.

"This is a pinnacle moment for American Frontier," he proclaimed. "They'll choose to do one of two things—the right thing or the easy thing. Either they'll act with honesty and integrity, doing whatever they can to pool resources to investigate how this happened, to establish safeguards that lessen the chances of it happening again, and to clean the mess up to the best of their ability. Or they'll do the easy thing, spinning the media their way and sidetracking the real truth."

Will's father had raised him with the admonition, "Might

never makes right. But if you dream big, do the right thing, set your direction, take your compass, and never stray from the path, you can accomplish anything you decide to do."

Will had watched time and again as his father had fought for what was right and never backed down. It was one of the many reasons that Drew, a picture of integrity himself, had stayed with the Worthington family for his entire career. When Bill Worthington said he'd do something, he did everything in his power to make it happen. He honored his promises, even when they were difficult. Whatever hard taskmaster he was at home—always demanding his kids pull their weight and not shirk responsibility—he was a symbol of trust and integrity in the media. Will was determined to uphold the reputation of the Worthington family and, even more, to always listen to the still small voice inside and do the right thing.

With his dad's continual reminder of doing what was right, paired with his mother's simple mantra of "family first in all things," Will had never wavered from either. He strove to do both to the best of his ability, even when it wasn't easy.

Like now. Personal worry for his risk-taking brother edged into Will's business thoughts about American Frontier.

Sean, as usual, was right there in the middle of the chaos. His message had been cryptic, but it got the job done so Will knew about the oil fiasco before any of the media. So typically Sean. The networking master. Will had to watch the rest of the details of the breaking news on TV. That was how Sean always was with Will in business details. Short and to the point.

To the rest of the world, Sean was a charming entrepreneur who lived in a fast-paced circle of money and friends and made things happen. He managed the Worthington Shares start-ups and was a good fit for the job, continually lining things up so he could stay at the forefront of events across the world. Will spent most of his time in boardrooms and black-tie events. That suited his personality.

But Worthington business always seemed to drive the brothers apart, and Will hated that part of it.

His next call was to his sister, who was working with the Department of Justice's Criminal Division. If there was an investigation into the oil spill, Sarah would be involved. Ironic how a single event was pulling all of them in from different angles.

Her response, too, was swift. "Yeah, I know. Could be big. We're working on it. You in the thick, bro?"

"Not yet," he said, "but I will be."

———————

When the initial furor had died down a bit that night, Will stood in front of the mirror and held up three different suits for his meeting with American Frontier. He finally picked the navy Armani one, then frowned. It wasn't the same navy as the color of the scarf that matched the topcoat. It would clash.

Just as he was debating the possibilities, his cell buzzed.

It was his wife, on Skype from Malawi. Once a day, they both stopped what they were doing and took time to discuss their days.

Her face appeared on his iPhone, smiling. She was as beautiful with tangled hair and a smudge of dirt on her cheek as the day he'd married her. "Hey there, good-lookin'. What are you up to? I can't wait to see you tomorrow!"

It only took a few words to explain about American Frontier and the spill. Her eyes grew sad, concerned. "This will affect a lot of people and animals, won't it? Change the water quality . . ."

He could always count on Laura to bring a larger perspective. It was one of the many reasons he respected her.

"And then there's what this means for Worthington Shares and you," she went on. "How are you dealing with all that?"

"Like usual. Examining all the angles before I make a move."

As they talked for an hour about all those angles, and his kids popped in and out of the screen with tidbits from their days, he smiled and laughed. The tenseness in his shoulders relaxed.

They weren't there in the room with him, but their presence still filled his heart and centered him.

"Will," his wife said at the end before she blew him a kiss and signed off, "don't worry. Just do the right thing. You always do, and you always will."

4

"You just never know," Will said the next morning over a quick cup of coffee with Drew at their usual pre-meeting breakfast spot, the restaurant on the ground floor of the Trump Tower at Columbus Circle. "Not really. Not until the votes, including the proxies, are in. You can't assume *anything* here."

Drew's keen blue-gray eyes met Will's. "True, but we both know where the votes are on this. It's inevitable. There isn't anyone else they can consider—not right now."

Will scanned the small restaurant to make sure none of his peers were around or in earshot. It wasn't likely. He always preferred to work out at exactly the same time every morning at the Reebok Sports Club on the Upper West Side in the city. The club was just down the street from his three-bedroom suite at 71st that overlooked Central Park on the west side. His Wall Street pals were rarely around, either at the club or at the restaurant. He could speak freely here.

"I know you're right. Probably right." But Will could feel the beginnings of a migraine.

"I usually am." Drew cocked his head and grinned.

"But this isn't Dad's company."

"I know," Drew interjected. "It's American Frontier, a very public company. The recent incidents mean all of Wall Street is paying close attention. More than usual. But you're still the only person for it, especially given the circumstances."

"Perhaps." Will pursed his lips and glowered at no one in particular.

It was an old habit. He'd done it since he was a young child. It had worked well to intimidate his brother and sister, even when he hadn't been trying, so they would do whatever he wanted them to do. It had even led his brother to say once, in irritation, "Oh, here comes God." After that comment, Will had swiftly regained the upper hand in a wrestling move, as he always did. His brother might have muttered it again under his breath, but he never did so to Will's face.

He was sure now, by the way Drew studied him, that the older man knew what the glower meant and kept silent on purpose for a while. Will was considering the odds in his head, calculating his rivals for the CEO job at American Frontier. In fact, he'd done nothing but calculate those odds for hours on end since Sean had broken the news of the Arctic spill . . . almost as if Will could control the outcome merely by focusing all his energies on it.

Will wouldn't admit it to anyone, except maybe Drew—certainly not to his father, who would only push him harder—but he badly wanted this position. It represented all he'd sought to date and was the pinnacle of nearly everything he might aspire to in life. He just hadn't thought he'd get a shot at it this soon.

There was nothing else in the world he wanted more than

to become the CEO of American Frontier at its gravest hour and turn it toward the top of the mountain again. He couldn't imagine anything more important, more prestigious, more significant, than running the most powerful company in the history of civilization.

The oil spill at the bottom of the Arctic Ocean had rocked American Frontier to its core. The stock exchange had even been forced to halt trading toward the end of the day, before its price slipped into oblivion. Everyone remembered the mess with BP. It had played out for weeks in front of viewers until the source of the gushing leak had been capped at the bottom of the ocean floor. Then there were the never-ending lawsuits with the Department of Justice, the communities and coastlines ringing the Gulf of Mexico, and environmental NGOs.

The Arctic spill was potentially much worse. The Arctic Ocean fed several other big bodies of water, and the currents could carry oil to the shores of nearly a dozen nations—all that would likely sue for tens of billions in damages. American Frontier, the company at the very center of the world's economy, was suddenly at risk, even with its vast reserves of cash and nearly impenetrable financial position. Any hint it might collapse could bring down governments around the world that were tied to oil wealth.

American Frontier shareholders, already nervous about the controversial decision to drill in the icy waters of the Arctic, demanded answers . . . and someone's head. The current CEO would certainly lose that battle. It would be played out in the American Frontier boardroom first and then in front of the financial press.

In that fallout, William Jennings Worthington VI was perfectly positioned to take over as the new CEO. It was a lock, the *Wall Street Journal* had reported. American Frontier's board of directors comprised CEOs from nearly all of the biggest companies in the world, along with former heads of state and the greatest wealth holders on the planet. Will's family controlled the Worthington Shares Equity Fund, which several years earlier had passed Warren Buffett's Berkshire Hathaway conglomerate as the largest equity holding fund in the world. Worthington Shares also held a substantial minority position in American Frontier. That alone gave Will a right to argue for a change in leadership.

But that financial incentive wasn't even why Will was the logical choice. He knew the reason. He was a natural leader.

"You know what your father would say," Drew added. "There's no position beyond your grasp, if you decide to go for it. You inspire confidence. You're easy to follow. And American Frontier and the world's energy economy rely on a steady hand."

It was true. Will projected confidence, whether he felt that way inside or not. He'd always been a star—valedictorian of his high school class, voted "Most Likely to Succeed," and captain of his lacrosse team at Harvard. But what he wanted most of all—for his father to be proud of him—hadn't changed since he was a little boy.

"And of course, you're not bad-looking either," Drew teased. "That helps. Love that *GQ* article: 'Six feet one, tantalizingly handsome with wavy, chestnut hair and riveting dark eyes. A man to watch.' And you've got the regal profile that spans the generations of Worthingtons." His face sobered. "There's speculation kicking up of politics for you." His keen eyes again studied Will.

Will sighed. There was always speculation. The Worthingtons couldn't get away from it.

As one of the five wealthiest families in the United States, with a legacy that reached back to the British blue bloods, the Worthingtons found it impossible to stay out of the clutches of the media. The press liked to compare the Worthingtons to the Bushes or the Kennedys. It was a bit like the fascination with royalty in England. Who even in the States hadn't followed the lives of Charles, Diana, Prince Harry, or Prince William and Princess Kate? The difference was that, in the United States, it was the wealthiest families who served as surrogates for royalty. People and tabloids were utterly fascinated with the lives of the rich and the famous—lives they could only imagine but loved to sneak peeks into. Like the Waltons, though—the founders of Walmart and the richest family in the world—none of the Worthington children had ever chosen a path in politics.

Yet the press continued to speculate. Someday, they said, a Worthington would be president of the United States, and Will, the firstborn in the sixth generation of Worthington wealth, seemed like the logical candidate. "He couldn't be more perfect for the job," one well-known journalist had stated.

But to get there, the press said, Will would have to start somewhere first—as either a governor or a senator from a state like New York, Connecticut, or New Jersey.

"Drew, you know I believe my calling is in finance—not politics," Will said.

"So you say." A smirk formed. "There is no doubt about it, sir," he said in a tone of mock seriousness. "There is no other candidate who brings more to the table than you do.

You can handle this crisis for American Frontier. You were built for this moment. This is the time when the Worthington name means something and isn't just an albatross around your neck. And when you get the ship headed back in the right direction, then perhaps you can focus on the only prize that's eluded the family for generations."

Will chuckled. It was a running, private joke between the two of them. They'd had long discussions about the value of the Worthington name—whether it helped or hurt. Drew had long ago given up trying to convince Will that it was worth considerably more than he believed.

He took a long, last gulp of his now nearly cold coffee. He pushed his chair back from the table, positioned next to the enormous window that overlooked Columbus Circle. He'd never glanced out the window once during breakfast, staying focused on the task at hand. "We'll pick that up another time. First things first." He grabbed his Armani suit jacket from the back of the chair and pulled it on. "But I will agree that at least the Worthington name doesn't hurt me right now."

Will loved the New York subway system, even though it was old, dirty, and packed. He could get anywhere in the city in a matter of minutes, regardless of traffic. And he wasn't alone. Google's cofounder, a billionaire many times over, had once been spotted taking the number 2 express train from the Upper West Side, wearing his new Google glasses. A passenger recognized him, snapped a picture with his iPhone, and tweeted about it. Sean, the networking king, had of course been the one to tell Will about it.

Will and Drew fought through the throngs of people on

the broad sidewalk at the circle and made their way to the massive subway stop at the 59th Street station. Will glanced up at the enormous CNN sign on one of the high-rises that looked down at them as they ducked into the subway station. There would be nothing easy about heading American Frontier at a time like this. Then again, he was always up for a challenge. His dad had taught him since babyhood to face them head-on.

They caught a local train south toward Wall Street. As he always did, Will wrapped his overcoat around his expensive suit and buttoned up, hiding his incredible wealth. Nobody would look at his 700-dollar pair of shoes, even though he was careful not to scuff them as he and Drew edged onto the crowded train. Will leaned back against the subway as the doors closed and focused his mind on the meeting ahead.

They were 45 minutes early by the time they'd left the subway system and walked the last three blocks to the American Frontier building in lower Manhattan. Not surprisingly, protesters loitered and picketed in front of the building. Will and Drew hustled inside. The protesters didn't connect either of them to the company—at least, not yet. But if today's meeting went as planned, that anonymity wouldn't last long. Will might shortly be in the eye of the hurricane.

The guards at the visitors' desk recognized them, though, and waved them through.

"Did you see some of the outfits the protesters were wearing?" Drew asked Will as they strode toward the elevators.

Will nodded. "Inventive. I especially liked the guy dressed in the bright orange American Frontier overalls."

They rode up to the fortieth floor of the building in silence.

By the time they emerged at the top, Will had steeled himself. His jaw was set. He was prepared for battle.

"Ready?" Drew asked him.

"I am now," Will said, then opened the door to the boardroom.

5

THE ARCTIC OCEAN

It was only a matter of time before Sean would be kicked off the USS *Cantor*, and the gap was closing fast. Today the American Frontier crews would arrive. The last thing they'd want is for nonessential personnel who weren't an official part of the American Frontier team to observe their cleanup efforts up close. And the Navy wasn't allowing any other ships in the area.

In the meanwhile, the scientists were hard at work, trying to gather all the data they could.

"In dealing with the currents and deep reaches of the ocean, there's only a single constant," Dr. Leopold Shapiro told Sean and Elizabeth as they stood by the railing on the deck overlooking the spill. "Prepare to be surprised."

But even Dr. Shapiro himself admitted he was more than a bit surprised at what was happening right in front of them. His research team had studied the Arctic Ocean circulation models for years, preparing for this first expedition. They'd also done as much research as they could about what might lie *beneath* the ocean in the Arctic. But it was geologists who were supposed to know what might happen in the event of this sort of rupture or leak, he'd told Sean, and none of them were on board yet.

"I'm convinced," Dr. Shapiro added, "that what happens with the Arctic currents actually regulates nearly the entire circulation patterns through all of the other oceans of the world."

"And now we're witnessing it firsthand and are powerless to do anything about it," Elizabeth murmured.

Whether anyone wanted to admit it or not, a whole lot of oil was escaping into the icy waters of the Arctic and hitting all sorts of circulation patterns in several directions at once. Every computer sensor on board was recording it in real time.

"We should go out and see it," Sean said.

"See it?" Dr. Shapiro asked, turning toward him.

"Yeah. Take one of the boats out, with a camera—before it's too late."

"What do you mean, too late?"

Sean peered over his shoulder. "I heard some of the Navy boys talking. They're gonna lock this place down real soon. Nobody's going to get near that spill. This may be our last chance to take some samples and pictures."

Elizabeth inhaled sharply. "We could drop a buoy right smack in the middle of it, with some of our best sensors attached."

Dr. Shapiro eyed Sean. "And I'll bet you have a plan?" The scientist grinned.

"I do." Sean lowered his voice. "We need to move one of

the small boats with a buoy inside out over the water, then motor out to the site."

"You know they'll come get us, bring us back in," Dr. Shapiro said.

"I know." Sean met his gaze confidently. "But at least you'll have some information firsthand, before they do."

Dr. Shapiro looked at the spill site and then back at Sean and Elizabeth. "Let's go. We don't work for the Navy, but I doubt they'll invite us back after this stunt."

"Oh, you never know." Elizabeth smirked. "Everyone knows scientists have an independent streak and don't take orders all that well."

"And we haven't been told not to go investigate, now have we?" Dr. Shapiro added.

"No, not yet." She wiggled her brows.

Sean, Elizabeth, and Dr. Shapiro had the small motorboat in the water within minutes and were quickly on their way toward the center of the spill site and the American Frontier platform. Shouts resounded from the deck as they motored away, but none of them glanced back. They'd agreed to simply plead ignorance later—say they'd never heard anyone tell them they weren't supposed to go out and visit the site themselves.

As they drew closer to the platform and then edged around to the side of it, where they wouldn't be seen, Dr. Shapiro reached his hand into the water as far as he could. The oil was already thick on top of the ocean, as long as his arm. "Good grief," he muttered. "There's clearly a lot more oil coming up than there was with the BP spill."

"Why, do you think?" Sean asked.

"There's a good reason American Frontier spent tens of

billions to get this platform out here in the Arctic once the ice had melted enough to allow for drilling," Dr. Shapiro replied. "I think there's more oil beneath this ocean than anyone knew about, and now they've ruptured something."

Elizabeth had already stashed some weights that would keep the buoy partially submerged and not so obvious to see from a ship. Now she turned on the buoy's sensors and dropped it over the side of the motorboat. Sean watched as it sank and bobbed once before settling three quarters of the way into the ocean.

Elizabeth checked her handheld and nodded. Dr. Shapiro blew out a breath of relief. The sensors were sending information back already.

"I have one other toy that I didn't think I'd get a chance to use on this trip. But I brought it along just in case." Dr. Shapiro winked.

"What?" Sean asked.

"An infrared camera attached to a weighted rope. It'll give us some interesting pictures. We can attach it to the buoy and let it hang down in the water."

"How far down will it go?"

"Quite a ways." Dr. Shapiro unfurled the rope.

"Hear that?" Elizabeth called to them both.

The roar of a second boat was headed their way, and it would bring a firm halt to their experiments.

Elizabeth attached the camera to the buoy while Dr. Shapiro worked swiftly to turn it on and sync it. Seconds later, he dropped the rope in the water and it sank quickly. The roar of the other boat was close now, but still out of sight.

"Let's get out of here—move over to the other side of the platform," Sean suggested.

Dr. Shapiro nodded. "Good idea. If we stay here, they'll spot the buoy and take it out as soon as they can."

Sean gunned the small engine, and they sped around the American Frontier platform. Taking out portable plastic containers, they started filling them with water as a diversion.

Several minutes later, a slightly larger Navy boat pulled up alongside them. "Dr. Shapiro!" a voice called sharply. "Who gave you permission to use one of the boats?"

Dr. Shapiro looked up. He smiled at the young Navy ensign who'd been their constant shadow for the entire research mission. "Just wanted to grab a few test samples of water," he offered lamely, holding up one of the containers. Oil and seawater sloshed around inside it.

"You should have asked," the ensign said.

"Sorry." Dr. Shapiro shrugged. "We will next time. We didn't think anyone would care, not right now when everyone is still on their way to the site."

"Follow us back to the *Cantor*, will you?" It wasn't a question, though.

"You bet," Dr. Shapiro replied. "Maybe we can fill up the rest of our—"

"Right now!" the ensign barked. "There will be time enough to fill up as many containers as you'd like once we've secured the area. But we don't know the risk or what's going on here. For all we know, this platform is dangerous."

Sean knew that was a bunch of bull. Any dangers posed by the platform weren't likely to be here but rather well below, in the murky waters. And they weren't a risk to the immediate ship's party. They were a risk to many other places on the planet that would be affected if the oil leak couldn't be stopped and it spread far and wide.

But now wasn't the time for that intellectual discussion.

"Got it," Dr. Shapiro said. "Sean, let's go. We'll follow them back to the ship."

None of them cast another glance in the direction of the buoy and infrared camera. The readings they were getting from Elizabeth's handheld were the only thing they double-checked as they made their way back to the *Cantor*.

6

NEW YORK CITY

A firm hand grabbed Will's shoulder as he and Drew stepped into the American Frontier boardroom.

"Ready to make history, my friend?" Frank Stapleton boomed.

"Are you?" Will asked.

Stapleton laughed and swiveled to look out over the boardroom, which was slowly filling up. There were more titans of industry assembled in this particular boardroom than with any other board of directors anywhere on the planet. American Frontier was the richest, most profitable company ever in the history of humankind. A seat on its board was one of the most coveted in the corporate world.

But at this moment Will knew all of them had the same basic thought: *Thank heavens it isn't us personally in the middle of this mess.* Initial reports coming from the geologists and engineers stateside who had been frantically pulling together every shred of data at their disposal were grim. This particular platform had drilled into one of the most promising fields at the bottom of the Arctic. In fact, it might even rival Ghawar in Saudi Arabia. And now it was leaking oil at a ferocious rate.

Will returned Stapleton's smile. The longtime CEO of City Capital had seen nearly every financial crisis imaginable, in boardrooms much like this in different parts of New York. Now that no one in Washington cared much anymore about how big companies got, City Cap had taken over all the major credit card companies and had swallowed up or consolidated nearly all of the regional banking chains. There was no bigger financial banking institution in the world than City Cap.

Stapleton was a towering figure, in more ways than one. He'd been a basketball player in college and had turned that athletic drive loose in the highly competitive world of finance after graduation. Height gave you an edge in the business world—people tended to respect you, whether it was earned or not. Stapleton had taken full advantage of that perception early in his career. Now his respect was earned.

Stapleton had taken Will under his wing years ago on another board and guided him through the ebbs and flows of boardroom politics. Will was grateful for the education and relied on Stapleton for advice and counsel on any subject he cared to discuss. Stapleton was a good 15 years older and wiser. There was literally nothing he hadn't seen at one time or another in the corporate, financial, or even political world.

The two men gazed across the room. Their eyes fixed on the current CEO of American Frontier, Eric Sandstrom, who was huddled with several of his executive vice presidents.

"Do you think he knows?" Stapleton asked.

"That he won't survive this meeting?" Will said.

"No, just how bad it will get for him very soon," Stapleton

murmured. "It's a given he won't survive. What he doesn't know yet is that this boardroom war will be followed by a shareholder lawsuit."

"How so?" Will swiveled back toward Stapleton.

"Criminal negligence."

Will stared hard at him. The board had been split for some time about the wisdom of drilling in the Arctic. They'd engaged vehemently behind closed doors for nearly two years on the subject. Will, with some help from Sean and his many contacts offstage, had led the opposition to the move. He'd assembled reams of scientific data and reports on the underlying threats. He'd presented endless arguments about how unwise it might look if something catastrophic happened. American Frontier could drill elsewhere. It didn't need the Arctic. It could substantially increase its pursuit of natural gas. It could race to develop oil shale in Israel and the western United States, which might ultimately be cheaper and faster than absorbing the risks of taking on the frozen but rapidly melting north. They were even dabbling in the massive, untapped offshore wind reserve along the Eastern Seaboard and could expand that.

Now that something catastrophic had happened, Will looked prophetic. But he didn't buy in to such a drastic next step as Stapleton was suggesting.

"Oh, come on," Will said. "There's no way. I'm no fan of Sandstrom or the Arctic drilling policy, but criminal negligence? That's utter nonsense. No one would possibly take it seriously."

"Your little sister is taking it quite seriously, my friend," Stapleton said in a low voice that only Will could hear. "Justice's Criminal Division is looking at that, and Sarah is going to head it up."

Will didn't dare ask how Stapleton knew that before his

sister had even had the chance to tell him. But he could guess. Stapleton had eyes and ears nearly everywhere, at almost every critical nexus in the financial, government, and corporate worlds. In this case, his source was likely the political appointee who headed the Department of Justice's Criminal Division.

For now, Will simply played along. "The shareholder lawsuit will be based here in New York, of course, and she has friends who will be involved. But there's no way criminal negligence is involved, or that Justice's Criminal Division will get in the game."

"Don't be so sure. I have it on awfully good authority that Justice will pursue criminal negligence charges. But your sister . . ." Stapleton shook his head. "I don't know why she wouldn't recuse herself. With your family connections to American Frontier . . ."

Will knew what Stapleton had left unspoken. *It would be a media frenzy.* He chose to gloss over the last part of Stapleton's statement. "I still don't see it. To quote you, 'So a few polar bears and beluga whales are coated with oil.' How's that criminal negligence?"

They shared a smile. This was a constant argument between the two of them, all of it polite and friendly. Stapleton didn't think much of the "loony left," as he liked to refer to it, or to the progressive environmental left either. Will argued with him every chance he could find, echoing information fed to him by his brother.

There were always political overtones in that friendly banter. Stapleton, a true kingmaker in GOP circles, had financed more than one Republican presidential campaign. And everyone knew that Will's family had been a left-of-center core of the Democratic Party for generations. Most assumed it was inevitable that a Worthington would become president. But the press and the kingmakers could never pin Will down. Was he a Democrat, like all generations of his family had been? Or could he be turned toward the Republican Party, as Stapleton and others hoped? When it came to politics, Will kept his heart and sympathies secret from everyone except Drew, Laura, and Paul.

"I'm not talking about the oil-covered whales. I don't give a rat's tail about them, as you know." Stapleton looked around, as if to make certain no one else heard that. "What I'm talking about is something else entirely. When you deliberately lie—to the board, to the White House, to Congress, to shareholders—that's criminal negligence. It doesn't matter who or what gets harmed."

Will hadn't thought about any of that. He would definitely need to connect again with his sister when things settled down. For now he said, "We've had immense fights and major disagreements over the Arctic policy, yes, but I've never seen deception."

Stapleton lifted his chin. "We'll see."

The room suddenly grew quiet. Every cell phone that Sandstrom and his executive staff had appeared. All stared down at their mobiles, trying to decipher the news.

The American Frontier CEO looked up from his own mobile device, conferred quickly with a nearby aide, and then pivoted to face the boardroom. "I'm sorry," Sandstrom announced to the gathering. "I fully realize that the board has called this meeting and that we have much to discuss. But we just received a command to meet with the president's chief of staff at the White House within the hour. I must leave immediately, though you all can meet, of course."

Well, that will make any sort of a board decision much more difficult, Will thought.

Sandstrom strode across the room, spoke briefly to the board's chairman, and then exited with his entourage.

He could feel it. This was his lucky day. The day his destiny was going to change.

Since his mama's death, he'd drifted into other pursuits that he'd pretended were somehow related to acting: appearances at seedy clubs, more appearances at private parties—his favorites were children's ones, where he wore costumes—and then personal, paid-escort gigs. He'd somehow managed to hang on to a semblance of his once-good looks, unless anyone took the time to peer closely.

His agent, who'd once lined up his appearances and gigs, seemingly had quite a decent network. He'd found himself partying on yachts and in penthouses—at least until he'd started spending most of his extra money on recreational activities that weren't all that healthy or productive.

In his lucid moments, he knew his mama wouldn't approve. But he couldn't stop. The recreational drugs made the dark haziness go away, if only for a while.

Then, at some point, the high-end work started to disappear, and his agent started referring him to fewer and fewer appearances. Not long after, his agent stopped calling and wouldn't take his calls anymore.

It had been more than two years since he'd gone to an audition, and even longer since he'd bothered to try his hand at real acting. He'd been living on and off the streets for most of that time, but he wasn't like the other bums, who wandered around with nowhere to go and nothing to do. He still had plans, goals, things to accomplish in life.

He had a little Brooklyn flat where he crashed when the street got to be too much. It belonged to someone else.

He hadn't been able to afford any of the prescription medication that had been useful once. So now he was paying for his habits and hobbies with anything that came his way, including highly unusual underground shows that involved metal bars on windows and bulletproof glass.

The previous night, he'd been at one of those shows when someone had gotten his ear and asked if he was interested in a two-hour gig that paid well. All he had to do, they said, was dress up in a polar bear suit, drop a backpack at a designated spot near a building, walk away, and then wait for instructions about where to drop the suit off after the gig was up.

No names had been exchanged. There were no business cards, no email addresses, no addresses of any kind. The young, slick-looking lawyer type who'd contacted him would be in touch if he was interested. When he'd found out how much it paid, he'd been interested. It was more money than he'd made in the past few months.

Now he saw the same guy walking toward him. The lawyer type handed him the polar bear suit and one of those off-the-rack cell phones. He received instructions about where to go once he'd dressed up. There was a backpack along with the suit, complete with some walking-around money.

"You'll be paid later for the gig," he was told.

Seemed easy enough. Strange, but easy.

Then again, in his line of work, he was smart enough not to ask any questions.

7

///

Sarah Katherine Worthington had gone to Harvard Law School on a lark. Truth was, she didn't have anything better to do. It wasn't like she *had* to earn money—not when her trust fund topped a billion dollars at least—or even pay all that much attention to what she was doing. She'd spent her entire undergraduate days at Harvard playing madam social butterfly. She'd thought nothing of running up 10,000 dollars in shopping debt at a mall in only one trip.

"Why worry? It'll just cause lines on my face," she would say half seriously to friends.

There was some truth to it, especially since she was 34. Her father had groomed Will to take care of all the big decisions for the family at Worthington Shares. Will was serious, thinking through every angle before making a decision. Then, once he'd decided, he was immovable. Sean, the Worthington entrepreneur, kept the company expanding and moving forward. Even while he finished one deal, his brain was already spinning out into the universe of his next one. Sean was smart, really smart, but understated . . . until he went public. Then he became the most sought-after and photographed Worthington, because he was doing something interesting or had a hot model on his arm.

So what was she supposed to do? What was her job, really?

Sarah had always been the baby of the family. The family still called her by her pet name—SB for Sarah Baby or Sugar Baby or Social Butterfly, depending on which family history you believed. It didn't seem like anyone would ever take her seriously. Sure, everyone cooed over her. Her curly chestnut hair, compliments of her father, and arresting green eyes, compliments of her mother, had garnered attention as far back as she could remember. First she was "cute," and then somewhere the transition to "beautiful" happened—at least in the eyes of the media. She was the life of every black-tie party and the entertainer at all of the family gatherings.

Sarah excelled at meeting and drawing in people. She'd been to every red-carpet gathering she could manage. But what was she supposed to actually *do* with her life? That was the question that had nagged her a bit, when she chose to think about it at all.

Which is how she'd ended up at Harvard Law School. Her dad had donated enough money to create a new wing at the law school library, and she was admitted to the school after graduating from the university. It wasn't supposed to work that way. Other folks had to work hard to apply to such a prestigious law school. But who cared? *Money buys all sorts of things*, she'd reasoned. *So why not go with the flow and try it out?*

Yet a strange thing had happened at law school. Sarah liked it. Flickers of a time she'd bested a bully and championed an underdog when she was young rose to the surface. Even more, she discovered she was actually good at law. She had always been a charmer and, she admitted, a little manipulative. She had wangled ways over the years to bend each of her family members around her little finger. She'd even charmed Drew, although he occasionally lifted a brow at her antics, especially in public. But his chiding expression never lasted long.

The dual traits of charm and manipulation served her in good stead in law. Arguing persuasively was something Sarah reveled in. And to be honest, she loved the limelight. After her first year, she'd interned at a big, influential law firm in lower Manhattan and discovered that every one of her natural skills made sense in the practice of law.

So she'd made a deal with herself. She'd play around with law school and whatever came after that for however long she felt like. If she got bored and wanted to take a year off and hang out in the south of France, well, that was what she would do.

It wasn't like she had to work. She could spend her inheritance on everything and anything, and there would still be many more fortunes left.

But she'd felt driven to work at law and graduated at the top of her class. Her last year she'd served as the editor of *Harvard Law Review*—and not because it had been handed to her. She'd earned it.

Upon graduation, she'd shocked everyone in her family and taken a position as an assistant district attorney. The pay was lousy—far less than what she gave away to charitable causes each year. After a few years in the DA's office in Manhattan, she'd shocked her friends and family yet again right after her twenty-eighth birthday by taking a career government position as the deputy assistant attorney general in the Department of Justice's Criminal Division.

Justice created the position and based her in New York. Her boss, the head of the Justice's Criminal Division, was a political appointee in a Republican administration, but he'd grown to trust Sarah and her instincts—despite her family connections and wealth. She earned $159,712 a year, which she donated to Goodwill charities.

Her family was a bit confused by it all.

But Sarah knew something no one else knew. Finally, at 34 years old, she had a life plan. Even saying *life plan* made her laugh. Drew's wife, Jean, a spunky lady Sarah admired, had a wonderful saying: "We make plans, and God laughs." Well, Sarah was sure God had laughed at her many times in her life, especially when she had lived in the moment.

Of course, Sarah didn't share her secret life plan with anyone. Not her boss and especially not her family. They were still waiting for her to "grow up." Still, it was a plan. And according to the deal with herself, she could bail at any moment . . . whenever she felt like it. In that deal was freedom. She could work as hard as she wanted, with no risk. She could quit at any time and jump off the treadmill.

With that freedom came the ability to try things that might be career limiting or risky for others. She could challenge principalities and powers. She could take on those in charge without fear. After all, what did she have to lose? She didn't have to worry about who she angered or who might try to stop her. She could always just quit the path she was on, if need be.

Sarah had learned quickly in the prosecutor's office in New

York that all manner of interesting cases walked through the door, and she'd started to develop a specialty in prosecuting bank, securities, and corporate fraud. It was that specialty that had gotten her the career criminal prosecutor's job, overseeing those same sorts of cases for the Department of Justice. Now, though, Sarah could see that her life was about to intersect with not only her big brother but her middle brother as well.

In the BP deepwater oil spill, Sarah's division at Justice had prosecuted a case against the giant oil company for criminal negligence charges related to obstruction of justice and lying to Congress. BP had settled with her division for 4.5 billion dollars. Their case had been first out the door.

A similar effort, which Sarah would spearhead, would emerge with this latest fiasco with American Frontier. But there might also be a massive shareholder lawsuit, which could include Will and Worthington Shares. And an environmental NGO that Sean contributed to and served as board chair for—the Center for Ecological Biodiversity—had led every NGO lawsuit on oil spills for more than a decade. Sean's NGO would likely sue to collect penalties based on the amount of oil that spilled into the Arctic Ocean and potentially harmed the species that made the Arctic their home. All of which meant that each of the Worthington siblings would, in some fashion, become entangled in the American Frontier spill in the Arctic shortly.

As soon as she saw the direction the legal disputes were heading, Sarah knew she had to try to recuse herself.

She stopped by her boss's office first thing that morning. "I can't do this," she told him. "My brother is on the board. He might become the CEO. Our family's fund has a great deal of stock in American Frontier. It's a massive conflict of interest."

"But he's not the CEO right now," John Barnhill, the Criminal Division chief, replied. "He won't be the target. He might even be the negligence remedy, in a manner of speaking. Where's the conflict of interest in that?"

Sarah was quick with her comeback. "What about the substantial minority holdings Worthington has in American Frontier?"

John stuck to his guns. "Immaterial. You'll hear material information about any shareholder suits, of course, but your job will be to prosecute criminal negligence. Shareholder value isn't in your purview, and it isn't your concern." He paused. "What's more, if I recall, didn't you remove any and all of your legal obligations to Worthington Shares when you took this job? You don't make any of the decisions. You're not involved in any of the financial decisions it makes or where money is invested, right?"

Sarah sighed. Her boss was right. She had extracted herself from Worthington Shares' decisions, precisely because she'd wanted to avoid any sort of complications, like the one she was faced with now. "Come on, John. You can't believe the press will let me get away with this, do you?"

"You let me worry about that," John said. "After all, it will be my neck on the line if we aren't serious about our criminal negligence efforts. I'll be the one in front of the cameras—especially if it gets ugly—not you. What I need to know is that we have the best information at hand . . ."

"And I can get that for you," Sarah said quietly.

"Yes, you can."

Sarah was silent for a moment. Truthfully, she'd been

looking for this sort of opportunity. It might make or break her boss's career, but it could do a whole lot more for her ultimate life plan if she could manipulate events in her favor. She wanted to sink her teeth into something big. Now she had that opportunity.

"Okay, I'm all in."

He gave only a brief nod, but the twinkle in his eyes revealed he'd already known what her answer would be.

8

Will was stunned as he and Drew exited the American Frontier headquarters. How could Sandstrom leave his own board meeting like that, even for a meeting with the president's chief of staff? It made no sense—unless he meant to use the White House as an excuse to delay any sort of board call on the question of his leadership. It was an interesting gambit, if that was what he was pursuing. And what was President Rich up to?

The current American president, Spencer Rich, had been elected to office only a few months earlier. This was his first big crisis, and he'd inherited it, though he had championed energy independence and Arctic drilling specifically in his presidential campaign. Like Will, Spencer Rich was the firstborn from a prominent, wealthy family that had long ago made its mark in presidential politics after a successful run in business—specifically the oil business. His father, Thomas Rich, had taken the presidential office when Will was a toddler.

The Worthington and Rich families went way back and shared some Irish roots. Thomas and Will's mother had been friends in their Harvard days. A common Irish heritage and their blue-blood lineages had drawn them together. Even though they were poles apart politically, the two continued their friendship after both had married and moved on to their respective circles. The two families had enjoyed each other's company until life had driven them apart—at least that was what his mother had once told Will wistfully.

By the time Sean was born and Will started his schooling, the two families were no longer spending time together. Will hadn't minded. He'd been quite a bit younger than Spencer and remembered him only as a hotheaded bully. The last time they were together was at Camp David, when Thomas Rich, midway into his first term as president of the United States, had invited the Worthingtons to spend a week with his family. Spencer's mom, Victoria, had arrived in a huff where the boys were playing baseball, whisked Spencer into a limo, and evidently took him back to the White House.

Being the only child at Camp David was preferable to having to spend time with Spencer. The days spent there were hazy in Will's mind, as he'd been only three or four, but he remembered feeling lonely. His father had been there just one evening before he was called back to New York City.

Now Spencer Rich was a strong, aggressive leader who naturally took charge and ran things. His father had paved the way for him, handing him a plum CEO job, followed by a successful run for governor in Texas, and finally his full support in the presidential primaries. Spencer was a lousy public speaker and survived a terrific hazing by the press, but in the end it hadn't mattered. He'd won by the slimmest margin.

The Republicans also won back the Senate, thanks to a nearly bottomless pit of spending from all of the major industrial, mining, agribusiness, and oil companies, including American Frontier, which had been frustrated by regulatory schemes in Washington for years and years. That meant the Republicans owned the nation's capital again, in more ways than one. Nothing was beyond their reach any longer in Washington, but they were much more careful, thorough, and discreet in their governance this time around. With little or no fanfare, they ratcheted back the reach of agencies and departments like the EPA, DOE, and DOI through the exceedingly boring budget process, while boosting the budgets of the Pentagon and Commerce. Meanwhile, K Street was fully employed with hundreds of business-oriented lobbyists, all working the appropriations process seamlessly.

People in the country had the impression that Washington was working like a business—largely because it *was* being run by the very same sorts of people who regularly managed big companies. Ayn Rand's many acolytes had finally gotten the Washington of their dreams.

Will admired most of his peers in the financial and business world who were mostly after one thing—sound management of resources and finances for the benefit of large, institutional shareholders who demanded steady, increasing value in publicly traded companies. Will himself was accustomed to such serious pursuits.

As a child, he'd been drawn to the sorts of things that adults did. He'd begun to read books about finance and business when he was only 11. While others read fantasy and science fiction, Will was drawn to thick books on banking and industry. As a Worthington family heir, he felt a much greater burden to succeed, to lead, and to understand the world around him so he could control it most effectively.

Now, as an adult and financial leader in his own right, he admired those who did whatever it took to seize control of the reins of power in Washington and run the country, the way a strong-willed parent might run a family or a powerful CEO might run a publicly traded company. He admired it, but he didn't necessarily have to agree with it.

Drew interrupted his thoughts. "Strange meeting, wasn't it?"

"To say the least." Will strode along the broad sidewalk south of Central Park. He'd wanted to clear his mind after the aborted meeting, and a brisk walk around and through the park made the most sense. Drew had joined him for the walk, as Will had known he would.

A horse pulling one of the expensive carriages that waited patiently for tourists rolled a lazy eye in their direction, then chose the moment they walked by to relieve itself. Will saw Drew wrinkle his nose and laughed. He didn't mind the smell, really. It was part and parcel of the allure of Central Park. You either accepted it or you didn't. And Will accepted it for what it was.

They turned left into the park on the East Side, opposite from the curious Apple retail store that was mostly just four big windows, two stories high. Tourists lined up to go inside, browse a bit, and then leave with a story to tell about the odd-looking store near Madison Avenue on the east side of New York.

"So what happens now, do you think?" Drew asked.

"I think Sandstrom intends to use the White House as a shield, to keep the board from sacking him just yet."

Drew lifted a brow. "Will it work?"

"It might. If the White House insists on accountability from the existing American Frontier leadership in the middle of the crisis, then it's impossible to press for a change now. And if the spill drags out for a time, which it might, and he does a good job managing the media firestorm around it, he might stand a chance of staying."

"But you doubt that, don't you?"

"I doubt he has the skills, either for the media or for the politics," Will said as he weaved his way around the tourists who always populated the sidewalks of the broad entrances to the park.

"So how . . . ?"

"Because the president's financial and political backers might insist on no change while the crisis is under way," Will explained. "Which is what I'd do if I were Sandstrom and if I'd been helpful in putting this particular president in his job in the first place."

"Sir, if I might offer an opinion?"

It was the "sir" that slowed Will momentarily because it was so out of place. One glance at the older man, whose brown hair was flecked with gray, told Will that was exactly why Drew had said it. Drew knew him well. That he'd stay on one particular mind track until presented with something that seemed out of order. Then he'd be startled into paying attention.

"Always welcome, Drew," Will said evenly. "You know that. So what is it?"

"If you are serious about pursuing this—and I'm reserving judgment on whether that's a prudent course or not—then I believe you should very publicly challenge the American Frontier CEO, regardless of whatever protection and comfort the White House might afford him. You should . . . how is it that you always put it . . . 'call him out into the street'?"

Will burst out laughing. "Very good! Yes, that's an apt way to put it. Good to see all those Westerns we watched being useful."

When Will was nine years old, he'd discovered old Western movies and had loved them so much he'd begged Drew to watch a few with him. *Three Amigos* had become one of Will's favorites. There was something black-and-white about Westerns that he loved. Maybe it was that the good guys always win and the bad guys are always punished. In the days of the Old West, calling someone out into the street was a quick and public way to take out an enemy . . . or, in this case, another candidate for your job.

"I think you should call Mr. Sandstrom into the street, so to speak," Drew repeated. "If you believe that he's led American Frontier on a path that threatens not only the shareholders—and you are certainly its most prominent shareholder—but the world's ecosystems and biodiversity as well, you should act on that belief."

"And how would I go about doing that?"

"Well," he offered slowly, "I might consider paying a visit to your friend, the financial editor at the very same *Wall Street Journal* that predicted you were next in line to run American Frontier. They are sure to follow this story closely from all angles, from the criminal negligence case your sister will almost certainly manage, to the ramifications for the global economy."

Will nodded. "True. This story is tailor-made for nearly every sort of reporting that they do. The owner isn't exactly a friend, but the editor has known me for years."

"Precisely."

"And when I meet with him?" Will allowed a glint of conquest in his smile as he swiveled his head toward Drew.

"I'd hand him a copy of a letter, just before you postmark it and drop it in the nearest mailbox, calling for Sandstrom to step down as CEO."

"And if he doesn't resign?"

"Then you call him out into the street and let it be known—very publicly—that Worthington Shares intends to join in the shareholder lawsuit against American Frontier."

"Is that wise?"

"I don't know if it's wise," Drew said. "But I will say this. It may be necessary, both for the value of the Worthington Shares holdings in the company and for your own ambitions."

Shortly thereafter, Will and Drew parted ways to head to their respective abodes. As Will pondered Drew's words, he was struck by the possibility of soon realizing his dream—to be the CEO of American Frontier. Before the age of 40, he'd reach the pinnacle of success he dreamed of. He would control one of the most powerful companies in the world. Such a position is what he'd been groomed for, what he'd always wanted . . .

Just then, though, a still small voice inside asked, *But is that really what you want, Will?*

He halted midstep, confused.

The voice didn't say anything else. Maybe he hadn't heard it after all.

But as he reached his building and headed up the elevator to his suite, the first niggle of doubt descended. Was the trajectory he was on the right one for him?

Stepping to the window, he peered out over New York

City—at the mass of humanity that moved in every direction like the fine threads of a spiderweb. He would have the opportunity to direct the forces that could influence the path of so many of those people walking below.

Straightening his shoulders, he shook off the doubt. *Yes*, he told himself. *It's what I was born to do.*

He'd come too far to question his destiny now.

9

A SMALL PORT IN ALASKA

Ever since getting kicked off the USS *Cantor* by the arrival of the Navy fleet and the American Frontier team, Sean had been restless. He hated not being in the center of the action. But as "nonessential personnel," he'd been given the boot. Thankfully, both Dr. Shapiros had been allowed to stay, and Elizabeth was still sending info Sean's way.

Now, though, seeing his brother's grim visage flashed across a TV screen didn't help Sean's frustration. Sean admired his elder sibling and wished Will well, but he was also a little jealous. He never spoke of it, except occasionally to his mother when he was at a low point in his life. So seeing Will's face on CNN and Fox News as speculation swirled around him becoming the next CEO of American Frontier only made Sean seethe all over again.

The lives and work of all three Worthington siblings were converging on one central event. Will and Sarah were both now in the middle of the fray. But Sean, once again, was on the outside looking in.

Though people saw Will as a natural leader, Sean was sure they saw him as just the party boy. Someone interesting to the tabloids but not to be taken as a serious player. Although Sean had billions of dollars at his disposal, he largely made his way through the world on his own, almost in the shadows in between parties and media blitzes while Will stayed in the spotlight.

So when did I know I couldn't compete with my brother? he asked himself.

He knew the answer instantly. *When I was 11. When I sneaked out of that Worthington social affair and nobody noticed I was missing.*

Later, he hadn't been sure whether to smirk or roll his eyes at the predictability of it. Nobody much asked his opinion anyway, at least inside his family. Any conversation centered on Will, the perfect one, and their entertaining little sister. So what did it matter that he wasn't there?

When that reality hit, Sean had decided he preferred to spend as much time as possible at his friends' houses. There, at least, he was noticed and mostly understood. Since then his close-knit group of friends had become more his family than his actual family. There, among that group, he felt he truly belonged.

Yet Sean had still been the dutiful son, carving out a massive, entrepreneurial role for himself inside Worthington Shares. He'd placed big bets on nearly 100 start-ups in more than a dozen industries in the past several years. A few, thankfully, were poised to break out in big ways now that IPOs were back in vogue, and both Wall Street and Silicon Valley were willing to roll the dice on big plays again.

The secret of a successful equity fund, even one as massive

as Worthington Shares, was the diversity of the portfolio of companies it had invested in. At one end, the stable end, were the shares in big, established, blue-chip companies like American Frontier. Will managed that aspect. It fit his traditional, non-risking personality all the way. But the real value—where big money was won and lost—was in the risky side of the business, where bets were placed on start-ups that had the potential to explode in value or crash big-time.

Sean had taken to that end of Worthington Shares like a duck to water. He loved the risk, the daring, the adrenaline rush he got from watching something that he'd identified begin its inexorable march toward an IPO or a big sale to a much larger company. And he craved the intermingling with others, gathering new people he grew to call his friends . . . part of his network. People who were loyal to him and could count on him too.

Sean already had three big wins in just the last five years, which was really all he needed to justify 100 failures in even a broad portfolio of start-ups. These three instances alone now delivered nearly a billion dollars in value. All of the other start-ups Sean managed could collapse or disappear altogether and it wouldn't matter. His end of the Worthington Shares business was an unmitigated success by any measure, even if that success was never good enough for his father.

This left him more than enough time to indulge all of his other many hobbies and pursuits. He'd sailed around the world with a group of friends and had been to the top of several of the largest summits. He had plans to compete in amateur bobsledding in Switzerland. Lately he'd set his goal to zip-line at some of the most amazing and beautiful spots in the world. Already he'd zip-lined over the Great Wall of

China in Simatai—a rush at a speed of nearly 100 mph—and in Labadee, Haiti, over a cove of sky-blue water. Now he was debating whether to do Gravity Canyon in New Zealand or Icy Strait Point in Alaska next.

Sean was also somewhat notorious for his single lifestyle, even though he was always seen in the midst of a growing circle. He'd been constantly photographed in the company of well-known actresses and supermodels, but there were the occasional wild rumors about why he was still single into his midthirties. Sean tried to ignore all the tabloid talk that swirled about the Worthingtons, especially him: "Keep an eye on Sean Worthington. Under that charming smile, could there be a devilish interior? A playboy who doesn't care about the consequences?"

When he'd seen the headlines of that tabloid at a newsstand, complete with a rakish picture of himself on the cover, he'd flipped the newsstand guy a 100-dollar bill, then flung the entire stash of tabloids into the nearby trash bin without even reading the story. "Inquiring minds want to know . . . right," he'd scoffed as he poured the remainder of his morning coffee over the papers.

As far as Sean was concerned, his personal preferences were his own business and not anyone else's. But every so often, he did think about ending the speculation and unasked questions. Someday he'd find the right woman to marry, settle down, and have kids.

Dr. Elizabeth Shapiro flashed into his mind.

Having a wonderful, brilliant daughter-in-law would certainly make his mom happy. He caught her glancing at him every once in a while with a wistful eye and knew what that look meant. She loved Laura and being a grandmother to

Will's kids. She'd even hinted that she wished Sean would find the same kind of happiness that Will and Laura seemed to share. Then again, Sean hadn't met anyone even remotely close to Laura. Not that he wanted someone exactly like her, but he admired her. A strong woman in her own right, she was perfect for Will. Made him lighten up. Put things in perspective when he got too intense. When Laura was around, Will was a much better human being.

And that was what Sean wanted out of a lasting relationship.

But even more, he wished for an end to the restlessness he continually felt in his heart. He didn't know why, but it was always there. As if a piece of him was missing somehow, and he couldn't be whole without it.

Now, however, he was on a mission. What he couldn't tell just yet was whether he'd be in a position to help or hurt his brother when all was said and done. It depended on a variety of circumstances and factors. But one thing Sean knew. This was his moment too, and he wanted to make the most of it.

Among his many hobbies, Sean was on the board of directors of a half dozen big environmental groups. As a wealthy donor, he could sit on almost any nonprofit board of his choosing. His favorite, though, was Green Justice. American Frontier officials and shareholders disliked Green Justice a great deal, which was all the incentive Sean needed to donate money and sit on its global board.

He was the only card-carrying member of the business community on the Green Justice board. Most of Green Justice's operations were funded on shoestring budgets by its individual members. They avoided corporate donations.

But Sean had long ago earned his bona fides as a stalwart individual donor to progressive causes. So his annual gift to Green Justice to fund its core operations was welcomed.

Sean pulled his mobile from his vest pocket and scrolled to the Bs in his hundreds of social contacts. He was looking for one name in particular—Kirk Baldwin, a crusty, bald-headed fellow traveler who'd been the head of research for Green Justice for nearly 20 years now. Sean hadn't spoken to him in a while, but it wouldn't matter. His comrade-in-arms would jump at the chance he was about to afford him.

"Amigo!" he almost yelled into the phone once he'd dialed the contact. "How's the battle?"

"Same as ever," his friend answered in a raspy voice. "And I'll bet you're busy right about now, huh?"

"Yeah, well, my brother certainly is," Sean said. "I'm just sitting on the sidelines, biding my time."

"Let me guess. You want in the game?"

"I do. How'd you know?"

"I know you way too well, dude," Kirk said. "You go where the action is. And the action, as we all know, is in the Arctic."

"That's the understatement of the century." Sean didn't mention that he'd already been there, in the middle of the action, right when it had happened. He'd save that information for a later date.

Kirk paused. "You know we're coming after American Frontier with everything we have, right? You *do* know that?"

"I certainly hope so. I wouldn't have it any other way."

"So, if you're calling on your brother's behalf to see if you can slow us down, get us to—"

"I'm most definitely *not* calling on Will's behalf, or American Frontier's, for that matter," Sean said much too loudly. "I would never do that. You know me, Kirk. I don't operate like that. Ever. Not even for my brother."

"I know." His friend chuckled. "Just had to put it out there. Worthington Shares is their biggest shareholder, after all. The entire financial community knows it, if not the rest of the world."

Sean rolled his eyes, even though Kirk couldn't see it. "Have I ever done anything that would make you think I'd try to get in the way of what you all do, just because my family's fund owns significant shares of the company? Have I?"

A slight pause, then, "No, you haven't. And it's what I've always liked about you, even if I don't completely understand you or your motivations. So, what's on your mind?"

"I have a proposition," Sean said.

"Which is?"

"How'd you like a new ship for the Green Justice fleet?"

"What sort?"

"The kind that can sail into the Arctic. With me aboard."

10

All is now right with the world, Will thought. *At least my world at home.* There was no place he'd rather be than here, now, surrounded with the happy faces of his wife and kids. As hectic as things were at the Worthington Shares building, he needed his family home to remind him of what truly mattered.

It was no surprise that eight-year-old Davy was the first to run straight into Will's arms. As the boy gripped his father's waist with fervor, Will ruffled his son's dark curls. But he didn't get a word out before Davy exclaimed, "Daddy! Guess what? We got to go swimming with a bunch of kids in a lake that had lots of really colorful fish, and . . ." Davy was off and running with an excited monologue, barely taking a breath.

Will couldn't help but grin. He caught the merriment in Laura's eyes and winked. She stretched her arms toward him and pantomimed hugging him. He moved toward her slowly, Davy still hanging on to his waist and talking.

Patricia stood nearby, arms crossed, patiently waiting. Her fair skin had a reddish flush. Clearly she'd given up on hugging her father until Davy was done. "Hey, Dad," she said. "I'm glad to be home. Do you know how hard it is to get a text signal there? I forgot that from last summer." And with those few words, she pulled her iPhone out of her shorts pocket and started texting like a mad woodpecker.

That was Patricia, his social networking queen. She and Sean had a lot in common. But Will knew that once she'd contacted her friends and he took her aside for some daddy-daughter time, he'd get a running commentary about the summer from her too.

Andrew stood back a few feet, looking taller than Will could remember. *Did the kid grow in the last few weeks? Unbelievable.* Always serious, Andrew was poised like a soldier on the outskirts, awaiting his turn.

Midstep toward Laura, Will cocked his head toward Andrew. She nodded and smiled. With Davy now hanging monkey style from his waist, Will shuffled across the floor to hug his oldest son as Drew carried the last load of luggage in the door.

Andrew returned the hug, stepped back, then hugged his father again. "I missed you, Dad," is all he said. But his thoughtful expression ensured he would share lots of new experiences later with his father.

"Incredible kids," Will mouthed to Laura.

She simply nodded again, but a mother's pride radiated from her eyes.

"Okay, kids, why don't you relieve Uncle Drew of some of your luggage and get it stashed away? I have a very special dinner planned—something you said you wanted as soon as you got home."

"Pizza!" Davy yelled and ran toward the kitchen.

"Whoa there, young man," Laura said, corralling him. "Get your suitcase put in your room first."

"Thanks, Dad." Andrew sniffed the air. "Sausage and mushroom. My favorite." He turned to Drew. "Thanks for picking us up at the airport."

Drew grinned. "You're welcome, William Andrew Jennings Worthington VII."

Will laughed and Laura sighed. It had been a long debate between them when Andrew was born. Will's father had insisted that he carry the William Jennings Worthington name to the seventh generation. Laura had balked against all the expectations that were set up for their son but at last had agreed. "If," she'd stated firmly, "he has something different added to his name—at least a name we love." That was when the given name of their trusted mentor, Andrew, had come to mind.

As a result, Andrew and Drew had always shared a special bond. Will hoped that when Andrew was ready to tackle his own career, Drew would still be able to mentor him, like he had Will and his father before him. There was no one Will could trust more to do right by his son.

"Ew, Dad, sausage and mushroom?" Patricia tapped her foot.

Will smiled. "Don't worry. I got you pepperoni." After all, he had learned something growing up with Sean. Sean always complained that he never got to pick what he wanted for dinner, and looking back, Will realized he was right. He didn't want Patricia to walk away from their home feeling that way, so he went out of his way to keep her interests in mind.

Satisfied, she ran at him full tilt. "You're the awesomest!"

Her hug was brief but crushing, and then their 10-year-old was off again, dragging her suitcase with one hand while using her iPhone with the other.

Andrew, right behind her going down the hallway, turned toward his parents and rolled his eyes.

Will laughed. It was so good to have them all home again. And finally . . .

Drew broke in. "Okay, think you all need to settle in now, and Jean is waiting on dinner for me."

"Thanks again for picking them up while I was finishing my meeting." Will clasped his hand. "Give our best to Jean."

When the door closed, Will at last moved unencumbered toward his beautiful wife. After a long, tender embrace, he drew back slightly. "You are my home," he whispered, "and I'm so glad you're home."

She reached up with both hands and cradled his face. "If I could, I'd choose you all over again, William J. Worthington." Warmth shimmered in her liquid brown eyes.

"And I you, Mrs. Laura Worthington." He gazed lovingly at her. "You know what my Irish grandmother used to say?"

"No, what?"

"Always kiss like it's the first time."

The smile he loved now hovered around her mouth. "Well, I think we can take care of that easily, don't you?"

Slowly, ever so slowly, his lips moved toward hers and claimed them . . . until a chorus of "Ew, yuck" resounded from the hallway.

11

A SMALL PORT IN ALASKA

Just before he left the little port in Alaska on a flight to New York City, Sean got the most long-winded call he'd ever received from his friend Jon Gillibrand, a journalist for the *New York Times*. Sean wasn't surprised to see Jon's number pop up on his screen after all that was happening in the Arctic.

Jon, a veteran reporter of 18 years, smart and persistent, had a nose for big news. He'd started out at the environment desk at the paper . . . until it was killed off. Then he'd simply asked to be reassigned to the science desk and kept moving. During the BP oil spill, the giant oil company had commissioned research aboard every available ship carrying out National Science Foundation–funded research, save one, in order to keep non-BP ships away from the Deepwater Horizon spill site. All of the research ships conveniently found other parts of the world to sail to for new research, funded by the company out of the goodness of its heart. Gillibrand had been able to talk his way onto that one remaining academic research vessel and report firsthand less than a mile from the site of the oil spill for nearly two weeks.

Sean grinned. He and Jon had a lot in common.

Jon jumped right in, not even saying hello. "You know Elizabeth and Dr. Shapiro never distort the truth or sugar-coat anything, and she's worried . . . in a way I haven't seen since we met. The Arctic spill is huge, planet-altering news. Consistent, ever-present, daily, front-page news. I need to be on the front lines, not trapped here at my desk, reporting on some claptrap propaganda fed from the press aides at the White House or the paid flacks at American Frontier."

"I know the feeling," Sean replied. "I want to be there myself again."

"Climate change isn't a hoax," Jon said. "It's real, big, complicated, and dangerous for the world over some unde-fined period of time. I know the facts. I've studied them. And after the facts Elizabeth sent me about the oil spill, I've got to get to the Arctic Ocean. I talked to the U of Washington about getting inside their research mission already there. No go. Called my friend at NSF to see if they're sending a research vessel that way. No go." There was a pause, then Jon plunged on. "I've heard rumors from one of my activist sources. Someone big is stepping up. There might be a ship available, but I'd be walking a bit across the line to join it. Then again, that's never stopped me."

Sean laughed out loud. Jon was gutsy and took his as-signments to the edge. He always said he'd never aspired to be an editor or a columnist, so he could basically do his job day in and day out without ever worrying in the slightest whether his output was elevating his status in the newsroom or the business offices of the *Times*. He'd been doing his job successfully for so many years that the editors cut him slack. If he said he needed time to develop a piece, they gave him time. If he said something wasn't actually a story, they didn't ask him to report it and instead carried a few paragraphs from Reuters, AP, or Bloomberg, if needed.

"So I talked to Frances. Pestered her relentlessly is more like it. She swears AF would have a stroke if they thought a national reporter was tagging along."

Sean could just imagine the conversation. Frances Blythe, the deputy science editor, was a climber, with her eye on greater horizons in the journalism world. So she always took the cautious, what's-in-it-for-me approach to any decision.

"I finally told her, 'Hey, let's say I *do* find a ship that's going that way and I catch a ride. But let's also say it's maybe, um, also headed there to cause trouble?'"

Sean broke in. "I'm sure that went over really well."

"She immediately assumed it was the Russians, since they are way ahead of the American military and geniuses in Congress on the need for ice-cutting ships in the Arctic. So I hedged a little and finally told her, 'I've heard about an opportunity, but it's a bit on the aggressive enviro side.'"

Sean propped his cell phone closer to his ear. He had a feeling . . .

"When I said Green Justice, she about passed out."

Sean wasn't surprised. If Green Justice got itself tangled up with American military types in the Arctic, it could be dangerous, and she didn't want to lose a great reporter. But Sean had great respect for Green Justice and folks like Kirk Baldwin. Green Justice was one of the few progressive environmental groups with both the resources and the courage to challenge authorities on the high seas. They sailed their aging boats in pirate-infested waters in the Indian Ocean, for instance, in search of whalers and dolphin killers. In one of their more notorious escapades, Green Justice had sailed a ship right in the middle of a Navy exercise to protest military maneuvers widely believed to kill perhaps millions of marine mammals routinely. The Navy had politely but firmly escorted the Green Justice ship back to harbor, but not before a news crew had filmed it all and reported on the confrontation.

Green Justice got things done. It was why Sean had gone to Kirk in the first place when he needed to make things happen.

"Frances claimed there was no way they had an ice cutter, only old rusted-out hulks that putter along," Jon said, interrupting Sean's thoughts. "But when I told her someone has stepped forward and offered to bring in a newly commissioned ship of sorts for Green Justice, she started waffling. When I said the paper would have the only reporter in the field reporting directly from the site of the spill on what would be the most covered story of the past decade, and that we'd have our own pictures, our own video—what no one else has—she caved in and approved the travel voucher. If I can find a ship, if it's safe, if I don't break the bank, and if I can get aboard before it sails for the Arctic."

"That's a lot of *ifs*."

"Yeah, but that's Frances. Covering all her bases." Jon's voice sobered. "Now I have to find the right connections to get on that ship."

"Well, buddy, I think I know just the person who can help out with that," Sean said wryly. "Me."

New York City

He'd been a bit surprised at the street-acting gig, even felt foolish parading around outside a building in Manhattan in the middle of a bunch of protesting nutbags.

But no matter. He had his instructions, and they seemed simple enough: "Walk around for a couple of hours in the full polar bear suit. Don't let on who you are or that you're an actor. Then drop the backpack off at the side of the building exactly where I've instructed." That was what the slick lawyer type had said.

Easy as eating a slice of cherry pie. It was something he could easily do even through the haze and a foggy brain. There was no heavy lifting involved. He knew how to follow instructions and hit his marks.

12

It was late morning when Will walked by American Frontier's New York headquarters after a round of meetings at Worthington Shares. He wanted to see what was going on with his own eyes. Like Occupy Wall Street, which had mobilized overnight and taken over a city block and a public park in the shadow of the World Trade Center site, protesters of the oil leak had mobilized within 24 hours.

It had started with pickets and signs and street comedy, Drew reported, but quickly grew into organized scenes and impromptu speeches. Now dozens of protesters camped outside on the streets. American Frontier had ordered additional security, and the New York Police Department had doubled its patrols nearby.

Will scanned the crowd and shook his head. It was natural. Whenever television cameras mobilized—and plenty of cameras regularly camped outside the American Frontier offices already—those groups whose only hope was getting their message of doom out to the greater public would find a way to primp before those very same cameras.

His eyes landed on a guy in a polar bear suit, wearing a bulky backpack. He didn't seem all that out of place, especially for a protest against an oil spill in the Arctic Circle. *Just one of the usual crazies*, Will thought, watching the guy trying to drink a Coke through the snout of his furry suit.

Like other major metropolitan cities, New York had its share of vagabonds, mentally ill transients, and the homeless. And they showed up in droves to mix in with the protesters at American Frontier. That made it tough for the NYPD to keep track of who was there legitimately to protest and who was just hanging out. And then, of course, add the tourists. Part of the intrigue around Occupy Wall Street was that it became a tourist attraction. During the movement's heyday, hundreds of tourists milled around the city block that included tents and vans and makeshift shelters, often outnumbering the actual Occupy protesters themselves.

So it was logical that much of the same kind of thing would spring up outside the American Frontier headquarters, albeit on a smaller scale. Whenever there was an event—something that galvanized the public's brief attention span—people would rush in to try to take the stage right alongside it.

Will's gaze caught the guy in the polar bear suit again. He paused under a windowsill up against the side of the American Frontier building, a good 100 feet or so away from the crowd, and set his backpack down. Then, after hanging out there for a while, the guy walked off and disappeared into the crowd, forgetting his backpack.

Yup, crazy, Will thought. Some homeless guy would doubtless discover the backpack later that day and appropriate what might be inside.

At that instant, his cell phone vibrated.

So how are the polar bears and Sean? his buddy Paul texted.

One's still in the Arctic. The other's on his way home. And some wacko guy is dressed in a polar bear suit in front of the AF building.

There was a pause, then: *Too much hard work makes you see things. Take a break, man. Pretend we're catching striped bass in Chesapeake Bay. Remember that 50 pounder?*

Will remembered, all right, and laughed. Paul still loved to rub it in that he'd caught the big one on that trip.

Glancing up at the bright sun that managed to filter through the congestion of the city's tall buildings, Will decided to do something that was rare for him. He spontaneously picked up lunch at a local deli and headed to Central Park by himself. There, among the squealing of toddlers playing in water and scooping sand and the laughter of school-age boys trying to outdo each other on the climbing net, he ate his sandwich and drank his bottled water, enjoying the sun's warmth on his face. Then he settled back against the bench and closed his eyes for a minute.

The respite wasn't nearly as good as a fishing trip with Paul to some remote location, but for now, it would have to do.

He chuckled. Funny how so many of his best memories in life had to do with fishing. Like his trips with Paul and the summers in Chautauqua Institution with his siblings, his mom, and occasionally his dad.

And then there had been the very special summer in Chautauqua, before his senior year at Harvard, when Laura had entered his life. He'd been lying on the grass, fishing pole beside him. His arm was flung over his face to block the sun, and he was breathing deeply of the scents of water and earth, trying to rid himself of the last stressful weeks of finals at Harvard. It was his way of both escaping the noise of the cottage and gaining some think time that was hard to get with his younger, very social sister tugging on his arm, always wanting him to take her places.

He'd complete his classes at Harvard within a year. So what was next? The family business, of course . . . but what else?

So he'd gone to Chautauqua to relax. The place appealed to him, had always appealed to him. He liked its history dating back to the 1800s, its cobblestone streets, its simplicity and beauty. As he lay there, dreaming and fretting about his future, he sensed a shadow, as if someone had entered his space and was blocking the sun.

Slowly he moved his arm and opened his eyes. There, haloed by the sunlight so her face appeared angelic, was the most beautiful, hazel-eyed, dark-haired young woman he'd ever seen.

He sat up so swiftly the blood rushed to his head, and he wavered for a moment.

"Whoa there, pardner," she said, grabbing his arm. "Didn't mean to scare you."

He opened his mouth, then shut it. Tingles shot up his arm to his head, making him dizzier. He couldn't believe he, William Jennings Worthington VI, was actually tongue-tied.

"You won't catch any fish that way," she continued, gesturing toward his fishing pole. Her laugh rang melodiously in the air. "Need some help?"

And that was his introduction to Laura, who was staying with some friends at Chautauqua Institution for the summer.

After they'd caught a few fish, which Laura insisted go back in to live longer, fuller fish lives, he gathered his courage and asked her if she was interested in going to an art show with him later that day.

He remembered even now the pounding of his heart as he awaited her response, like he was some teenager who didn't know how to ask a girl out on a date. Then again, he'd never really had to worry. Will's money and looks had always attracted girls in prep school and at Harvard, and they flocked around him. But none had ever interested him. Paul had said once, "Yeah, cotton-candy girls. All sweet on the outside but nothing on the inside." He and Will had laughed, because it was so true.

He had always known he wanted someone like his mom, who treated family as her top priority. But he also wanted someone who could stand on her own two feet and think for herself—no offense to his mom or her generation, who tended to allow males to do all the thinking. Someone who was passionate about making the world a better place. Hopefully his wife-to-be could even cook a little too. It was a tall order, and Will still hadn't found anyone even close by that summer.

Then Laura said yes to his art show offer. As they wandered the Chautauqua show together, he was amazed by the depth of her knowledge and the solidity of her opinions. They extended the art show to ice cream afterward, and then a walk along the cobblestone streets until it was so dark they couldn't see each other's faces.

After that, he'd escorted her to her friend's house.

That was only the beginning. The rest of the summer they attended concerts and many intriguing lectures, and yes, fished together.

Their romance bloomed—all within the beautiful setting of a historic lakeside village.

Before they left Chautauqua that summer, Will had no doubt Laura was the woman for him—or that she would wait for him to finish Harvard.

The day he graduated from Harvard, he asked her to marry him.

At the end of that summer, they said their vows in a lovely outdoor ceremony, on the banks of the Chautauqua Lake, where they'd first met . . .

Will sighed and sat up. He checked his watch. Lunch was over. Time to stop dreaming and get back to work.

He texted Paul: *Took a break. Happy?*

Do it once a day, his buddy prompted. *All work and no play makes Will a dull boy. How's polar bear suit doing?*

Maybe Will would do another quick run by the American Frontier building to check things out before his next meetings at Worthington Shares.

The bomb went off at 1:00 p.m.

Windows shattered with loud pops, falling into thousands of crystal shards to litter the street.

One side of the American Frontier building caved in.

Debris sprayed in multiple blasts, like gunshots.

People screamed and fled in mass panic, leaving their protest signs and possessions behind.

Smoke billowed in a huge cloud, enveloping the people on the street.

Terror reigned.

13

"Seriously? They bombed the American Frontier HQ? Was Will in the building?" Sean hadn't heard from his brother yet, who had promised to call him back after lunch, so he was worried and had phoned Drew.

"Will called right after the blast, since I knew he was going by AF. He says NYPD thinks it was a backpack, left up against the side of the building," Drew said.

"Like Boston?"

"Yes, like Boston."

"The same sort of bomb?"

"No one is saying, not yet at least. The blast wasn't nearly as big, though. I've heard a few reports that it was maybe a couple of sticks of dynamite, triggered remotely."

Sean couldn't believe it. Like everyone else, he saw the news as it came across multiple television networks in JFK. He too was riveted by the aftermath of the explosion. Just as the Boston Marathon bombings had dominated worldwide news coverage for days afterward, this bombing would likely dominate news coverage for the foreseeable future.

He frowned. It seemed a bit too convenient. He wasn't one to go in for conspiracy theories, especially given that the Worthington family had been the focus of more than one of those rumors of conspiracies over the years when people raged about the Bilderbergers or the Trilateral Commission. But this particular bombing sure did come at an opportune time for American Frontier, he mused. And right when the company needed the diversion.

Their CEO, Eric Sandstrom, had literally walked out of his meeting with the president's chief of staff at the White House to a bank of cameras established just outside the press office briefing room and had commented live on the act of domestic terrorism.

Yup, too convenient, Sean told himself again.

As his dad used to say when they were fishing, "If something stinks like a dead fish, it probably is one."

So instead of a steady stream of highly negative coverage of the Arctic spill, the coverage had swiftly turned to run-of-the-mill but still over-the-top disaster coverage that the American press had become skilled at over the years. CNN had already branded the domestic terrorism act as that of the "Polar Bear Bomber" and had created an associated graphic to go along with their round-the-clock coverage that showed what looked like a white grizzly wearing some sort of military head gear.

"And Will's okay?" Sean asked again.

"He's fine," Drew assured Sean. "He wasn't anywhere near the building when the blast occurred."

"Good. That's a relief."

Sean would never tell his brother, but he'd always worshiped the ground Will walked on, even though he knew he'd never measure up. But he'd purposefully chosen to go another direction. There was no competing with Will, ever. Sean had stopped trying long ago. Still, he would never want to step into his brother's place in the family, especially now. He saw all the pressure Will was continually under, all the expectations heaped on him. That was why Sean liked to live on the fringes of his family—to come in and touch base when he was needed but otherwise to handle life and business on his own.

But that didn't mean he didn't care.

"And you? Can I assume you're about to jump into the fight publicly, as only you can?" Drew pressed.

Sean hated being pinned down by anybody. He liked keeping his feelings and his thoughts to himself. But Drew was the one person who knew how to wrestle answers out of Sean and didn't give up until he got them.

Sean chuckled and tried his typical ploy. "I can't keep anything from you, can I?" He'd read once that the surest way to avoid answering a question you didn't want to answer was to offer up a question right back. It worked with most people.

It didn't work with Drew. "You didn't answer my question."

Sean paused. "I didn't, did I? All right, yeah, I've decided to get in further on the game. I've arranged for a lease."

"A lease?"

"Yeah, one of the Russian ice-cutting ships. I've leased it for exploration purposes for the month. I'm heading out within the hour to meet up with the crew we just hired."

"Oil exploration? Like in the Arctic?" Drew's voice was suspicious.

"Sure, why not?" Sean said breezily. "It's international waters, after all, even though the entire ocean has been carved out for commercial purposes already. It's a Russian-flagged ship. Not like anyone can deny us entry to the waters."

Drew persisted. "So it's not your Green Justice pals?"

Sean had to give it to their family's advisor. He didn't miss a trick. "Well, not exactly, but yes, a couple of the Green Justice folks will be on board."

"Anyone else?"

"Uh, well, dunno, maybe a few others." Sean hedged. "A *New York Times* reporter is joining us."

He heard Drew's sharp intake of breath. "Do I have to say it?"

"What, to be careful? Have I ever *not* been careful?" Sean bristled. "I know what's at stake, for our family, for my brother—"

"Your sister's involved too. So be careful what you say around that reporter. There's an awful lot at stake right now for Worthington Shares. Will is considering joining the shareholder lawsuit against the company."

"And you're worried about me, what I might say to some *Times* reporter?"

"I'm only saying be careful," Drew said gently. "That's all."

"No worries," Sean tossed back. "I'll be careful. But I'm trying to evaluate the situation from all sides, and if I'm on-site, I can help Worthington Shares all the way around with firsthand information. Don't you think I can help bring something to the table that way when needed?"

"Sean the peacemaker." Drew laughed.

"Yeah, that's me."

"Except when you're causing trouble." A small sigh escaped.

Dr. Kevin Leman and Jeff Nesbit

"Never. I simply like coloring outside the lines every so often. It's worked before."

"Promise you'll watch what you say and do? And update us?"

"Always, and often," Sean vowed.

But he didn't promise how much he would tell and exactly when.

14

NEW YORK CITY

"I'm in deep here, bro," Sarah told Will. He could hear the stress in her voice. "And I can't help but think that explosion was a little too convenient."

Will wondered the same thing himself. Miraculously, not a single person had been killed by the explosion. Unlike the Boston Marathon bombings, which had killed three people and injured many others, this explosion only damaged the American Frontier building. Even there, the damage was minimal, since the bomb had gone off next to an unoccupied storage room. The only people injured were those on the street who had stepped on the glass from the broken windows or suffered twisted ankles or bruises after being shoved to the ground when the crowd started running.

"And to have a CNN field producer right there on the spot, hanging out with a camera when it happened? Talk about timing for a rookie fresh out of Columbia University's Journalism School. Catherine Englewood's career has definitely launched. Within 30 minutes of the explosion, her footage was used by everyone in the media—even Fox News, CNN's rival." Sarah blew out a breath.

"So you think she might be a plant, a setup?" he asked.

"No. My sources tell me she was only there interviewing as many of the protesters and hangers-on as she could. Doubt she thought her footage would ever be used. But I have to hand it to her—she's tenacious. She kept right on rolling the camera and asking questions."

"So she just happened to get those shots of the guy in the polar bear suit, the same one I told you I saw." His mind flashed back to the crowd at the American Frontier headquarters and zeroed in until he saw the guy in the polar bear suit with perfect clarity. It was a gift Will had. Still, there was something not right in the picture. Something out of place. But he couldn't put his finger on it . . . yet.

"Yeah. And when she went back through all her shots, she found some with the polar bear suit guy in the background. She even had video of him carrying a backpack. The same backpack that has now been identified by bomb disposal experts as what housed the bomb. This whole thing now makes my job even tougher."

He understood. Within a few hours, the entire world knew about the crazy ecoterrorist in the polar bear suit who had bombed the American Frontier headquarters to protest the oil spill in the Arctic. Public sentiment shifted a bit in sympathy for the poor, beleaguered oil company. No longer was AF the 100 percent bad guy in the media. That meant the work Sarah was doing had ramped up. The explosion and shift of public opinion also muddied the waters for Will's own moves to take control of the board at American Frontier.

After he'd dropped the backpack off, he'd wandered away from the building as the man had explained and waited until he was in an alley to strip out of the polar bear suit. He'd bundled it up into a brown plastic garbage bag and then walked around carrying it for the rest of the day.

He'd checked the disposable cell phone with preloaded minutes they'd given him nearly every five minutes since the incident at the American Frontier building. He wasn't sure whether he'd get his instructions via text or a phone call. Either way, he hoped the instructions would come soon.

That evening he heard about the bombing at the American Frontier headquarters. It was hard to miss—the story was blaring almost everywhere anyone looked. When the news started to report that maybe some guy in a polar bear suit had been responsible, he panicked. He was pretty sure they were talking about him. He needed to get rid of that suit.

15

Elizabeth kept Sean informed via email and text as he was lining up his and Jon's ride through Green Justice. Her news wasn't good.

She had linked in by satellite to the one and only super-computer ever built to study the entire Earth system. It had been built in Cheyenne, Wyoming, and connected by a massive Google dark fiber network to the National Center for Atmospheric Research in Boulder, Colorado. She and her father and the rest of the scientific team had huddled for hours aboard the USS *Cantor* to link up all the hardware, then sync it all through the laptop connected to the wireless network on board the ship, getting every piece of data moving in the right direction.

So far the Navy hasn't cut off any of our ongoing research. We're still permitted to gather streams of data from the buoys we placed and then feed it back to the supercomputer. The data's pure gold.

No one else has had this kind of steady stream of data from the Arctic, ever.

For decades, research teams had to guess at what might be transpiring in the Arctic region. Sure, they'd tagged a few polar bears and beluga whales to study land and sea migration patterns. NASA satellites could take pictures from space, and others could extrapolate from there. But hard data from sensors in strategic places in and around the Arctic waters, ice, and land masses? Not available, until now. That had been the entire purpose of the research mission—one Elizabeth said her father had talked about for years.

What they'd not anticipated, of course, was the bizarre turn the mission had taken since the oil leak occurred. Besides Elizabeth, her father, and the tight research team, Sean and Jon were the only ones who knew the team now had access to both underwater images from the infrared camera and linked data about where the oil was traveling in the Arctic, based on flow rates and currents.

We think the highly unusual and novel subsea platform that American Frontier built and anchored broke free at the floor—not somewhere along the pipe.

Your Green Justice buddies are going to have a fit. The few whales not tainted by the spill have fled the area. The only ones left are the dead and dying.

Sean knew her well enough to realize how angry that made her. Elizabeth hated seeing animals die because of mistakes humans made or accidents that could have been avoided if the research beforehand had been thorough. But she was also enough of a scientist to realize that some things just happened, and even those who were careful couldn't have guessed when or how the resulting events would take place.

> After the supercomputer linked all the available worldwide ocean circulation patterns together into one software coding stream, we plugged in data from the linked buoy system so we could estimate where the spilled oil might go as it migrates.

> Before this is over, the oil will reach many shores. How bad it gets will be based on the flow rate, how long it takes AF to diagnose the problem, and how long it might take to seal the break. All we can do is guess on those fronts.

The Arctic wasn't self-contained, Sean knew. It fed ocean systems in several different, separate directions. The Arctic Ocean was literally at the top of the world, and what happened there spread out to the rest of the planet. At that moment, Sean realized he had to loop in his brother on the data. To manage the mess at American Frontier if he became CEO, Will would need every bit of front-end information he could get, even if he couldn't reveal his sources or it might end what Sean had in motion next.

Though Will's controlling nature often rubbed Sean the wrong way, he wasn't about to let anyone in his family get caught in the crossfire. Not if he could help it.

Speaking of which, he'd better call Sarah too.

It had been 12 hours and still no call or text. He kept checking. Every minute he kept the polar bear suit with him here in the basement of the Baptist church on Madison Avenue that he'd crashed in was another minute that he anticipated the police would arrest him. He didn't dare go back to his crummy, one-room flat in Brooklyn. They'd find him there.

He was glad they were going to pay him in cash for the street-acting gig. He could at least take that with him if he had to run. But the waiting! It was killing him.

16

Will could sense a storm approaching—and an enormous opportunity as well, if it was managed properly. And now Drew had done something he'd never done before in all the time he'd served the Worthington family. As soon as Sean's plane had landed at JFK, Drew had maneuvered each of the three siblings into a family dinner before the three of them went their separate ways back into the firestorm of the Arctic situation.

To anyone who didn't know the Worthington family, a dinner with three siblings might seem like an easy thing to accomplish. Just set a date and people show up.

But each of the Worthington siblings had more scheduled in a day than most people would schedule in a month. And because of their roles, few of the scheduled meetings could be bumped.

Will kissed Laura before he headed out the door. "Something's up. You know I have a sixth sense about these things. Just sorry you and the kids won't be there."

She looked him straight in the eyes. "We're happy to be home and landed for a while. I'd already promised the kids Chinese takeout and a movie night, and I can't go back on my word now, even as much as the kids love Drew's family. Besides, I get the feeling it needs to be only you, Sean, and Sarah this time." She grinned. "Maybe I've got a sixth sense of my own."

"Or maybe," he teased back, "Jean called you separately and let you in on the news."

She gave him a little push out the door. "Well, you never know . . ."

So there is an ulterior motive, and she knows what it is. He wasn't surprised. Laura and Jean, Drew's wife, were tight. Both strong-minded women, they were also moms with kids still in the home, and they shared a die-hard view of family first, just like Will's mother. But how that played out looked different in each home. Laura had decided to stay home with the kids until Davy was at least in high school. Jean had continued working full-time. A few years younger than Drew, she was a force of nature in her own right and had carved out a career for herself, first on the trading floor of the New York Stock Exchange and now in one of the most prominent brokerages on Wall Street.

The dinner invitation had been spontaneous, even last-minute—completely unlike the meticulous Drew—and Will wondered how Jean was dealing with that. Usually family dinners were held at Will's posh place overlooking Central Park or the Worthington summer home in Chautauqua. If he'd told Laura that he'd invited his siblings over for dinner at the last minute, she would be a trooper, plunging in, getting the job done, and being a gracious host to their guests. But he'd hear about it later. Of that he was sure.

Maybe Drew had taken into account the fact that Laura had been gone for two months and just returned, so he didn't want to dump the dinner on her. Or perhaps their wise financial advisor was trying to get them all on neutral ground. But why?

A picture of Jean filtered in, and he grinned. Jean was probably ready to string Drew up right about now for inviting the Worthingtons to their place in the village. But she, like Laura, was a trooper and was used to the Worthington craziness.

He knew they'd have a great dinner, even if she ordered food from FreshDirect and had it delivered.

One thing he could guarantee. It would be served on her best china.

━━━ /// ━━━

"Seriously? Tonight?" Sean had sputtered when Drew invited—no, more like commanded—him to come to the family dinner. "You know I'm just getting home now, and I'm in the midst of securing the ship. I have to pack up to—"

"Even more reason to be there," Drew said in a mysterious tone.

Finally, after a debate Sean knew he wouldn't win, he agreed. Only because it was Drew. He understood Sean more than any other person—even his mother. If he could count on any person to hold a confidence, it would be Drew. Squashed between two older sisters and a younger brother in a home where both of his parents worked, Drew had been the frequent mediator, especially between his warring sisters. Sean had teased him that it was good preparation for launching his career with the strong-minded Worthingtons.

Sean understood what being stuck in the middle felt like, and it wasn't easy. The mantle of leadership in the Worthingtons had been handed to Will seemingly without a second thought. And their social butterfly sister had been financially irresponsible for years, with no repercussions. Neither were positions Sean was allowed to have. His was best summarized by the family photo album, which had hundreds of baby pictures of Will but a whole lot less of Sean, and he was almost always paired with his brother. When baby Sarah, the only girl, came along, pictures abounded. Still there were hardly any of Sean, except when he was squeezed in between his brother and sister.

It wasn't easy being a middle kid in a family, especially one like the Worthingtons. Everyone across the nation knew about the Worthingtons and made lots of assumptions about them. There were plenty of whispers about their comings and goings in the press and constant rumors in the tabloids. Will tortured himself by reading all the articles. More than once, Sean had overheard Sarah telling Will to lighten up. "Why are you even trying to set the record straight? It won't do any good. It'll only fuel the gossip fires more."

Sean publicly ignored the hoopla. He stayed unruffled most of the time until the pressure built up too much. Then he'd have a moment like he did when he tossed that whole stack of tabloids in the trash. Usually, though, he was good at acting like what the media said didn't touch him. But underneath it all, what they said hurt—especially when they compared the two brothers.

He'd already done that himself for years and always came up lacking.

Now Sean started kicking himself. Drew knew Sean flew

by the seat of his pants. Why didn't he put his friend on hold for a minute, make a quick phone call, and arrange a dinner date? Then he'd have had a good excuse not to go.

But underneath all the arguing he did with himself, he realized one fundamental truth: because Drew had asked, Sean would go.

Sarah was on the fly between meetings when Drew called. "Sure, I'll come. Count on it."

She'd have to talk her way faster through the meeting scheduled right before the dinner, but that shouldn't be a problem. *Spontaneous is my middle name*, she told herself and laughed.

Still, it was strange. Drew had sounded far more solemn than usual.

But she couldn't ponder that thought anymore now. Her next meeting was in less than a minute.

When the text did finally arrive, he knew right where the bar was. He'd been there often when he crashed at the Madison Avenue church. The bar was rather nice, right around the corner near 20th and Madison. Plenty of high rollers stopped there after work.

When he got there, he took a seat at the bar, as the text had explained. At one point, the bartender leaned over and asked if he wouldn't mind moving down a few seats to make room for a new group of customers. He moved without a word and took the seat the bartender indicated, next to some guy who was nursing a drink and had been there a while.

Sean still hated the thought of the family dinner. They were never his favorite affairs. But after finally agreeing to go, Sean had said he had to take care of a business commitment first and would be late.

An executive from one of the start-up companies Sean had invested in on behalf of Worthington Shares had had his secretary call. She said her boss had some important questions and wanted Sean to meet him in a bar near 20th and Madison.

So Sean went in, sat at the bar, and nursed a drink for nearly an hour. The guy never showed. But while Sean waited, he chatted up all the usual suspects who kill time at local establishments after work in the city. One guy, sitting on the stool next to him, was talkative but seemed a bit off his meds, or maybe slightly drunk.

At least it had been a pleasant wait.

Then Sean got a second call from the secretary. The executive wouldn't be able to make it after all.

Disgusted, Sean got up and made his way out of the bar to hightail it over to Drew's.

He knew he'd catch an earful about his late arrival. He always did.

17

That night Will showed up first—prompt as always.

The Simons place was a nice venue for such a get-together with the Worthingtons. Years ago, at Will's insistence, Drew had purchased two condos side by side and combined them into one big place. It had an enormous window that extended from the kitchen to the living room and overlooked the village. At night, when the city was lit up, the view was magnificent.

"Didn't I just see you?" he joked to Drew and then headed straight into the kitchen. He'd been to their place on so many occasions that he knew his way around. He reached into the closet, took out an apron, and put it on.

"Don't even think about it," Jean said without looking up. "I have this well in hand." Then she chuckled. "And FreshDirect helped a lot too."

"I'm sure you do," Will offered, "but I'm still here to help." He took a knife, pulled a cutting board over, and grabbed a handful of the fresh vegetables that hadn't been diced yet.

Leave it to Jean to add more to a ready-made salad, he mused. But he started in without saying another word.

This time Jean didn't object. She simply said, "Sounds like Laura and the kids have a fun evening planned. Pajamas and downtime in front of a movie. Chinese food to boot. Even FreshDirect can't compete with that." She swept a hand toward the delivered food.

He laughed. "Agreed—at least in our kids' eyes. But yes, she's glad to be home. By the way, where are your two?"

"Figured that since your kids couldn't come, I'd send the girls out for a fun dinner and an outing with Robyn so they wouldn't have to listen to us adults talk all night. They already left."

The Simons daughters loved their live-in nanny, Robyn, who had been with them since Emily, now 15, was a baby. Three years later Eliza had come along—an added blessing Drew and Jean hadn't expected since they'd started their parenting journey at a later-than-usual age.

"Our kids are starting to think of their time in Malawi as a permanent thing since we've been doing it for so many years," Will said. "Now they assume they're going there for a couple of months after school lets out."

Jean nodded. "That's a good thing. Gets them out of their comfort zone. Heaven knows we could all use that."

"Especially for our family," Will added. "We've tried almost everything we can think of to not allow them to just be tagged as Worthingtons. It's not easy. Everyone assumes things about them because of their last name, the wealth, the privilege, all that comes with it. Everywhere they go, whatever they do, they can't escape the glare of the spotlight and the pressure that comes with being a Worthington." He sighed. "You always feel the pressure—to carry everything out exactly right, to never make a mistake, to do everything that's expected of you."

Jean glanced up. At 51, she was a looker. Five feet seven, with long brown hair and a trim physique that looked like she hadn't borne children, she was a prize. Drew had once admitted he wasn't sure why an ordinary-looking guy like him had gotten a beauty-and-brains combo like Jean. But even more important, she loved him, put up with him, and considered him "brilliant" from time to time. They were a good match.

Just like Laura and me, Will thought.

Jean met his eyes with a startlingly sky-blue gaze that pierced through his soul. "Hmmm. Sounds like someone else has thought a great deal about this." The question was unspoken.

Will smiled. He could always count on her to shoot things to him straight, with no waffling. He liked that. He knew where he stood with Jean. She and her husband were not only advisors to the family but their oldest, closest friends. It wasn't easy to let people inside the Worthingtons' circle, but it was easy with Jean and with Drew. Will trusted them implicitly.

"I guess," he replied. "A little."

Mercifully, there was a second knock at the door before the straightforward Jean could continue the conversation. Will wasn't certain he would have had a response, for he was grappling with it himself.

Sarah bounced into the kitchen a moment later, still dressed in her Saks Fifth Avenue business suit but carrying her pumps and Louis Vuitton briefcase. She dumped them unceremoniously on the kitchen floor, then advanced to give Jean a quick hug. "So, may I help?" she asked.

"Sure, why not?" Jean laughed. "Like brother, like sister. Your mama sure did train you well. No one can say you Worthingtons aren't helpful, so you might as well get to work. We can put everything either in the oven to warm up or in the fridge to chill and sit a bit before dinner."

"Sean will be here?" Sarah raised a dubious brow.

"He'll be a bit late, but yes, he'll be here." Drew stepped into the kitchen.

"And this was your idea—to get us together?" Sarah asked Drew before shooting a glance at Will.

Will chuckled to himself. His little sister had turned into a great attorney. She was certainly persistent, and she did have a point. Will was normally the one who pulled strings to get all the siblings together.

"Yes, it was," Drew stated. "I thought it made sense. I've talked to all of you separately, and it became obvious that we all needed to talk together."

"Compare notes?" Will asked.

Drew rubbed his chin thoughtfully. "Yes, that."

"Well, good." Sarah crossed her arms and tapped her foot. "I could use some advice right about now. There are more than a few things about this American Frontier situation that aren't making sense to me."

18

It was typical of his brother, Will thought. Arrive late and try to spend as little time as possible at a family dinner. Will loved his brother, but sometimes he didn't get Sean at all.

Sean arrived right after they'd put the food into the oven. He apologized for not being there earlier to help out but said it hadn't been easy to change his plans at the last minute. He didn't offer any other explanation. By now, Will and Sarah were used to it, so they merely nodded and didn't ask for details. But Drew lifted a quizzical brow.

Sean simply shook his head and headed to the living room with the others.

"So, Drew, this was your idea," Will said when they'd settled in. "What's the urgency? Why are we here?" He didn't miss the knowing smirk exchanged between Sean and Sarah as he moved comfortably into his role of being in charge. By now he was used to it. But someone had to get the discussion going.

"I have a pretty good idea what each of you is doing related to the American Frontier situation," Drew began, "and I think we can all agree it's going to get a whole lot worse before it gets better. Beyond my usual advice that I'd provide to Worthington Shares about what its stake in AF means, there is also what all of this means to each of you individually. I think you know I have your best interests at heart—"

Sean jumped in. "Drew, you can rest easy. We all know where your heart is. So just tell us. What's weighing on your mind?"

"Yes, Drew, spill it," Sarah chimed in. "We've seen numerous crises roll through the door. Why is this one any different? Because it's AF? Because it affects Worthington Shares? Because it's the kind of crisis that can cause untold financial, political, and environmental damage?"

Drew looked toward his wife. Jean nodded almost imperceptibly.

He took a deep breath and plunged in. "I believe this very situation will define each of you in your own way and shape your destinies. This isn't simply another corporate event, or environmental disaster, or something that can impact Worthington Shares' bottom line. It doesn't matter whether we sell off the shares in AF or hold them and fight for control of the company. It doesn't matter how this all plays out in Washington and whether it helps define or shape the Republican Party that has done the bidding of industrial giants like AF for a long time. It doesn't matter how all of this might play out in some courtroom as the shareholders sue the leadership for decisions they and the board made to allow the company to drill in the Arctic, putting AF at grave risk. No, that isn't what I believe matters. Those are merely things we all work on daily in our professional lives.

"But this time, it's clear to me that what happens next will change each of your life paths. It will define each of you personally. That's what I wanted to make sure we all understood before each of us goes about our business. You all know me well enough to realize I have both the family's and the company's best interests at heart. So when I say that the fate of American Frontier—and Worthington Shares' involvement with it—is just business in the end and not something we should really worry about all that much, you know what I mean by that. I will fight with every ounce of my being to protect the Worthington business. But what I most care about is how this will affect you—each of you."

Again Drew peeked at his wife. Jean gave another encouraging nod.

He gazed directly at Will. "Until the events today, I would have predicted that there was a clear path forward for you. You were almost certainly going to be asked to take over American Frontier, either as its CEO or possibly as its board chairman. In another time, for other reasons, I'd have supported that. But right now I'm not so sure that's a good idea for you. Events will almost certainly play out in such a manner that anyone associated with the decisions AF made to build platforms in the Arctic will, at a minimum, be on the wrong side of history. No one will look kindly on the people responsible for those decisions, which would be hugely unfortunate for you, considering that you opposed the decisions at the board level to drill in the Arctic."

Will opened his mouth, but Drew put up a hand. "Please wait. I need to say this."

He swiveled toward Sean. "Things are a bit murkier for you. But the risks to you may be even greater than they are for your brother. You may not be on the AF board or under consideration as the company's leader. But knowing you as I do, I can only imagine you are going to join this fight in the way that suits you best—as someone who sees all the angles, plays them all, and brings in a vast network of people and resources to highlight what's happening in the Arctic.

"I'm quite certain that the Center for Ecological Biodiversity will sue AF as they've sued every other oil company over spills. And because you're well known as a fierce environmentalist, and you're about to head to the Arctic on a Green Justice ship that the entire world will ultimately know you paid for, the fight there will become your fight. Not Worthington Shares' fight, but your own personal fight. Should you lose that fight in the eyes of the public, there will be consequences to you, Sean. Never mind the consequences to the company.

"Make no mistake: AF will use everything at their disposal—every public relations ploy, every investor relations gimmick, every political favor owed or assumed, and every legal or regulatory maneuver they can possibly engage—to win this fight in the public, the boardroom, and the halls of power in Washington. If you, Sean, are perceived as a lone warrior on the front lines, tangling with the world's largest company in the midst of all that, there is a grave risk of being vastly misunderstood and mischaracterized by the press. There is no peace to be found here, only unavoidable conflict. Any attempts on your part to obtain some sort of a peace will be seen as naïve at best and misguided and personally damaging at worst."

Drew focused on Sarah next. "But the gravest risk, in my opinion, may rest with you, Sarah. If what we've heard is true—that questions about criminal negligence are about to surface and that you and your office will be prosecuting what could become the largest such case in years—you'll have to make an exceedingly difficult decision. Do you take on that case, one that could involve discussions and decisions made at the American Frontier board level by your brother? Do you take part in some sort of a challenge that drags in your own family? How do you separate yourself, the prosecutor, from the little sister and member of the Worthington family? The press will eat you alive if they suspect you might play or grant any favors to either your older brother or your family."

Drew straightened his shoulders. "I wanted to make absolutely certain each of you understands what's at stake. Please take this fight seriously. Ignore what it means for the family business. That will all play itself out, one way or another. AF's stock price and Worthington Shares' holdings will go up or down. But none of that matters nearly as much as how all of this may play out for each of you *personally*. Given that, I want to make some recommendations. I fully expect that you'll ignore them." A smile flickered across the older man's face. "But I still want to make them—if only so you have them in front of you as you deal with this.

"First, I'd encourage you, Will, to stop trying to become the CEO of American Frontier. Give it up. I know it seems like the pinnacle of your career, something that makes perfect sense to you and that you've worked toward for much of your adult life. Yes, there is great prestige and honor in leading the largest company in the world. But there may be a bigger prize at hand someday, one that no Worthington has ever aspired to, and you would be placing all of that in jeopardy if you take AF's considerable troubles on board in your own professional life. You'll need to make a decision about that, whether you're ready to or not.

"Second, Sean, I'd ask you to stand down from your effort to sail to the Arctic. I don't say this lightly, knowing your passion for that fight. But there's almost no way you can win this thing in the public's mind. So let others take on that fight. Give them the ship if you must, but don't take the fight on board yourself. There is no peace to be had here.

"And finally, Sarah, recuse yourself. I know you've always wanted to prove yourself, and you see this as a worthy fight where you can do that. But it's the wrong fight. And it can cost you dearly. For that reason, I'd urge you in the strongest possible terms to get out of it now, before it's too late to do so."

Drew sat back in his chair, and Will had to close his gaping mouth. It was by far the longest single speech he'd ever heard Drew give in his life. And it had been given only to an audience of four.

Sarah was the first to react. "I didn't think you had that in you, Drew. So how do you *really* feel?"

They all laughed. It broke the ice.

"Yeah, Drew," Sean chimed in, "I can't believe you delivered all that in one fell swoop. What's the deal? You been saving that up all these years?"

"It's how I feel," Drew stated matter-of-factly, "and *someone* needed to say it. Might as well be me."

"Well, thank you," Sean said. "I don't know what the future holds, but I'll certainly consider what you've said." He looked over at his brother and sister. "And I'll bet that Will and Sarah will take everything you've told us seriously as well."

"Absolutely," Sarah replied.

Only Will hadn't yet spoken. At last, when Sarah gave him the eagle eye, he said, "I've heard what you said, and I do indeed take it seriously. But what we each decide is something else entirely. I may not have a choice, whether I like it or not. I get the feeling that Sandstrom is going to fight for his job, which puts me in a vastly different place."

"And I don't have a choice either," Sarah reported. "The head of Justice's Criminal Division told me today that his job is on the line on this, and he wants me involved. I'd have to come up with an awfully good reason to walk away from the fight altogether. But I will consider the risks you've explained. I really will."

"And I will too," Sean added. "The last thing in the world I want is to be perceived as some Don Quixote type tilting at windmills—although I feel that way sometimes." He laughed. "That isn't my style or my wish. If I don't think I can make a genuine difference in the fight, I'll walk away. I promise."

Drew seemed to relax now that his thoughts were out in the open. "That's all I'm asking. Go into this with your eyes wide open. The business and financial side will take care of itself. What I care about is how this affects each of you."

Will stared at his brother and sister. "Trust me, Drew," he said slowly, "we're all wide awake right now. We get it."

He'd been at the bar for nearly 30 minutes and had managed to avoid anything other than a casual conversation with the guy on the stool next to him when he got a second text, directing him to another address. The money would be delivered to him once he'd dumped the suit, the text said. He still wanted the money, but he wanted to get rid of the suit as fast as he could.

He carried the brown plastic bag with him over his shoulder and walked the entire 30 blocks to the address displayed on the text message. When he got there, he heaved the bag into the dumpster out behind the dilapidated office building, looked around to make sure no one had followed him there, and then ambled away.

He hung around a bit, hoping that yet a third text would arrive, telling him where he could go to pick up his pay for his gig. When it didn't arrive, he left and walked aimlessly back in the direction from which he'd come. He wasn't sure where he'd wind up for the night. But at least he didn't have the suit with him any longer.

It never occurred to him to take even a peek at the names of any of the nonprofit environmental, social justice, and civil liberties organizations that all shared the office complex by the dumpster. It wasn't like he'd know even one of the names anyway.

19

Sarah had gone right back to the office after the family dinner, without even going to her penthouse suite first. She'd already felt the conflict between her job and her family in the American Frontier crisis, but now, after Drew's speech, the even greater dangers to her pressed in. Now that she, Will, and Sean had discussed all the angles of the American Frontier situation—though she was certain Sean, per usual, was holding back—she had calls to make.

The first was to Darcy Wiggins, a feisty Department of Homeland Security field agent. There was no doubt in Sarah's mind that her friend would still be in the office. If anyone had started to figure out what really happened during that explosion, it would be Darcy. After 15 years with the ATF and then as a DHS field agent for more than a decade, she had seen it all. And she was a bloodhound on the trail.

Enough to scare all the guys in her unit. Sarah smiled to herself. Nobody messed with Darcy. She got a job done and done right, even in the midst of a male mecca. A long time ago Darcy had learned that law enforcement, whether you liked it or not, was still a good ol' boys' club. It wasn't going to change anytime soon, she'd told Sarah. So Darcy went out of her way to outdo them when it suited her. For that reason, the club left her alone, to her work.

Sarah knew what that felt like. It was one of the things that had connected them as friends and fellow crusaders. She too wanted to prove herself—not only to the men in her office but to her father and to the world.

The domestic terrorism unit at the Department of Homeland Security had certainly been busy in recent years. People naturally assumed all would be well in the world when Osama bin Laden had finally been killed at the top of his private home complex in a city in Pakistan. Hardly. If anything, things had gotten a whole lot more complicated for the DHS domestic terrorism unit.

First, there had been the online magazine created by a couple of al-Qaeda zealots in Yemen who had taught lone jihadists how to make homemade bombs anywhere in the world with tools and materials that were commonly available. That was what had inspired the Boston Marathon bombers.

The truth was that the Homeland Security domestic terrorism unit had a vastly more complicated job than the international terrorism experts at Langley and the Office of the Director of National Intelligence. Most of the al-Qaeda leaders had been killed over the years. Iran's Shia leadership had, after considerable pressure from both Russia and China, chosen to stop sheltering al-Qaeda leaders within Iran. Once that decision had been made, ODNI and the CIA had found that their efforts to track and kill al-Qaeda leaders with unmanned drone strikes became vastly easier.

But inside the United States, the situation was murky. Unlike the international counterterrorism effort that had grudgingly forced several agencies to share resources, people, and information on a regular, real-time basis, the agencies with authority over acts of domestic terrorism had not learned to play nicely with each other in the sandbox.

Sarah had heard Darcy complain about it all nonstop. The federal ATF agency did its own thing. The FBI likewise pursued its own agenda, its own suspects, and its own leads. And to complicate matters, the INS had its hands full at the borders and generally chose not to cooperate with cross-border threats that might feed domestic terror operations and cells.

Homeland Security did its best to try to coordinate among ATF, INS, the FBI, and other assorted agencies that all had a hand in efforts to ferret out domestic terror plots. But some of the groups that they tracked were, well, "just this side of complete and utter crazy town," Darcy was known to say. And when you didn't know if someone was operating off an agenda or merely mentally unstable, it made it truly difficult to know when to intercede and when to only sit, listen, and wait.

Now that Darcy was assigned to the New York office, where everyone always seemed to think they could just show up in Times Square and set off bombs, her life was even more insane.

"It doesn't add up," Darcy told Sarah over the phone. "I've reviewed the security footage until I'm blue in the face."

"Any suspects—beyond the guy in the polar bear suit with his face covered?" Sarah asked.

"Not a one," Darcy declared.

"And the video from that CNN field producer?"

"Englewood? Yeah, I've looked at that, matched it up with all the other security and cell phone videos we have from the scene. And . . ."

"And?"

"Nothing. That's what's bugging me."

"But isn't that standard? Finding nothing, until something pops and you can start to connect a few dots?"

"That's the thing," Darcy fired back. "We have all the dots in front of us right now. We don't have to search that hard for them. We have this guy in the polar bear suit, with a protest clearly and publicly displayed. He hangs around the bombing scene long enough to guarantee almost everyone around remembers something about him and connects him with the environmental protest. We have the backpack he was carrying in a whole bunch of the videos that we can cross-match, and we can easily link it to the bomb that went off. It's the guy. We know it's the guy, and he did his level best to telegraph his motives for the bombing."

Sarah leaned back in her office chair. "So what's the problem? You have a suspect, a motive, and a weapon. Now you just need to find the guy and put him away for good before he does something like that again and actually kills people."

"See," Darcy said in her gravelly voice, "that's what's bothering me. I don't like someone else doing my job for me. I prefer it when I have to go find it—not when someone hands it all to me like it's my birthday, and I only have to rip off the wrapping paper."

Sarah laughed out loud. "So you're *complaining* that you haven't worked hard enough to put the pieces of this case together?"

"Not complaining." Darcy exhaled. "Just wondering. Unless the guy shoots off his mouth to someone about his role in it, or we get lucky and someone remembers seeing something about the guy getting ready to blow up the AF building and calls us, we aren't going to find this guy. He'll be a ghost. We don't have DNA matches on anything. We don't have a face to hunt for. We don't have a group to tie him to. Yet we have the guy, his motive, and the weapon in full view. We know who he is, sort of, and why he did what he did. We have plenty to go on at the center of the investigation . . . but nowhere really to go with it. Honestly, it seems like it was created for the TV cameras."

"Isn't that why all these nutjobs do what they do?" Sarah asked. "At the end of the day—whether they're shooting through the fence at the White House, trying to blow people up at the finish line of the Boston Marathon, or bringing down an oil company—isn't the thought lodged in their pea brains that this is their one and only chance at infamy? Isn't that what drives most of them?"

"Yeah, I guess." But Darcy didn't sound convinced. "But I've looked at a lot of footage of this guy in the polar bear suit. He was awfully deliberate about where he was walking. He made sure lots of folks in the crowd saw him wandering around, like he was some kinda street actor. But when it came time to plant the bomb, he didn't case the building. He knew right where to go, like he'd either cased it before or somebody told him. Left his bag and exited off the stage."

Sarah was thinking hard. "You're right. That is weird."

"And it also wasn't near any office in the building. That section of the building was on the other side of an old storage area that no one ever visited, except to drop off used furniture or boxes. It's why no one was hurt in the blast. That, and the fact the explosives in it were self-contained and the bag didn't have other stuff, like nails, in it to spray into the crowd. And the place where he planted that bag wasn't anywhere near the crowds or the protesters. It's like the guy wanted some attention but went out of his way to make certain no one got hurt."

"So we've got a terrorist with a conscience. Or maybe he's really just a do-gooder. Maybe he's precisely what he seems to be—an environmental activist who crossed the line, wanted to make a statement against the fossil fuel industry and this particular oil company, but didn't want to inflict any actual harm. Make the statement, get some TV coverage for the cause, and move on."

"You mean like Green Justice? Or one of those groups that likes to go after other groups physically and isn't shy about confrontation?"

As soon as Darcy mentioned Green Justice, Sarah's thoughts flicked back to Sean. He was in deep with Green Justice, and she had been certain he was hiding something at the family dinner. Could Sean know something about the explosion? Or did one of his Green Justice buddies?

"Hey, you still there?" Darcy barked.

"Yes, just thinking."

"Well, I still don't buy it. I'll certainly pursue that angle hard, as fast as I can. But things aren't matching up."

"You'll figure it out," Sarah said. "You always do."

20

Sean checked his messages as he left Drew and Jean's. Elizabeth's message from the USS *Cantor* was cryptic:

> The CEO of AF is here to inspect the drilling platform for himself. His helo landed right on the platform, and he was hustled below to their operational room.

"Wow," Sean muttered. It was highly unusual for the CEO of a major multinational company to go out in the field to oversee a disaster such as this firsthand, but Sandstrom wasn't an ordinary CEO, and likely he didn't want to suffer the same fate as the CEO of BP after the Deepwater Horizon incident. Sandstrom had been a wildcatter at the start of his career, and he was used to taking risks. He was known for hating to sit behind a desk when there was work to get done. Though Sean had no love for any of the oil magnate CEOs, he could identify with wanting to be actively in the field.

Will had told him it was widely known at AF that staff needed to be prepared for two types of meetings: the 15-minute senior staff meeting where everyone was required to stand and deliver reports to the CEO in a minute or less and then answer questions in rapid-fire fashion, and the "walking" meeting through the halls of AF's corporate headquarters. This second type of meeting was a Sandstrom favorite. It was rumored he'd sometimes put in 10 miles or more a day just walking and talking through a series of rolling meetings.

> He has a lawyer with him. Jason Carson. I get the feeling he's not to be trusted. Maybe it's just my bad experience with lawyers, or maybe there's something there. If you listened to him for a minute, you'd think this "leak" is a really small thing and easily fixed. But we both know that's far from the truth.

Carson, Sean thought with disgust. Will had spoken of the man rather heatedly on more than one occasion, saying he'd brownnosed his way into rising quickly through the corporate ranks at AF. Rumors flew that he did things Sandstrom didn't want anyone else to know about. It was Carson's specialty, and he was very good at it.

Will needs to know Carson and Sandstrom are on the Cantor. Sean's hand moved toward his cell phone, then halted.

He liked being a lone warrior, on the front lines. He couldn't and wouldn't stand down from sailing back to the Arctic, even though Drew had suggested it. Sean had never backed down from a fight and wasn't about to now. But after Drew's long-winded speech, Sean realized anew a critical truth: his siblings were also on the front lines, and this war that involved all three of them could best be fought together.

He speed-dialed his brother's number.

"Sandstrom and Carson are where?" Will barked at his brother.

"Hey, don't kill the messenger," Sean said.

"Sorry." Will paused to adapt his tone. "That means this is very, very bad. Worse than Sandstrom is letting on, worse than the media is portraying. We already know that this isn't just about a leak. It's about the whole subsea platform anchored on the ocean floor. Elizabeth has to be right. It must have fractured."

And the fact Jason Carson was there meant that Sandstrom had secret plans that weren't on the up-and-up. Carson, a too-smart-for-his-own-good Harvard-educated lawyer on detail to the CEO's office from regulatory and government affairs, had a firm grasp on the liabilities AF would likely be facing and also ran point on their relations with the White House. But he also was a climber with no conscience, and now Sandstrom's constant shadow.

It was one of the reasons Will was working so hard to take over the CEO position. American Frontier needed new leadership, honest leadership. Leadership that a Worthington had been groomed to provide.

What are they up to? Will wondered. *And is Drew right in saying there's even greater risk in taking over AF at present? That I should give it up?*

"Rumors are that Sandstrom was pretty ticked when the Navy cutter was still anchored next to his oil platform," Sean added. "Elizabeth said some of the USS *Cantor* crew were talking about how steamed he was. Carson evidently tried to smooth it over with Sandstrom by saying the Navy and science teams had been very helpful in providing real-time info as the events unfolded, but . . ."

"I'm sure that went over well."

Sean laughed. "Carson told him that the White House had asked the Navy cutter to remain in place, so they didn't have a choice. Sandstrom flung back a snippy remark about the Russians and Chinese showing up next. Guess that ended the conversation. Okay, gotta go." Sean abruptly hung up.

So, Will translated in his mind, *Sandstrom is worried about one or two things. Getting caught lying about the reason for the spill or the severity of it.*

The oil industry had believed that AF's engineering marvel would be the salvation for their efforts to drill in the harsh Arctic conditions. Stock in the company had soared as a result. The crew of ex-NASA engineers and technical experts who'd moved over to AF after the US space agency had downsized and laid them off took immense pride in their creation. They'd believed the platform was capable of withstanding anything in the Arctic and could handle the load on the ocean floor. But they'd been vastly wrong. If the subsea platform was fractured and hopelessly beyond repair, that changed the game. It might be days before the American Frontier crew was able to isolate the precise location of the leak and contain it. From what Elizabeth had said, they had no real idea how much oil was leaking, or even how they might ultimately contain it.

Worse, winter was coming on, and even the unmanned submersibles that had constructed the subsea platform and would be called on now to either repair it or deep-six it permanently might conceivably struggle to work properly for months going forward.

So what now? Will asked himself.

That was a very good question. And he wasn't certain there was an immediate answer.

Even as he wondered what Sandstrom and Carson's next steps would be, a warning went off in his mind. *It pays to stay out of Jason Carson's way, because he can be . . . direct.* Will knew good people whose careers and public image had been shattered by Sandstrom's young gun when they'd failed to get out of the line of fire.

Though Will had Worthington money behind him, he didn't want to be one of them.

21

"Enough," Will said that night after he watched the latest news report.

He flipped off the television and exhaled loudly in disgust. Settling against the back of the couch in his living room, he addressed Laura, who sat next to him. "So that's the way Sandstrom and the White House have decided to handle it. Control the truth. Dad was right. At AF's pinnacle moment, they could have chosen to do the right thing or the easy thing. They chose the easy thing."

"Did you expect anything else? And keep in mind Sean's going to sail right into the middle of that supposed 'truth'—complete with Green Justice and a *New York Times* reporter." She eyed Will. "Kind of makes what you've decided to do seem like a cakewalk."

Will laughed. Laura had a way of bringing a lighter perspective to any problem.

"So they decided to lie," he said bluntly. "The president's largest financial backer is Eric Sandstrom, so President Rich has to back him or else. Especially since the Department of the Interior's decision to allow drilling in the Arctic in the first place was driven by the White House."

Whether they admitted it or not, the spill was clearly the White House's problem. And just as the Obama administration had done during the BP oil spill, the Rich administration was doing everything it could to control the information pipeline to the media and, ultimately, the public. The difference this time was that AF and the Rich administration weren't adversaries. They were collaborating or, quite possibly, conspiring with each other to control information to the public. What made it easier was that the spill occurred in a remote location, where TV crews couldn't easily camp out and film what was happening. That meant the White House had the luxury of sifting through the information at hand and releasing as much or as little of what they had to the press. They'd announced that they would provide two briefings every day, at noon and then 4:00 p.m.—plenty of time for the broadcast networks to prepare something for the evening news.

Laura broke into his thoughts. "It was easy to tell that footage had been filtered through AF's media officers. Even down to the four main points. You couldn't miss them." She ticked them off on her fingers. "One—no ruptured pipe on the ocean floor, just some leaking. Not gushing. Which, of course, we know from Sean and Elizabeth is a big lie. Two—the platform has not been toppled." She grinned. "Nice touch when they said the CEO was himself directing operations from the platform. So it's safe and nothing scary is going on if American Frontier's CEO would risk his life there. Three—there's no evidence the oil is moving beyond the Arctic. Not technically a lie since it hasn't moved yet, but the Shapiros' work shows where the oil will end up. And finally, four—American Frontier is cooperating fully with the White House to resolve the problem as swiftly as possible. So everybody is in the same court. The message all around? 'Don't worry. Be happy.'"

"So everybody is going to think this will be quickly contained when that's far from the truth." Truth was important to Will, just as it was to his father. It didn't always make them popular with those who liked to twist things even a little, but Will had chosen to walk the straight and narrow. To take his compass and never stray from the path.

Laura snuggled up against his shoulder. "You know the truth will win out. And when it does, you'll be in a position to make even more of a difference than you can now. Sandstrom and his cronies will be revealed for who they are. If not now, then sooner or later."

He knew she was right, but that didn't make the waiting any easier.

22

When Will thought things couldn't get worse or any more convoluted, they did. The call he received from Drew was disturbing indeed. Especially because James Loughlin, the tough senior senator from New York, was involved. Loughlin was an old, traditional Republican who had somehow managed to balance both Tea Party and Wall Street types to stay in office for three six-year terms. Now, however, he faced a primary challenge from the Right, when he was most vulnerable and up for reelection in less than two years.

It was Will's business to know a lot about Loughlin. Especially since party leaders had talked to Will on and off about challenging the senator. But Will had never shown much interest.

Those in the know joked about how much Loughlin hated fund-raising calls, even when his campaign finance director made it as simple as he could. Rumor had it that the finance director printed up the names of wealthy donors on three-by-five cards, with their personal cell phone number, net wealth, what they did for a living, their history of giving to GOP candidates in the past, and fun, personal facts about them that Loughlin could throw out casually in conversation.

At the beginning of each day, Loughlin's senate administrative assistant handed him 10 cards to put in his suit pocket. All the senator had to do was dial the cell number in between hearings or Senate floor sessions, start a casual conversation, and then make the pitch for the person on the other end of the line to max out contributions, from both him and his wife, to Loughlin in both the primary and the primary election.

Loughlin's job, put simply, was to suck up to wealthy people and promise them access that he would rarely, if ever, grant to them on any issue of substance. He was warned frequently what he could say and not say on each of those calls, and he had to make the calls from a cell phone that was part of the campaign—not part of his regular Senate office.

But rumor also had it that Loughlin had been cutting corners for years. He'd developed a small cadre of folks who would deliver for him when he asked—a select group of CEOs who ran defense companies that relied on the Pentagon for their livelihood, banks that needed help with SEC regulations in Washington, tech and media companies that needed access to the FCC, and oil and gas companies that relied on subsidies and federal leasing permits to do business.

"On Loughlin's list is Eric Sandstrom," Drew reported, "who now has a tiger by the tail with the Arctic spill. So Loughlin decided to remind Sandstrom about how helpful he'd been in establishing a little line in the interior appropriations bill last year that had paved the way for exclusive drilling rights in the Arctic."

"And?" Will prodded.

Drew laughed. "Loughlin must have figured a big ask right now would be timely. Probably had to do with the fact he figured Sandstrom was down in public perception, so he needed somebody in Congress in his court. So he gave Sandstrom a call in the Arctic. Evidently they made some kind of deal, because Sandstrom promised him 25 million for his reelection campaign, and he'd help get another 25 million for Loughlin through the other oil and gas companies."

So, Will reasoned, *I wonder how much Sandstrom told Loughlin about what's really happening up there in the Arctic. Or if he sold him a bill of goods too.*

23

ICELAND

The family dinner had gone so late into the evening, Sean had decided to just charter a plane to Reykjavík that night. He'd flown all night and slept on the plane. As a rule, he didn't like to do that. He traveled a lot and almost always flew commercial, though first class, no matter the destination. He liked having lots of people around him when he was on an airplane. But he didn't want to burn any more time. They'd secured a ship, and it was ready to sail. Sean had picked up the tab for Kirk Baldwin and the Green Justice crew's airfare, part of a brand-new philanthropic research gift. They were already in Iceland, waiting for him to arrive and join the crew.

By the time Sean finally caught up with Kirk, the burly Green Justice veteran had already managed three cups of coffee. It was only nine o'clock in the morning.

"Dude, took you long enough. I'm about ready to jump out of my skin. And can I say, you look like you had cats screeching outside your window all night," Kirk said as Sean arrived at the coffee shop where they'd agreed to meet.

The rest of the crew was on the ship, choosing their berths and bringing their gear on board. But Kirk had insisted he wanted to see Sean first. Even after all these years of knowing Sean, Kirk was still cautious. He wanted to take Sean's temperature a bit and gauge his expectations for the journey ahead.

Sean scratched his grizzled chin. "You have no idea. I took a direct flight and slept on the plane."

"No worries," Kirk said. "Plenty of time for sleep once we're on the ship. We have a bit of a trip in front of us before we get there."

"Speaking of that, any chance we'll get anywhere close?"

Kirk shrugged. "Probably not real close, but who knows? They haven't had a chance to bring in all the heavy artillery yet. It *is* open water, after all, and in international waters. It's not like they can arrest us or keep us too far away from the spill. We're not pirates."

"Yeah, maybe. But they'll try."

"I would if I were them," Kirk agreed, rubbing his bald head. "And with the Navy involved and this being so critical to the White House, who knows what we're likely to run into?"

"Is the captain a hired gun?"

"He is, but we've used him before. Good guy. He'll take some calculated risks to get us as close as he can."

"Good. We'll need that sort of an attitude."

Sean had known Kirk for nearly 15 years. They'd been on campaigns several times, including a harrowing trip into a cove where dolphins were slaughtered. But Sean knew he was being evaluated, and he could tell what Kirk was thinking.

This guy isn't your typical wealthy plutocrat. He's a

campaigner at heart. He just happens to have several billion dollars in his bank account.

Still, Sean could tell Kirk was uneasy.

"So, Sean," he said tentatively, "you know me. I don't usually ask a lot of questions. I'm game for any grand adventure, especially when it comes to taking on the biggest oil and gas company in the world while they're trying to deal with an environmental disaster. We have a ship all gassed up and ready to go. I'm on board. But I gotta know. What gives?"

"What?" Sean frowned. "You're asking because Worthington Shares owns more shares of American Frontier than just about anyone else?"

"That and the fact the whole media is reporting that your brother is a sure bet to step in as CEO to take charge."

So that's it. He's now laid his biggest card on the table.

Sean glanced over at the waitress behind the counter of the coffee shop before answering. "Can I get a coffee to go?" he called out. He pulled a 20-dollar bill from his wallet and placed it on the table, then hesitated. He eyed Kirk. "They take dollars? It's all I have."

Kirk shrugged. "Probably."

Sean finally answered Kirk's probing question. "On the first point, that's why I'm here—to see for myself how at risk our stake is in American Frontier. Think of it like my own personal due diligence. On the second point, I wouldn't be so sure Will is going to take over anytime soon. Sandstrom is digging in his heels. What's more, my brother may not be all that interested. Depends a bit on what we find . . . and what I tell him."

Kirk nodded.

Sean knew from experience that the grizzled Green Justicer wouldn't probe further. There was already a bit of an uneasy partnership going on. Green Justice, as a rule, didn't take corporate donations. But Sean wasn't corporate, not exactly. Only an extremely wealthy guy who had inherited a whole lot more money than he knew what to do with, and he was generous with it. But his family's company also owned all or some of the very same companies that Green Justice took on publicly and privately. That meant there was a fuzzy gray line, and now, as in the past, Kirk probably didn't know where he stood in relation to that line with Sean. But that fuzziness wouldn't stop Kirk from carrying on with their plan.

"So let me just ask this and we can be done with it," Kirk said. "You're not going to ask me at some point on this trip to do something I'd regret, are you? If so, then maybe we'd better bring a life raft for you—in case I need to kick you off the ship."

Sean laughed but didn't answer immediately. Kirk was kidding about the life raft, of course. But he wanted to know Sean wouldn't pull rank and order the Green Justice crew to do something they wouldn't otherwise consider merely because he was the wealthy donor funding the effort.

The waitress brought Sean's coffee over and grabbed the 20-dollar bill from the table without saying anything.

Kirk smirked. "Guess they do take dollars."

Sean grinned, and their eyes met for a moment. "You're in charge, Kirk. Really and truly. I'm just along for the ride. You call the shots. I may have some questions and a suggestion or two. But there will be no orders from me. None. You do what you think is right, as you always do."

Kirk nodded again. He grabbed his Windbreaker from the back of the chair and headed for the door. "Glad to hear it. The team will be relieved to hear it too."

24

"It isn't that easy," Will said into his iPhone. "I wish it were, but it's not. I can't make a decision that quickly."

He'd stopped to take the call during his daily run through Central Park. His first mistake was running with his iPhone, and his second mistake was stopping to check the caller ID. Once he saw who it was, he'd decided to bite the bullet and deal with the call. He knew Kiki Estrada, the executive director of the Democratic Senatorial Campaign Committee, well enough to know that she'd just keep calling until she got him . . . and his answer. Will had to hand it to her—she was persistent and a straight shooter.

"I know the primary is soon," he said, "and that you don't have anyone with the resources or a decent name ID interested in the race. I'm not even sure *I'm* all that interested. I'm really focused on something else right now. It comes first." He tried to calm himself, slow his breathing. He'd been about halfway through his run and had started to hit a decent pace.

Kiki wasn't easily dissuaded, though. If she had been, her party would never field any first-tier candidates like William Jennings Worthington VI. Everyone in Washington knew she was relentless once she had her target in sight. And now she'd clearly focused her sights on the Worthington family, Will in particular.

"Come on, Will, don't tell me there's anything more important than taking back the Senate," Kiki said. She'd been a Senate chief of staff and then a Democratic National Committee official for more than 20 years before finally agreeing to run the DSCC in an attempt to bring control of the Senate back to the Democrats.

Kiki was well known for recruiting more diversity into the Democratic Party single-handedly than almost anyone, ever. Nearly every Latino in either the House or the Senate had Kiki to thank for something memorable in their campaign life. In only six short months at the DSCC, she already had six strong female Senate candidates lined up. That kind of record was unheard of.

Kiki really only needed four good candidates who could flip incumbent seats to take a good run at winning back control of the Senate, and Will was near the top of her wish list. A Senate campaign in New York was as expensive as they came, and very few candidates could challenge an entrenched incumbent and raise the money necessary to run a credible campaign. That certainly wouldn't be a problem for a Worthington.

Even more, right now there were a couple of third-tier candidates with no money, no name recognition, and no chance whatsoever in the general running in the Democratic primary. Will knew in his gut that he, with his immense wealth, connections, and network, was their best hope to unseat James Loughlin. So it made sense that Kiki was determined to do whatever it took to get him at least interested in the possibility. If that agenda didn't work, she'd try to lock in his financial interest for their efforts to take back control of the Senate.

"You're more interested in running American Frontier? Some giant oil company? Seriously?" She sounded skeptical.

Will had heard all the arguments before, and he wasn't inclined to go through them again with Kiki. Big Oil was every bit as evil to the progressive wing of the Democratic Party as Big Tobacco. Except that he believed they weren't. For years, until it had become apparent that burning fossil fuels was killing the planet, nearly everyone respected the American oil companies that strove for new, creative ways to make the United States energy independent. The demonization of the big oil companies was a relatively new phenomenon, and Will had never bought into it.

He could do a great deal more good from inside the oil and gas industry than he ever could from outside it—at least, that was what he rationalized. Part of his plan as CEO of American Frontier, should that come to pass, was to put an end to the company's longtime anti-environmental stance and bring it fully into the twenty-first century. He would create a highly entrepreneurial venture group inside the company with a mission to find and develop a broad, efficient renewable energy portfolio.

AF was already aggressively pursuing natural gas development and was now making a considerable sum from natural gas to go along with their oil exploration. Will fully intended to accelerate that progress and make certain they were researching and developing new technologies to capture and sell methane that leaked in the natural gas mining and development process. That would also help out with environmental questions.

Though he had never shared his vision with anyone outside his own family and advisors, Will fully planned to define American Frontier as a whole energy company—not simply a big oil company that made money drilling for expensive oil in hard-to-reach places like the bottom of the ocean floor. The world needed lots of cheap energy, and Will was convinced that American Frontier could lead the way toward solutions for providing cheap, abundant energy that didn't rely solely on burning fossil fuels.

"Look, Kiki," Will said, trying not to sound exasperated. He came to a complete halt in Central Park. He looked up, a bit disoriented about where he was until he saw the tennis courts on the north side of the park through the trees. "Don't you start in on me too about how evil the big oil companies are. I don't have the time, and I don't want to hear it. Not right now. It won't help you in your arguments with me."

"I wasn't, actually," Kiki said. "I admire American Frontier, if you want to know the honest truth. I've always liked them. You don't become the biggest, baddest, toughest kid on the block without learning how to win a street fight. And AF pretty much wins every street fight they get in. No, what I was going to say is that I don't know why you'd want to be their CEO when you don't have to. You're already their largest shareholder. You can tell them to jump, and they have to ask you how high."

"Right." Will laughed. "You and I know it doesn't work that way."

"Maybe. But you have more to say about their direction as their largest institutional shareholder than you ever would as their CEO. You don't need the money or their salary. You're on the board of directors right now—you tell the executives what to do. Why would you ever want the job that Eric Sandstrom has—so that your peers on the board can tell you what to do and how high to jump? *That's* what I was going to say."

Will couldn't help but grin. The woman was good. "That's not bad, Kiki. But tell me this. Why would I want to win a job as just one of 100 senators, all of whom believe they're the single greatest gift to humanity? Who have egos as large as the Grand Canyon, yet virtually no real power in a dysfunctional town that has no knowledge any longer of what actual bipartisanship looks like?"

"Because I said so? That works with my kids, by the way." She chuckled.

"That's nice. It never works with mine."

"Look, how about this?"

Will rolled his eyes as Kiki tried one more direction.

"Don't turn me down right now," she cajoled. "See how this American Frontier thing plays out. See how you feel about all of it after this situation in the Arctic has had a chance to play itself out on the evening news for a bit. But keep your options open. You may decide you'd like to be a United States senator after all, if they don't give you a chance to run AF. Because—and this is the only real incentive I can ever offer someone like you who doesn't need the money, fame, or power that comes from being in the Senate—it may be the right thing for you to do for the good of the country. And it also may be the right stepping-stone for you to consider if you'd ever like to consider running for that place on Pennsylvania Avenue. So think about it. Okay?"

"I have no plans to ever run for president," Will replied.

"Said like a true candidate who'd like to keep his options open."

"I'm not keeping my options open. I am genuinely not interested in running for public office—*any* public office." Will had thought about running from time to time, but he'd always been too focused on the AF CEO position to explore the idea fully. Perhaps it was because he wasn't really a Democrat. Not in any meaningful way. His heart and sympathies actually lay with the values of the Republican Party. He simply didn't like big government solutions. Instead he trusted corporations to create wealth and employ people. He was an entrepreneur and a calculated risk taker, as well as fairly conservative in his moral outlook. So he didn't fit fully with either the Democratic Party or the Republican Party.

"That may be," she fired back. "But circumstances change. From everything I'm hearing, this thing with AF is likely to get really ugly really fast. It's going to get everyone associated with it dirty. Not even someone like you, Will—who has a pure heart, no ulterior motives, and nothing more than a sense of duty to run a great company correctly—could keep from getting dirty when mud is flying from one corner of the room to the other."

"I'm interested in running American Frontier," Will said firmly. "I believe in its mission and what it stands for. I believe I can make a difference while running it. That's where my focus is."

"Fine," she said. "I acknowledge that and respect it. But

if it doesn't happen, for whatever reason, can we talk then? Can you give me at least that much?"

Will smiled. He knew Kiki wasn't going to give up. But this was as good a stopping place as he could manage right now. "All right, sure, I'll give you that. If it becomes apparent I'm not going to be running American Frontier as its next CEO, we can talk again. But you really are wasting your time. No Worthington has ever run for public office in New York, and I seriously doubt that the first one to do so in six generations is going to be yours truly."

"There's a first time for everything, Will—even for the Worthingtons. So, go do your thing. We'll talk soon."

"I have to hand it to Kiki," Will told his wife later that day as they sipped decaf coffee at the kitchen table. "She's determined. She doesn't give up. She goes after what she wants."

"But what do *you* want, Will?" Laura asked, her expression thoughtful. "That's what matters to me. You've spent your whole life doing what you think you ought to do. To uphold the Worthington name. To make your dad proud. But what do *you* really want? If you could go after anything?"

She sure knew how to hit the nail on the head. He grinned weakly. "I'm thinking about it."

She rolled her eyes. "Sounds like a way of avoiding the issue."

He sighed. "Okay, you got me. I can't help but think about what Drew said—about the risk, especially right now, not only for me but for all of us. The entire family. I—we—could be caught in a firestorm."

She lifted a brow. "So? You have before. It's one of the costs of being a Worthington. What makes this one different?"

"Ironic, isn't it?" He frowned. "I'm the one who opposed the board decision to drill in the Arctic. Now I might be the one who has to clean the mess up."

"You're a pro at cleaning messes up. But that's not the real issue here, is it? Is it because you're not sure if you should pursue the CEO, or you're wondering, as Drew stated, if there's a 'bigger prize'?"

In that moment his resolve solidified. He would follow the trajectory his life had been on, rather than sidetracking himself with what-ifs. "I believe I can make a difference right here, right now, as the CEO of American Frontier," he said slowly. "But Sandstrom isn't going to go down without a fight."

"So," she replied, aiming a one-two fist move in his direction, "give it right back."

He laughed. It was so Laura.

25

EN ROUTE TO THE ARCTIC OCEAN

Elizabeth's message to Sean was pointed. He could hear her frustration through her words.

> We've cross-checked everything we're receiving from the buoys and correlated it with what NASA's satellites long confirmed about what the Arctic connects to. That, along with the visual confirmations from the infrared camera, leaves only one conclusion. The amount of oil in the water is growing thicker by the hour. And you know what that means.

Sean knew the oil spill itself wasn't what worried Elizabeth and her father. The truth, not widely known truth but that Sean had learned through Will's work at AF and through the Shapiros, was that even truly bad oil spills and accidents like the Exxon *Valdez* and BP represented only about a tenth of the amount of crude oil that regularly seeped into the world's ocean systems from millions of places. But accidents got headlines. A massive oil spill concentrated in a critical marine system like the Arctic Ocean, which was not only pristine but linked to nearly every other ocean and marine system in the world—that was unknown and largely unstudied.

Because no one had ever considered that there might be massive amounts of oil under the Arctic or that anyone could get at it, there had never been a need or demand to study or model its effects on the ecosystem. It was hard enough to get research money to study climate change in the Arctic, where global warming temperatures were two to three times higher than the rest of the planet. People had scoffed at re-searchers predicting an ice-free summer in the Arctic, until it had actually happened less than 20 years after the start of the twenty-first century. Then the rush to extract oil in the Arctic began, and AF got involved.

What happens in the Arctic could have repercussions almost any-where on the planet. If critical food chain elements are damaged, the effects will ripple throughout most ocean species. Just as coal ash and soot from China substantially reduced the albedo effect in Greenland, causing the entire sheet of ice to nearly completely melt one year, the same sort of thing might happen if oil changed the Arctic. There's no way to predict what might happen or how bad it could get. The world has a right to know what's going on. Marine scientists, geologists, and others could then offer advice and research so we can get answers as swiftly as possible. The longer anyone waits to get the word out, the more dire the effects will be.

That was one of the reasons Sean was there. To see and hear the facts for himself so he could figure out a way to make a difference for good in this situation.

But the instant we write up anything like this that's different from the official line coming from either AF or the White House, they'll yank those buoys and the infrared camera right out of the water.

Our team is torn. After all, we're not here to study oil. We're here to study water, which now has oil in it. We have data, even though it's limited. What is science supposed to do when that happens? It reports what it observes. Discoveries can be happy—or unhappy—accidents.

So we've decided to simply email a bunch of science friends with some very specific questions before we write and post a single word on our research blogs. The first one I'm going to ask is what anyone happens to know about methane hydrates in this part of the Arctic Ocean.

But with social media, as soon as they penned their first questions, the top would be off Pandora's box.

Was Drew right—was there no winning this thing?

Still, Sean hated bullies. Especially government bullies. He'd never back down in doing what he knew was right.

26

NEW YORK CITY

Right before lunchtime, Sarah received a call from Darcy Wiggins and immediately dashed out of her office building. She hurried down the street into a sub sandwich shop to grab two of their specials and Diet Cokes, then hailed a taxi.

Darcy, looking as intense as ever, was pacing on the sidewalk in front of the Homeland Security Midtown office. She didn't even say hello. She just peered around briefly as if ensuring no one was in earshot, tugged Sarah farther down the block, then plunged in. "My colleagues think I'm the luckiest agent in the history of Homeland Security."

Sarah handed her a sub. Darcy ripped the paper open and took a big bite. "Mmm, haven't eaten anything since midafternoon yesterday. Things have been too wild."

"So why the luckiest?"

"Let's put it this way. For the two Boston Marathon bombers, my colleagues had to go through over 100,000 pictures and then 1,000 more security camera videos and pictures once they knew what the bombers looked like so we could put them at both bombs and find the backpacks. And *then* DHS had to interview dozens of potential eyewitnesses who may or may not have seen those two in the crowd. They did nothing but that for almost two days. After that, some homeowner found one of the guys hanging out in his boat, right under our noses, and did all our work for us. But at least we had to work for it." Darcy huffed and looked Sarah straight in the eye. "But I got the American Frontier bombing handed to me on a platter. The guy was even wandering around in everyone's cell phone videos for a couple of hours so no one could miss him."

She took another big bite of her sub and chewed for a second. "Then, like a bolt from the blue, a social worker finds the polar bear suit in a plastic bag out behind a set of wacko progressive offices, including at least three of the more radical environmental activist groups that like to go after oil companies." Darcy waved her sandwich around, frowning. "I mean, come on. The next thing I know, the guy's gonna walk in the front door and handcuff himself to my desk."

"So the case is wrapping itself up with a big bow, and you're not falling for it," Sarah said.

"Exactly. I haven't been able to sleep for two nights running. It's driving me more than a little crazy." Darcy leaned her back against the cement of the nearby building, set her now-empty sandwich wrapper on the ledge, and scrubbed both hands through her close-cropped blonde hair.

"I get it. I feel the same way. Something is wrong about all of this."

"No one would be so stupid to ditch such a suit where they worked. Not even radical eco-fascists, as my Republican friends like to call them, would be that boneheaded." She grinned.

Sarah laughed. Darcy had been spouting off on that subject over the long years they'd been friends. It bothered Darcy that so many people felt like they had to be either Republicans or Democrats because, well, that was who they felt most comfortable with and who so many of their friends and neighbors were. She said once she wished that people would stop equating their religious beliefs with their political beliefs. After all, Billy Graham, the most revered pastor in America, had been a lifelong Democrat. "Then again," she'd say, "no one cares what I think, and that particular ship sailed in America quite a while ago."

Darcy slumped. "I spend my days chasing down leads that invariably dead-end at white extremist 'Christian' groups who have some sort of a grievance against the FBI, the ATF, or another federal entity. I have to separate out my own biases and focus instead on the underlying psychology. What are these extremist groups doing, thinking, and plotting?" She narrowed her eyes. "Whenever anyone starts talking about God's wrath and judgment, then mixes that in with guns and hatred aimed at this agency or another group, I know I have to at least pay attention. If I can't anticipate and understand their psyches, I can't get ahead of potential domestic terror plots."

Sarah nodded, patiently waiting. She knew Darcy needed to process and blow off a little steam first before presenting her case.

"This particular case is so baffling. It doesn't fit any pattern I've ever seen. No note about why the bomb went off. No group has taken credit. No group is even a likely candidate. People generally don't like big corporations, but the corporations are rarely the focus of domestic terror plots—that's reserved for the government. Some lone environmental activists have committed fraud against oil companies or disrupted commercial activities on occasion, but none fits this profile."

Sarah leaned forward. "What about the Unabomber?"

Darcy waved a hand in dismissal. "A deranged type who hated technology and progress and had littered the landscape with letter bombs. But even he took his time and spread out his acts over months and years."

"And the Polar Bear Bomber materialized overnight and then vanished like a ghost. I see what you mean."

"Honestly, I doubt we'll ever hear from the Polar Bear Bomber again . . . assuming we don't catch him."

Sarah cocked her head. "So what's your next move?"

Darcy straightened and jammed her hands on her hips, feet spread apart like a determined policewoman. "I want to go talk to Catherine Englewood, the CNN field producer who gave everyone their first lead and exclusive video footage of the Polar Bear Bomber. And I want you to go with me."

Sarah brushed sandwich crumbs from her business suit. "Done."

They tossed their wrappers in the trash and headed out on their mission. The CNN building was only a five-minute walk. Once there, Darcy and Sarah didn't flash their badges at the visitors' desk in the lobby. There was no need. They only wanted to talk to the field producer, so the desk clerk called up to the newsroom. Catherine Englewood, a slim redhead who looked to be in her early twenties, showed up in the lobby a couple minutes later and walked briskly across the spacious foyer toward them.

"Darcy Wiggins, with DHS?" Catherine held out her hand,

which Darcy took, then extended her hand toward Sarah. "And Sarah Worthington, with Justice?"

"Yes, we spoke by phone, after the incident at American Frontier," Darcy said.

"I remember," Catherine said. "And I sent you my video. I hope it was helpful."

"It was. Thanks." Darcy glanced around the lobby.

"I know a place," Catherine said, as if sensing what the agent was looking for. "A quiet coffee shop that *isn't* a Starbucks less than a block from here."

Sarah had to laugh. Trying to find a seat at a Starbucks in New York anymore these days was a complete waste of time. They were always jammed, with lines out the door. And she knew Darcy's opinion: "Why people pay five dollars for coffee in a dark, crowded, brand-name joint that never has any open seats is beyond my comprehension."

Darcy gestured toward the door. "Lead the way."

The shop Catherine took them to was lovely. It wasn't actually a coffee shop. More like a combination ramen noodle and herbal tea place. But they had private wooden tables tucked away in different places, and they did have coffee as well.

"Can I get you something?" Darcy offered.

"A small coffee, black," Catherine said.

"Anything to eat?"

She smiled. "No, but thanks. Coffee tends to be my breakfast. And lunch, for that matter. Learned the bad habit at journalism school."

Sarah laughed. "Learned the same bad habit at Harvard Law."

All three got small black coffees, then found a table next to the window.

"So I'll bet you're wondering why we're here," Darcy said.

Catherine tilted her head. "It crossed my mind. I figured I'd pretty much given you all at Homeland Security everything I knew about the case."

"You did. We have no complaints there whatsoever. You were incredibly helpful. Sarah here is handling the American Frontier oil spill incident. We've been wondering if you can go back over that day some, what you saw, what you can remember about the Polar Bear Bomber."

Catherine lifted a brow. "Are you any closer to finding him, by the way?"

"We're making progress," Darcy said. "But I'm curious. You refer to the bomber as *him*. Why is that, do you think? As far as I can tell from all the footage I've seen, the bomber was like a mascot at a college football game. No one ever saw his—or her—face."

Catherine sat back in her chair and cradled her coffee in both hands. "You know, that's interesting. I assumed, I guess. I mean, he was taller . . ."

"Women can be tall too," Sarah mused.

"Yeah, they can, but this guy was taller than me. And I'm five feet nine. So that seemed to make me think he was a guy." Catherine's brown eyes turned thoughtful, as if she was remembering something. "But I don't think that's where I got the idea from. It was from something else . . . another conversation."

Sarah's investigative instincts kicked in. "After the bombing, you mean? Nearly all of the reporting talked about the bomber as a man. I think you even referred to him that way in one of your early reports."

"I did," Catherine agreed. "But no, I don't think it was

afterward. There was some reason . . ." She stared out the window for several seconds. Pedestrians streamed by in multiple directions. "I know I talked to a lot of people that day. I did a ton of interviews with folks who were there protesting."

"So maybe it was one of those protesters?" Darcy asked. "Maybe one of them pointed out the person in the suit to you?"

Light sparked in Catherine's eyes. "Now I remember. No, it wasn't them. I'd been so busy with different interviews. I'd been laughing with the American Frontier press guy about the funny signs some of the protesters were carrying. He pointed out the polar bear suit and referred to the person as a guy, and I assumed from there. But there's no way the AF press guy knew anything. He's right out of college himself, like me. He was only there to babysit me."

"Babysit?" Sarah asked.

"Yeah, you know." Catherine waved her hands in the air. "Make sure I didn't try to interview some AF employee without permission or try to take my camera inside the building. That kind of thing. He was clueless. He knew less about the oil spill situation than I did. If I remember, I spent more time telling him about what I knew than the other way around. He wasn't very good at his job as a flack."

"You're pretty sure that's where you got the idea from, then?" Darcy pressed.

Catherine paused, then stated confidently, "Yeah. But I'm telling you, he's a nobody. There's no way he could have known anything. We were both merely joking about whether the polar bear suit guy was sillier than the homeless lady with a Statue of Liberty hat on, or some other guy who'd come dressed up like Poseidon."

"Poseidon?" Darcy asked.

Sarah nudged her friend. "You know, the god of the sea?"

"Oh yeah. *That* Poseidon. So there were lots of those folks around during that protest?'

Catherine nodded. "For sure. A number of them. It was like a party, with all the typical New York street-actor types. Happens all the time whenever there are cameras and an event. People get dressed up in wild and crazy getups and mug for the cameras. I interviewed a bunch of them myself that day, for fun. None would ever make it on the air, but I figured, why not? I had plenty of time to kill, and it's all digital video anyway, so I can dump it at the end of the day."

"But I'm assuming you never interviewed the guy in the polar bear suit, right?" Darcy asked. "I'm sure you'd have told us if you had."

"Absolutely. But no, I never interviewed him. I even went back over my field notes to double-check. I kept a running tally on interviewees. That guy definitely wasn't one of them."

"I see." Darcy had a glint in her eye, and Sarah knew what that meant. Darcy now had a thread to pull on and see where it might unravel. It might be something, or nothing. But it was one place to start. "So the guy from American Frontier you talked to, the one who'd pointed out the guy in the polar bear suit—can you send me his contact information?"

"Sure. I'll email it to you first thing when I get back to the office. But seriously, he's just a know-nothing suit. He was clueless." She laughed. "About nearly everything."

"I understand. I'm only trying to get a better understanding of what happened that day, that's all. Every bit of information helps."

Catherine put a lid on her coffee cup and prepared to

leave. "Didn't I hear that they found the polar bear suit out behind some environmental activist offices?"

"We're headed there next," Darcy said.

"But we wanted to stop by here first," Sarah added. "Fill out the picture. Make sure we were asking whatever questions were hanging around."

Catherine pursed her lips. "I know what you mean. Reporters are like that too. We keep on asking questions when things don't make sense." Her brown eyes twinkled. "And we especially ask questions when things continue to not make sense."

Now she's singing our number, Sarah thought. She had to hand it to the young journalist. Catherine was a smart one, even this early in her career. And she had definitely been in the right place at the right time.

27

No one could live in New York City for long without running into a crazy—people who dressed in ridiculous getups and acted so insane that they drew notice to themselves. Some worked at it. To others it seemed to come naturally.

And that was what bugged Will. He couldn't get his brief glimpse of the man in the polar bear suit out of his brain.

So what's the deal? he asked himself. He saw crazies every day—on the street, in the subway. It was New York City, for heaven's sake. But this particular crazy lingered in his thoughts. Finally, Will did one of the things he did best. He allowed his laser-like focus to zero in on the picture he remembered of the Polar Bear Bomber. Anybody who would wear a polar bear suit in a crowd—unless they were hired by a company to do so—was slightly crazy. But this guy's wandering wasn't just wandering. He was casual, yes, but very precise in the way he'd laid the backpack down by the building. He seemed to be going out of the way to be noticed by the cameras.

Will's own thoughts circled back around and intensified. *That's it—he was hired by a company.* Why else would a guy act the way the Polar Bear Bomber was acting—crazy but precise?

But if he was hired, who hired him? Will didn't figure the ecological people who picketed buildings for things like oil spills could scrape up enough cash. And he knew enough about Sean's Green Justice friends to know that wasn't their way. They'd confront a situation head-on, not have some guy dress up in a polar bear suit.

What option did that leave? Will focused again. No one had been injured. And the location where the bomb went off was by a storehouse in the building, so nothing much was damaged.

A hard thought stopped him cold. Would Sandstrom stoop so low to get public sympathy back that he'd try something that crazy? Hiring a guy to blow up part of his building?

Just then his cell phone rang. It was Sarah. Usually she texted, unless it was something he needed to know right away. Then she called.

After concluding their short discussion—her report on the visit with Catherine Englewood—he mused, *So things don't make sense to DHS, Justice, or CNN. Maybe, just maybe, I could be right.*

But he had to take a long, hard look at the facts before he shared the possibility with anyone—especially his sister, who was supposed to go after AF with everything she had.

28

The Arctic Ocean

The Russian ice cutter that was carrying Sean, Jon, and Kirk toward the oil spill had definitely seen better years. Sean could imagine what his sister would say. Something to the tune of, "You're going to travel on that rust bucket? All the way across the Arctic Ocean? With no way to get off? Are you nuts?"

Well, yes, he was, but he'd made a career and a lot of money for the Worthingtons out of being just a little nuts. It was part of being an entrepreneur. You had to think outside the box and take some risks. Or, in his case, a lot of risks.

He laughed to himself. Over the years of growing up, Will had always tried to rein him in. But Sean wasn't a cautious, precise Will clone, and he wasn't about to let his older brother control him. In fact, Sean went as far in the other direction as possible. He couldn't compete with his brother's perfection in business and brilliant mind, but he had something Will didn't—the ability to take phenomenal risks and go along for the ride. If he succeeded, great. If not, he simply tried another way.

So when his US contacts hadn't worked out to get him and Jon a space on an American ship, he'd quickly contacted the Russians—a place where big American money really talked.

Now here he was, hands braced on the railing, catching up on life with Jon as they set out from the port at Reykjavík.

From the moment they'd met at the environmental symposium, the two men had hit it off. Truth was, even though Sean and Jon had vastly different careers, they were an awful lot alike. Both had older siblings who were like gods in their respective families—they'd always gotten straight As, were teacher's pets, and were generally the types of older siblings that no one could measure up to, so why bother trying?

In Jon's case, it was a sister who'd even been allowed to babysit him, though he was only two years younger. Jon had been stuck with almost every teacher she'd had in middle school and high school. There were a million pictures of her as an adorable baby in the family albums and "three of me, all of them with her hanging around in the background," Jon had once said, shaking his head. "I don't think I remember one of just me anywhere."

Naturally, Jon's older sister had gotten into an Ivy League school. Their parents had paid for her education. Jon, to be different, or maybe ornery, had gone in state to the University of North Carolina on a cross-country scholarship and hadn't even bothered to ask his family to help out with anything other than some room and board. Even then he'd bailed out of the dorms after two years and paid his own way by working odd jobs and living off campus.

Sean had told Jon that Will had been the captain of every

team in high school and then had captained an NCAA national championship lacrosse team at Harvard. He'd ruined any relationship Sean might have had with teachers as he came through. Everyone expected Sean to be a cookie cutter of his older brother, which he wasn't, and that seemed to make them angry, depressed, or grumpy.

While Sean was used to it by now, it still bothered him from time to time that everyone simply paid attention to his older brother like it was Will's birthright. He'd spent years feeling like a speed bump on the road to his older brother's success, though he'd never mentioned that in public. But he had complained to his mom more than a few times about it. He didn't dare complain to his dad, because he knew Bill Worthington would always back Will.

Still, Sean did have one thing that his older brother had no prayer of matching, and it turned out that Jon did too. Sean's network of social and professional friends was deep, loyal, sophisticated, and almost endless. They would run their cars through a brick wall for him if he asked. In fact, Sean was like Kevin Bacon squared. He could access anyone on the planet with only three emails or phone calls.

As the men stood on the deck of the cutter, they fell into their usual pattern of comparing their social networking skills for fun.

"Okay, give," Jon said, grinning. "How many contacts?" He pulled out his mobile phone and aimed it toward Sean like a weapon.

Sean took his out of his pocket and peered at it. "1,737."

Jon's face fell. "1,513." Then he brightened. "How about LinkedIn? I'm at more than 1,000."

Sean lifted his chin triumphantly. "More than 2,000."

Jon sighed. "Twitter?"

Sean shrugged. "Only a couple thousand."

"Yes." Jon fist-pumped the air. "More than 30,000."

"Unfair, man, unfair!"

Their favorite competition ended with comparing Facebook, where they were about equal.

Sean couldn't resist a little taunting, though, as the cutter crunched its way slowly through some unexpected ice on their way toward the Arctic Circle. "You're a *New York Times* reporter, for crying out loud. Aren't you *supposed* to have a bunch of followers on social media? Isn't that part of your job?"

"Yeah, kind of—though it's a mixed bag."

"Why?"

"'Cause it's still a daily newspaper," Jon said. "The editors actually hate social media. They hate anything online, to be honest."

"Because it's ruined your industry?"

"Yeah, that, and . . ." Jon hesitated. "There's this thing that all journalists have in their veins. We want to see our stories *in print*, not blinking away on some screen."

Sean nodded. He'd heard the same complaint from a few of his author friends. He actually knew quite a bit about the newspaper, magazine, and publishing business. He had investments in six new digital or online news ventures right now. One was a potential game changer.

"But you don't have a choice, do you?" he asked. "I mean, doesn't the industry have to figure out the business model going forward if journalism is going to survive?"

"They're trying," Jon said. "Everyone has more viewers and readers, thanks to online. But we have a tenth of the ad revenue, which kills every business model. That's why the publishers get crazy when you talk about online, and why the editors have this love-hate relationship with social media." He smiled wickedly at Sean in the gathering darkness on the deck. "But I hear that some smart investors have money in some interesting, new digital aggregation companies . . ."

"You caught me." Sean laughed. "You must have done your homework. Yeah, I know a bit about this subject."

"Are we gonna make it—the news business, I mean?"

"You will." He shrugged. "I mean, the *New York Times* will. People will always value branded content. They want to know where the information is coming from, who's behind it. But there are other content creators that people trust as well, such as academics at universities, or scientists. The news media has competition now in the world of trusted sources of information, and it just has to get used to it."

"But a blog isn't a news story," Jon said a bit halfheartedly.

"Of course not. But most readers don't care much anymore. If you're transparent, that's what matters. They only want to know the motives and agenda behind a story. They want to know that it's a real effort, not propaganda."

A door slammed behind them. Kirk Baldwin and one of the ship's crew members came toward them. The wind was starting to pick up.

"Captain says we need to get inside," Kirk told them. "A storm's coming on. The winds could be strong, like hurricane force."

"Seriously?" Jon asked. "Will we still get to the site in the morning?"

Kirk nodded. "He says we will. They're not planning to

stop. There's no point sitting out here when the winds hit. We might as well keep moving forward, cutting ice as we go."

Jon squinted out over the deck of the cutter. It was now so dark that they could barely see each other in the dim light from the deck. "You know, that's one of the things I want to get into when we get to the spill site. I mean, look at this weather—high winds, ice everywhere, pitch-black dark at night earlier and earlier as we head into winter . . ."

"Not to mention that no one knows what oil does to the species like beluga whales that mostly hang out in the Arctic and have never had to contend with oil in their water," Sean added. "And what that then does to the rest of the food web."

"Right, there's the food web question we haven't answered yet," Jon said.

"And don't forget the methane hydrates everyone is all gung ho to start drilling for here in the Arctic and a few other places. If we thought oil spills were bad, imagine what might happen if you guess wrong about *that* sort of drilling."

"Exactly! And what happens when one of those massive hurricanes comes rolling through here right about the time the oil spill occurs—"

Kirk held up a hand as if he was sure this could go on all night if he didn't step in. "Careful." He laughed. "Doesn't sound like you're being an objective reporter here. There's that 200-page oil spill and restoration manual that the Arctic Council put out before the eight countries in it gave the big ol' thumbs-up to deepwater exploration in the Arctic—"

"Which is a worthless piece of you-know-what." Jon scowled. "Booms and skimmers don't work in ice. And if I'm not mistaken, I'm seeing and hearing a whole bunch of ice all around us. Plus don't forget what happens when oil gets up under the ice as it forms."

"No, Jon, tell us," Kirk said wryly.

"It just hangs there! You can't get at it. You can't recover it. Seriously, it could be years and years before anyone gets at any of that type of spilled oil. Who the heck knows where it might go, how much of each marine species it might kill in a pristine environment that's never had to absorb this sort of toxic shock to the ecosystem? I mean, come on! Didn't anyone think this stuff through beforehand?"

Sean reached out and gave his friend a pat on the shoulder. "Don't get all wound up, Jon. We aren't even there yet. You've got miles to go and lots of notebooks to fill up before getting to all that. So let's move inside. Tomorrow will be a big day."

That night Sean shot an email to Elizabeth:

On my way. What a weird mix we are. A reporter, a die-hard Green Justicer, and me—whatever I am. ETA, don't know.

He worried when he didn't get a response, even hours later. Then he shook it off. Of course Elizabeth would be head over heels into her project.

NEW YORK CITY

Sometimes he wondered if he was going crazy. The guy had said he'd get paid for the gig, right?

And he was bad off. He needed some meds.

He'd been scared of his shadow ever since the bombing

was announced. Sure, he'd done some crazy and bad things in his life, but he'd never bombed anybody before.

But you didn't know what was in that backpack, he told himself.

Yeah, right, like anybody would believe you.

He needed to disappear—get out of the city.

But first he needed that money.

29

Will couldn't get the Polar Bear Bomber or his suspicions out of his mind. So he mentioned them to Laura.

"Mmm," she said, "you've got a point there. But that would mean . . ." She drew in a breath.

"Yes, that Sandstrom and his cronies committed a criminal act to try to save his hide. I'm not a fan of Sandstrom's, but I still can't imagine him going that far."

She lifted a dark eyebrow. "Seriously? You've never seen anybody make a bad decision when they were squeezed?"

He sighed. "You're right, as usual. I've seen even really good people cave under pressure and do things they'd never normally do." He gazed unseeing at the wall.

"Speaking of things people would never normally do . . ."

He jerked his head toward her. She frowned at him with that you-better-pay-attention look. "What do you mean?"

"Right before you got home, your mom called. She was definitely not herself. Went on and on about what your dad was saying . . . about Kiki trying to talk you into running."

"Dad called me too. I didn't tell him, but the word still got around somehow. Dad knows everybody. He insisted again it was time to take the bull by the horns and turn the country around, and that I was the one to do it." Will scratched his head in frustration. "I told him Kiki and I had just talked. Nothing else."

"Well, your mom seems to think it's a done deal. And she seemed really worried. There was a tone I've never heard in her voice. Worry for you, yes, but something more. Fear, maybe?"

"Why would Mom be afraid of me making a run in politics?" Will asked. "That doesn't make any sense."

"I'm only telling you what I heard. Something's up. And I aim to find out."

Now he chuckled. "Good luck with that. Mom married into the Worthington family. She's a keeper of more secrets in the highest levels of society than you could ever imagine. You won't be able to worm anything out of her until she's ready to give it up."

"Maybe not," Laura said with a determined tilt of her chin. "But I certainly plan to try."

30

THE ARCTIC OCEAN

The bright sunshine was deceiving. The night had been bitterly cold, and the wind was fast approaching hurricane strength. The captain of the Russian cutter ordered everyone to stay off the deck while he navigated his way through the last remaining miles to the American Frontier platform.

Sean and Kirk sat in the mess hall while the ship made its final approach. The wind still howled outside the ship, but at least the grating crunching of ice had gone away as they'd managed to sail into ice-free waters. Now they were moving along at a decent clip.

"Should we be nervous?" Sean asked. He hadn't been able to sleep during the night. It wasn't that he was worried. It was exactly the opposite. He felt a bit like a pirate—ready for a fight, though what that would look like was anyone's guess. "Do you think anyone will approach us?"

"Who would that be?" Kirk asked.

"Don't they have a Navy ship out here?"

"Yeah, and what might they object to?"

"Stop answering my questions with another question!" Sean shot back.

"And why—oh, never mind." Kirk grinned. "Seriously, though, I can't imagine why anyone would keep us away from the platform."

"Maybe because we have no reason to be here?" Sean threw in.

"We may not have any reason, but we certainly have a right."

The mess door slammed open, and Jon stuck his head in. "We've got company," he said, out of breath. "I was up on deck. That cutter—the Navy ship—is headed our way."

Kirk bolted from his seat. Sean wasn't far behind.

They took the stairs to the deck three at a time. Half the sailors and the captain were out on deck when they got there.

"Whoa," Jon exclaimed as they spotted the USS *Cantor*. "I've been on the *Healy*, the ship the Coast Guard operates on behalf of NSF. But this?" His eyes widened. "It's gotta be three times bigger than that."

Kirk whistled. "Looks like it can cut through even the thickest ice too."

Both the Russian ship and the USS *Cantor* slowed their engines as they approached each other and then came to a halt 100 feet or so apart.

Sean peered out over the horizon, trying to spot the American Frontier platform. But they were clearly some distance from it, because all he could see was water and floating chunks of ice in front of them.

"Wow, that's a mother of a ship," Kirk whispered to Sean and Jon. The Russian crew shuffled uneasily on the deck. To

Sean, this had the feel of a confrontation. The Navy ship had clearly positioned itself in their path. But what did it mean?

Everyone stood awkwardly on the deck of the Russian ship for what seemed like an eternity. All waited for something—a signal about what kind of play was about to happen. From his vantage point, Sean could see that the crew aboard the *Cantor* was also mostly standing around waiting.

"Maybe they don't have our mobile number," Sean joked.

Jon kept his gaze focused on the *Cantor*. "They have it. My guess is that they're waiting to see if we're going to try to move past them, and then they'll react. If we just sit here, they might simply wait as well."

"Well, that seems silly," Sean said. "Not to mention a big time waster."

He could have dealt easily with yelling and chaos on both sides. After all, he was used to being in the middle of the standoffs and wars between his big brother and little sister. He'd somehow become the family peacemaker over the years. But this? Nothing was happening. The two ships were merely staring each other down. Neither side had stated their position verbally, so there was nothing to mediate. No decision to reach. Nowhere to go. Talk about frustrating.

"Look at it from their perspective," Jon reasoned. "We're in international waters. This is a Russian-flagged ship. The Russians have as much right to sail these waters as the Americans. It's not like they're going to stop us if we choose to go by, or fire a shot across our bow, so to speak."

"Then what are we waiting for?" Sean asked. "Let's tell the captain to move."

"No!" Kirk said forcefully. "Not now—not yet. We don't want to provoke an international incident if we don't have to."

"So what then?" Sean crossed his arms and leaned on the ship's railing.

Kirk didn't say anything further. He turned and walked over to the captain. They talked briefly, then left for the comm center. When Kirk returned about five minutes later, he wore a grim expression.

"I think we're at a standoff for the time being," he announced to Sean and Jon. "I had the captain call them, explain that we were here not under a Russian flag but as part of a research mission for a US-based nonprofit organization. The captain told them of our intention to sail to the site of the spill for research purposes."

"Great," Sean said. "So why aren't we moving in that direction?"

"Because," Kirk answered, "they then told us that they were operating under the parameters outlined in the Arctic Council oil spill recovery plan. Until they'd secured the safety of the area, no other ships were allowed in. That recovery plan, he told our captain, carried the full force and weight of the eight signatory nations on the Arctic Council, and Russia is one of those. The *Cantor* captain said we could get by only if one of the eight nations granted us permission to sail on and join in the recovery efforts, even if it was only for research. Otherwise, no go. Boys, we need to round up a letter of permission from one of those eight countries. Otherwise, the *Cantor* is going to hold us here—for our own safety, they say."

"Safety!" Sean almost shouted. "There's no safety problem, except maybe to the marine life in the area."

Kirk exhaled heavily. "Maybe so, but there's not much we can do about it at this point. We need a letter from someone. Any ideas?"

"Don't look at me." Jon shook his head. "I'm just a reporter."

Sean really hated this kind of regulatory game playing. But if there was one thing he'd learned in life, it was that sometimes you had to play within the rules—up to a point.

That night Sean emailed Elizabeth.

It's the standoff at the O.K. Corral. We're simply standing here facing each other with guns drawn, and nobody will let us in the saloon.

I really, really hate Westerns. Especially when they happen in real life.

31

NEW YORK CITY

It certainly helped to have connections in high places, Will mused the next morning. And Drew was the king of that. This time his information came from the highest of circles in the NSA.

"Know that Fact Sheet President Rich put out about the AF oil spill?" Drew said over the phone. "Well, he'd hoped it had at least some semblance of the truth, especially since Sandstrom had contributed heavily to his presidential campaign. Word is, though, the president was not in a good mood when he got off the phone with Sandstrom, who's still in the Arctic. The spill isn't contained, and they can't even identify where all the oil is coming from. Top that off with a winter storm moving into the area . . ."

"Of course, we already knew some of that from Sean," Will replied.

Drew laughed softly. "Let's just say I bet President Rich

wishes he could replay the day the CEO warned him against allowing any sort of deep drilling in the Arctic until we had better oil recovery and containment options. He brushed them off. Now this mess is going to haunt him all the way through his reelection."

"Unless, of course, he makes it someone else's problem."

"You got it," Drew said. "Seems there are only two good things about the whole situation. One—the platform hasn't fallen into the ocean yet. And two—unlike BP, there are no deaths . . . at least not yet."

"So what's Sandstrom's next move?"

"He and the White House have to convince the public that the spill can be contained and managed and it's not really a big deal. So they're going to make a big show of either fixing the subsea structure or capping the well, recovering the oil, and providing help and money for any Inuit villages that suffered a bit of hardship from the spill."

Will blew out an exasperated breath. "You and I both know that spilled oil isn't something anyone can do anything about. So you're saying the real battle isn't the oil cleanup. It's a public relations one."

"That's what I'm saying. It's a brilliant, tough, risky ploy, but if there are no eyewitnesses, it'll work. It isn't like the media is going to fly up to the Arctic and report from the scene of the crime, so to speak."

Will had to admit, Sandstrom's crazy genius made a lot of sense.

"But here's the sticky part," Drew said. "Sandstrom told the president that there was a fly in the ointment. That one of the Worthingtons—the one who's on the board of directors for a bunch of the greenies—was on board the Green

Justice ship that's now facing off with AF in the Arctic. Not only that, but the Worthingtons paid for it."

Once again Sean had put himself in the middle of a disaster waiting to happen. Will hadn't heard from him yet about the face-off.

Drew continued. "The president wanted to know how that squared with the Worthingtons' shares in AF . . . and in your interest in Sandstrom's job."

So what Drew predicted—the drawing of the Worthington siblings in to the line of fire—was already happening.

"That's just the press spinning their usual guesses. Not really—"

"The truth isn't what matters here," Drew said. "It's what people believe based on what the press says. Anyway, Sandstrom gave you a compliment. He said you were mostly a straight shooter but a bit too aggressive for his tastes. He's worried that your efforts to come after him will gain some traction. If they do, he said, and I quote"—there was a sudden rustling of papers in the background— "'Then I'll have to make some moves I already have in motion.'"

Will frowned. "What moves? Did he say?"

"No. But he said something rather odd. That the Worthingtons have never exactly been able to control Sean. That he's a bit mysterious and does his own thing. And that it's going to get him in trouble one of these days, like maybe right now. 'We're monitoring that situation closely,' Sandstrom said."

What does that mean? Will's thoughts raced. If his brother was in the middle of the Arctic, in an explosive situation because Sandstrom was worried about Will taking over his job . . .

"You know our family has never been especially political.

We haven't made a run for the White House in six generations," Will said. "And nobody's ever made a bid in New York."

"Yes, but with your wealth and connections, you could be formidable if you ever engaged in any meaningful way, either financially or as a candidate yourself." Drew laughed. "President Rich just told Sandstrom in a not-so-nice tone to let sleeping dogs lie—in this case, the Kennedys, he said."

It wasn't the first time anyone had compared the Worthingtons to the Kennedys. Will brushed the comment off. He was used to it by now.

"Sandstrom clearly thinks he's got the situation covered, though."

"What do you mean?"

"He said the Green Justice ship can't get anywhere close to the platform or the spill without a letter from one of the eight nations that are part of the Arctic Council and signed the oil spill recovery plan. As of right now, the council has authorized the American military to keep the site secure. So no ships except AF's are getting anywhere near the spill, at least for the foreseeable future. Especially since Sandstrom claimed direct access through AF's government and regulatory relations office to every member of the council."

Sandstrom doesn't see any cracks, huh? Well then, he doesn't know Sean Worthington very well.

Will couldn't help but grin when he clicked off his phone.

32

For as long as he could remember, Will had always known what to do. He'd never doubted his path. He'd always believed that everything was for the best, that even dire circumstances eventually led to proper outcomes, and that there was nearly always a reason for something.

Though born into incredible wealth, he wasn't conflicted about it the way Sean was. He wasn't frivolous or carefree about it either, the way Sarah had been growing up. No, he believed that wealth wasn't so much a privilege as it was a burden.

To those who are given much, much is required.

Will wasn't a religious person ordinarily—that was his little sister's department, and her interest in it had ramped up over the past several years—but that verse had lodged itself somewhere deep in the recesses of his brain years ago and never let go. He genuinely believed it. He acted on it, even if he never told anyone about his motivations.

Sarah and he had argued about religious stuff for years.

She was always after him to actually sit down and read the Bible, if only so he could dismiss it for himself rather than merely disregard it in casual conversation because most intelligent people in their circles didn't take it very seriously. But that particular verse haunted him somehow. He didn't want to reach the end of his life and realize that he'd squandered what he'd been given in life. "Much is required," it said.

Okay then, God, he thought, *please tell me. What exactly is required?*

At the moment, though, Will was completely at a loss. The American Frontier opportunity was slipping through his grasp, and there was virtually nothing he could do about it. And if it went away, then what?

Much is required.

But what if he had no chance to act on that requirement? What was he supposed to do then? Was there, as Drew hinted, a potentially larger prize out there? One that Will should pursue?

Will knew how the real world worked. He wasn't naïve. With Sandstrom physically away from New York, running the spill recovery operationally on-site in the Arctic, the board couldn't act in his absence. Even if a majority now had decided they wanted to replace Sandstrom and that it made the most sense for the head of the largest shareholder to take over in such a turbulent time.

There had to be a change in leadership at AF. Will had argued against the deepwater drilling effort with everything he could bring to bear at the board level. He'd almost won the fight. But Sandstrom had staked his entire reputation, and the company's with it, to get the board to go along with the exploration effort. It had taken two years of failed efforts and billions of sunk costs, but Sandstrom and his executive team had gotten platforms built in several locations over some of the biggest potential deposits in the region.

But that was before the accident. Now the board realized too well that Will had been right and Sandstrom had been wrong. The decision threatened to pull the company, and much else, under with it.

Even so, Will was powerless to take any decisive action, and it was killing him. It was now two in the morning, and he'd never come close to falling asleep. He got up and walked through the darkened bedroom in their Central Park apartment and turned his laptop back on.

He shook his head. Old habits died hard. He'd grown up seeing his dad constantly working, and he was trying to change that about himself. To always be present in the moment, even if the rest of his world was poised on the edge.

A gentle hand descended on his shoulder. He swiveled his chair and looked up.

"Couldn't sleep, huh?" Laura's shoulder-length dark hair was mussed. "I've been thinking about what you said too, and reading up on the AF situation and the bombing. I'm so sorry. It sure looks like you're right."

Leave it to Laura to take a few facts he'd told her, add her own research, and then sift through the information for herself. The one person whose judgment he valued above all others believed him. Maybe he wasn't crazy after all. "But being right doesn't get us much."

She squeezed his shoulder. "You do what you have to do. Don't worry about me and the kids. Just save the world for us, okay? Get American Frontier—and your brother—out of the Arctic. Your mom is worried sick about that too. I think she worries more about Sean than the other two of you."

He chuckled. "She has reason to. Some of the things he's pulled . . . Dad's been at his wit's end. I still remember him yelling once, after Sean blew up the neighbor's trash bin, 'This boy cannot be from my loins!'"

They both laughed.

Then Laura's brown eyes turned serious. "But you know Sean's heart. He may not act like it, but he'd do anything for you. He loves you and worships the ground you walk on."

"Yeah, maybe a little too much. It's torn us apart over the years. And Dad hasn't helped. He's hard on all of us kids, but with Sean, there's always an edge. Like the two of them can never see eye to eye on anything. Dad and I could always work together on Worthington Shares, but Sean had no choice but to go off on his own and work with the start-ups."

"Which he's doing a great job with," she interjected. Then she softened. "Just take one thing at a time."

"I'm tryin', babe, trust me. But right now I'm at a loss. I honestly don't know what to do, and I feel like time is slipping away from me. I know I need to do something, to act. But for the first time in my life, I can't sort out what that might be. And I'm having a hard time believing the truth I'm seeing right in front of my nose."

"So tell me about it. Give me the options, and we'll sort it out together."

Will filled her in on the latest information he'd received that day, including what his contact had told him about the standoff, and the continuing inquiries from the DSCC for him to make a decision about running for the Senate in New York. Laura had been playing catch-up the last few days after being in Malawi, and with the AF crisis, he hadn't seen as much of her as he wanted. It felt good, even at two in the morning, to get it all off his chest. Sometimes simply getting the questions out on the table was helpful.

When he was finished, Laura wagged a playful finger at him. "Come on, Will. You know what you need to do. Your options seem pretty clear to me. And if you think it through a bit, you'll see them too."

He shrugged. "So tell me."

"First, is there any reason at all that AF should be drilling in deep waters in the Arctic right now? Does that make any sense?"

He pondered the questions. "No, it's what I've been fighting at the board level for months now."

"They didn't heed your warnings or take your advice," Laura stated emphatically. "So it's time to get beyond that fight. You lost it. I know you have your heart set on using the situation to take over the company and lead it in a new direction. But Sandstrom isn't going away quietly, if at all. He's clearly fighting, maybe even in a dirty, underhanded way. So you have no choice, especially as the head of Worthington Shares. You have to go public with this fight. You have a right, as a big shareholder, to call the question publicly. Demand that they get out of the Arctic. Don't worry about whether you then get the chance to run the company. You have to do the right thing first and see where that path takes you."

Will sat back in his chair. "Wow," he murmured. "In all the years we've been married, that's the longest lecture you've given me."

"Well, you're being a big baby," she chided. "You know what you need to do. I know you think being the CEO of this big company is what's required of you. But what if it's not? What if the thing that's *really* required of you is to do the right thing at a critical moment, and that you need to use what's in your control—what's been given to you—to get that job done? What if *that's* the job you need to do, not become American Frontier's CEO?"

When he was silent, thinking, she added more softly, "Will, are you afraid you'll fail? Because you've never failed at anything you've done? Honey, the only way you can fail is by *not* taking the risk to do what you know is right. Nothing is a failure if you learn from it and come back even stronger."

He exhaled heavily. "And then once that fight is over? What's required of me then?" he asked with both palms extended upward.

"Run for the Senate, Will. Why not? You've thought about it for years." She laughed. "Even if you've told everybody else you haven't. So quit thinking about it. Yes, I know your mom's worried, but she's tight-lipped about her reasons. You're right. I can't wangle them out of her until she's ready to spill. So call back that woman, Kiki, and tell her you're in. Tell her you'll put your name into the primary."

And there it was again. The clarity Laura brought to his life.

Marrying her had been the single best decision he'd ever made.

33

Sarah was in a cab partway to her office when Darcy called.

"That CNN field producer has been incredibly helpful. She already sent me the contact information for that press aide at American Frontier. Not only that"—Darcy's voice increased in fervor—"she was kind enough to scan in her shot list and field notes and give me a link to the raw video footage that she'd uploaded to a password-protected Vimeo site."

Sarah was taken aback. That was way beyond the call of duty. Reporters and producers, as a rule, didn't do that sort of thing. At least the ones she knew. Everything tended to be a one-way street with them. They were in the job of vacuuming up information, not doling it out.

Except . . .

Her thoughts flashed back to when she'd met Sean's friend Jon Gillibrand. Of average height with dark blond hair, he didn't stand out from the crowd. And he certainly wasn't the usual type of guest who showed up at Worthington events. But Jon's keen blue eyes revealed a quick intellect. The kind of person who studied situations from all angles and knew when to keep his mouth shut.

He'd also selectively shared information with Sean when it would affect the Worthington family, but without revealing his sources. Lots of people shared information with the Worthingtons, but they expected handouts, favors, or to be paid. Jon wasn't pushy. He just slid the details into a conversation because he was Sean's friend and cared about the Worthingtons.

Sarah was no pushover with men—she had a lot of her mother's feisty Irish spirit in her—but Jon had slowly earned her respect. Even more, he'd always treated her with respect, instead of as the baby sister of his friend.

Jon Gillibrand was a quiet force to be reckoned with, she thought, yet totally trustworthy. He intrigued her. She'd had enough of the Harvard Law guys and all others of their ilk.

Darcy's voice interrupted. "So what are you waiting for? Get back here."

Startled from her reverie, Sarah said, "Yes, ma'am," and hung up. Darcy wouldn't have heard anything else she said anyway. Her friend was clearly on the track of something and intensely focused.

So the young producer was both smart and helpful. Probably figured it didn't hurt to have contacts inside DHS and Justice's Criminal Division if there were going to be any further developments in the Polar Bear Bomber case.

When Sarah swept into the door of DHS and hightailed it to Darcy's office, her friend already had her nose close to the computer. "So what have you got?"

"The shot list . . . whatever that is." Darcy peered even more intently at the screen.

"That's what TV producers shooting out in the field create for themselves so they remember what they took pictures of with their camera." When Darcy swung her chair around and gave her friend a blank stare, Sarah added, "Let's say you're on assignment for five hours, and you run the camera for most of that time. You'd need to be able to go back in and know what to look for and when to look for it."

"And how exactly did you get to be that smart?"

"Dated a producer once." She shrugged. "He was a jerk and my parents hated him—with good reason, I found out later—but I learned some of the terminology."

Darcy looked her up and down. "That, I didn't know about you."

"Hey," Sarah teased, "there's a lot you don't know. We Worthingtons keep our secrets."

Darcy nodded sagely. "I bet you do."

Together the two women went through the entire shot list. There wasn't a single American Frontier official anywhere on the list. It was all random people, one after another, who'd shown up for the protest.

But one entry intrigued them. *Tried to get interview with polar bear protester. AF press guy said likely wouldn't work. So B-roll only, no interview.*

"AF press guy," Sarah mused. "That's probably the same young aide Catherine talked about. The one who'd expressed an opinion about the guy in the polar bear suit for whatever reason."

"What's 'B-roll,' oh brilliant one?" Darcy asked, smirking at Sarah.

"Shorthand for video footage shot so it can be used as background in a news piece," Sarah replied.

"Well, aren't we smart?" Darcy scrolled to the timeline marks for the polar bear suit guy in the raw footage.

Catherine Englewood had been there by herself, without a camera operator beside her to shoot film. Clearly CNN hadn't felt like there would be anything of use there and had sent Catherine only as cannon fodder. So the journalist shot all the video herself. For those shots that would wind up only as B-roll, she either talked into the camera mic as she was shooting or left it open for natural sound.

She only had one extended shot of the polar bear suit guy. He was still carrying the backpack at this point.

"I already saw a segment from this that passed among law enforcement earlier in the investigation," Darcy started to say, but then stopped talking. She was silent the rest of the video as they both watched.

It was fascinating to Sarah for two reasons. First, the guy was walking around, gesturing, talking, and interacting with people. He wasn't trying to hide. He looked like one of those characters who wandered around at Disneyland and had their pictures taken with kids. The guy—if he was a guy—had either done this type of thing before or was pretending he was a street actor. Clearly he either thought he was there for that reason or wanted people to remember him like that. It was hard to tell which it was from the video, because the guy appeared to have no plan whatsoever. He seemed to wander aimlessly, accosting one group then another, and the next minute veer off into space for no good reason.

Second, she could hear the AF press guy in the background for most of the video. He'd obviously been standing right next to Catherine as she'd filmed the bomber. She'd left the mic open, and they'd kept up a cute running dialogue the entire time. The guy was obviously hitting on Catherine, but she wasn't having anything to do with it.

Sarah grinned. *Good girl. I could hang with her.*

At one point, the press aide had rather unartfully checked with Catherine to see if she maybe felt like grabbing a cup of coffee. She'd brushed it off with an "I've had too many cups of coffee already" comment, to which the aide had come right back with a lunch offer, prompting her to counter with an "I don't usually eat lunch while I'm in the field" comment. The guy had kept pressing, finally getting to a "drinks around the corner" gambit, which Catherine had parried with an "I've got to get back to the studio and edit" comment.

But neither the bomber's wanderings nor the inane conversation intrigued Sarah. What did was the simple fact that the AF press aide had, for whatever reason, come out of the building to point out the polar bear suit guy to Catherine. At one point, as Catherine had indicated in her shot list notes, he mentioned that he and some of his press office buddies had been watching the polar bear suit guy from the tower because he looked so goofy, and that he hadn't stopped to talk with anyone for any length of time.

So why did he bring the polar bear guy, of all people, to Catherine's attention? To make sure she got him on camera?

When Darcy sat back hard in her chair, Sarah knew her friend was thinking the same thing. They didn't even need to discuss it.

Together they lined up some questions, then Darcy placed a call to the AF press office and asked for the young press aide Catherine had spoken with.

Darcy rolled her eyes when the receptionist who'd answered the call put her on hold. Five minutes later, she was still on hold and raging. "How can a press office function with such a sloppy, nonresponsive receptionist?"

Sarah tilted her head. "Maybe it's how they deal with anyone who calls for information."

At that, Darcy frowned even more. Then all of a sudden, she waved her right index finger in a circle. Their signal for Sarah to quietly pick up the other line and listen in.

"Hi, this is Jack Canton," a deep voice said, "the executive vice president for external relations here at American Frontier. Is there something I can help you with?"

It wasn't all that uncommon to ask for someone junior and get their supervisor instead, especially when you were asking for information. As a general rule, any investigator made offices nervous. But Darcy's scowl showed her clear frustration that she'd have to go through a gatekeeper. "Well, hello there, Jack Canton, Mr. Executive Vice President for . . . what was it again?" she asked sweetly.

Sarah rolled her eyes. Darcy? A sweet tone?

"External relations," he answered. "My office handles inquiries from outside the company, like from the media or investor analysts—"

"Or nosy investigators from the Department of Homeland Security?"

"Exactly," Canton said. "So. What can I help you with?"

"I was hoping I could speak to one of the aides in your press office. I was given his contact information from a CNN field producer who had some footage of the Polar Bear Bomber, and I just wanted to ask him a few questions."

"I see. Well, as you know, we've been cooperating fully and completely with every investigator who's been through here. We've answered every question you've had and given you all of our emails from anyone who's ever threatened the company. I believe we've thoroughly exhausted all of those questions, but we do want to be as helpful as we possibly can and certainly hope that you catch the perpetrator as soon as you're able."

"I only have a couple of follow-up questions," Darcy said lightly. "Harmless, really, and routine. So maybe if you can just put him on the phone, we can get this out of the way rather quickly and all get on with our day."

"Ah, if only that were possible. He's actually out on assignment. He's in transit right now, as we speak. So he's not available."

"In transit?"

Yeah, right, Sarah thought.

"To Alaska. Or, to be more precise, to a small village on the coast of eastern Alaska. We've had to set up a press operation there to handle the care and feeding for the reporters who are gathered to cover the oil spill."

"They're in a village in Alaska, covering an oil spill in the Arctic Ocean?" Darcy asked.

"It's the closest physical location to the spill," Canton explained. "We're staging spill recovery from there. We have ships with booms and skimmers leaving that port. So he's on his way to babysit the media on the ground to cover things."

"But surely he has a cell phone with him and I can give him a call?" Darcy pressed. "So if you'd be so kind as to give me that direct number, I'd appreciate it."

"Well, here's the thing about that. We don't as a general rule give out personal cell phone numbers of employees. You can certainly send him an email and ask him. But I'm afraid it's company policy not to give out personal information like that. Our general counsel's office says we have to abide strictly by those HR policies."

"I see. So even with federal investigators . . . ?"

"It's a privacy violation thing. We get dinged if we don't observe the privacy rights of our employees. You understand. You are, of course, more than welcome to visit with him when he gets back to the city, or you can visit him there at our temporary office in Alaska."

"A bit impractical, wouldn't you say?" Sarcasm dripped from Darcy's voice.

"It's the best I can offer. I'm sorry," Canton said. Sarah didn't buy the apology for one minute. "Or you can send him an email, see what you can arrange with him that way. Conversely, you can send me your questions and I can relay them. We do that with media requests all the time."

"I'll bet you do," Darcy said.

"Actually, it tends to save time all the way around. The reporters get answers on deadline, and no one gets their feelings hurt by sitting around waiting by the phone for a callback."

And you can totally and completely control your responses back to the reporter asking the questions, Sarah thought. *How convenient.*

"I think I'll drop him an email," Darcy concluded. "As I said, they're only a couple of routine follow-up questions. No big deal."

"Great. Let me know if you don't connect with him, or if there is any way I can help further."

"You bet." Darcy looked livid. She didn't say a word when she got off the phone—merely attacked her computer keyboard with gusto and penned a memo.

"You know what kind of response you're going to get back, right?" Sarah asked.

"Yup. But they are stonewalling. What I want to know is *why*."

"You mean simple paranoia . . . or more?"

"Exactly." Darcy whacked the Send button. An instant later, an automatic reply message flashed back.

I'll be out of the office in Alaska for the foreseeable future, with limited cell phone access and email coverage. I'll respond to your inquiry when I get back, or you can phone the office directly in New York and someone else can help you with your inquiry. Thanks for contacting the American Frontier press office. Have a great day!

"You could always submit your questions in writing to Canton . . . ," Sarah began. When she saw Darcy's glare, she added, "Or maybe not."

"That would be a complete waste of time. All I'll get back is a whole bunch of corporate speak, with zero substance and no real answers." She huffed. "What I want to know now, though, is why did they ice the press guy? I mean, come on. I don't have to be an investigator to figure out that's what they did. But why? Why hide the guy in Alaska? It doesn't make sense—not if the company really wants to help investigators get answers to the case."

"Or maybe it's all innocent and aboveboard, and they've just given the guy a chance at learning the ropes by throwing him to the media sharks in the middle of a crisis. Could be."

Darcy shook her head vehemently. "Nah, doesn't feel right."

"But what exactly can we do about it?" Even as Sarah asked the question, she wished she had an answer. But none was forthcoming.

34

When his phone buzzed and Sarah's number popped up, Will excused himself from the top-floor conference room of the Worthington Shares building and stepped out into the hallway.

It took two seconds to realize his sister was on a roll. He grinned. He'd learned the hard way that when she got her high horse up, the best thing he could do was listen. So he did. He headed down the hallway toward his spacious office and closed the door, waving his assistant away.

"It doesn't make any sense, Will," Sarah claimed. "But I know what I saw on that video, and American Frontier is giving us the complete runaround."

As she was talking, he was putting the pieces together logically, and the puzzle was starting to become clear.

So American Frontier *was* somehow involved in the bombing. But how far or how deep that went, he had no idea. Did the decision stretch to the top, to Sandstrom? Had he really stooped this low? To attempt to control the destiny of the largest oil company in the world in such an underhanded manner?

Will's sense of injustice rose, and he had to battle to stay calm, to keep his thoughts crystal clear.

He needed to have a serious discussion with his sister, to fill her in on the rest of the pieces he was figuring out, but now was not the time. He still had a Worthington Shares meeting to finish.

Strange sometimes how the mundane could go on, even in the midst of a crisis.

35

Kirk Baldwin was incredulous. "You really *are* Kevin Bacon squared."

Kirk and Jon had just watched Sean, who was done with any waiting, place two phone calls to contacts in his network, which in turn led to a third call that linked him directly with the executive director of the Aleut International Association, one of the six permanent NGO observers to the Arctic Council.

On that third call, thanks to some persuasive and fast work by Sean in describing the situation, AIA's executive director agreed to intercede with her counterparts on the Russian side and start the process of introducing them to the staff who coordinated Russia's involvement with the Arctic Council. They weren't able to move past the Navy ship yet, but they at least had their foot in the door.

After nearly an hour of waiting, AIA's director called Sean back on his satellite phone. After listening to her explain the situation, Sean tried not to get impatient. But he wasn't smiling.

"All right, dude, what gives?" Kirk asked as soon as Sean was off the phone. "Did you get us a hall pass?"

"No, not yet, but I will have the chance to talk to the Russian ambassador to the United States shortly."

"And will that help?" Jon asked.

Sean ruffled his hair in frustration. "Perhaps, but perhaps not."

"So explain," Kirk said. "First off, who the heck were you talking to?"

Sean sighed. The Arctic Council was in charge there. Eight countries, including Russia and the US, were permanent members, along with the other countries that ringed the Arctic: Canada, Denmark, Finland, Iceland, Norway, and Sweden. The spill recovery plan they'd just voted on had the support of all eight countries.

"The whole thing is highly political," Sean said. "Some of the smaller countries in the council, like Sweden, have talked on and off about cutting their own side deals to allow access to the Arctic. As we see right in front of our own eyes—in the middle of all this ice, wind, and hurricanes—there may be a whole lot of money at stake. China and others have pushed like crazy to get invited into the Arctic Council, and a whole slew of countries now have been invited in as 'observers.' But there are also six permanent NGO observers that represent the indigenous native population—all of whom have excellent relations with the Arctic Council staff. AIA, the place I just talked to, is one of those six. One of the foundations that the Worthington family trust often partners with had given AIA funding to study Arctic biodiversity in the past three years. So they put me in touch with the executive director, who promised to intercede for us and at least get an audience with the Russian staff. That got us the call with the ambassador."

"Whew," Kirk said. "I take that back. You're Kevin Bacon quadrupled."

"Not yet I'm not," Sean fired back. "We haven't gotten a promise of much of anything. We may still be dead in the water. The AIA director had a quick chat with the Arctic Council staff before calling me back. This whole situation is sitting at the highest possible levels—and not only in the US. It has the personal attention of the Russian prime minister right now as well."

"Which means the Russian ambassador can't do much of anything without clearing it," Jon mused. "It's above his pay grade, as they say."

"Yep, unfortunately, that's the case," Sean said. "But I'm not done yet. I have other aces up my sleeve. I also have my staff at Worthington Shares making calls to other partners with connections to Sweden and Finland. We're not out of the game yet, even if the Russian government doesn't cooperate because they don't want to cause trouble with the US."

Over the course of the next two hours, Sean made or answered more than a dozen calls. The Russian ambassador to the US did, in fact, call him, but promised only to take it to his superiors. Sean wasn't hopeful. The director at AIA called back three times. She'd talked with representatives in Sweden. There was some progress there, but it would take time. And his staff at Worthington Shares had managed to talk to the Arctic Council liaison to Finland. There was at least a dialogue going there.

"So there's some hope?" Jon asked when Sean took a break from his calls.

"Some, but none today. All of this will take time." Sean turned to Kirk. "You should tell the captain that he can shut down for the day. We're not going to be moving away from this spot anytime soon. Even under the best of circumstances—and assuming we're able to get one of the eight countries to tell us we can sail—it will be at least another day."

Kirk didn't say anything, but his disappointment was obvious as he turned and left.

Sean walked over to the edge of the deck, Jon trailing behind. At that moment Sean wanted nothing more than to board the *Cantor*, to see firsthand what was really going on with the spill—and, he had to admit, to see Elizabeth in person. She'd been strangely mute in her emails. She was probably wrapped up in her work, especially during something as big as this. Still, it was unlike her.

"So close," Sean muttered, staring out over the water. "Yet so far."

"Bureaucracy sucks, doesn't it?" Jon said.

"It does when it's used for these purposes—to get in the way and delay. That's when I dislike it the most."

Neither said anything for quite a while. There wasn't much *to* say. They could only wait for some break in the system, for something to change the equation. Without it, their trip may have been nothing more than expensive vanity.

When Kirk returned, he was practically running. It took him a second to catch his breath. "We gotta go," he said finally.

"What do you mean, 'go'?" Sean asked.

"We have to leave the area. The captain is ready to haul up the anchor and move out."

"Did he get permission to proceed somehow?" Jon asked.

"No. The weather did it for him." Kirk's eyes blazed with intensity. "There's a hurricane headed our way. Like in the next 24 hours. And we have to make a choice. We can either try to ride it out here or head to the nearest coastline. But if we do, we need to leave right now . . . before it's too late."

Sean shot a glance Jon's way, and his friend gave only a simple nod.

Even Mother Nature seemed against them achieving their goal to board the USS *Cantor*.

But Sean was sure they weren't the only people who were unhappy right now. *Bet ol' Sandstrom is about to blow a gasket.*

He'd never much liked the guy. Sandstrom was a little too slick, a little too corporate. Sean vastly preferred the Kirk Baldwins of the world. You never had to wonder what they were thinking or doing because everything was right out front. No deception. No coddling. Straight-out truth.

That was a refreshing concept in the complicated world of a Worthington.

36

It was a curious thing. Will had spent most of his adult life believing that everything he'd ever worked for would logically culminate in attaining one goal—being the CEO of the world's largest company at a great time of need. He'd been so certain of that path. He'd almost come to believe there was a measure of fate or destiny involved.

He'd spent so much of his life looking over his shoulder, worrying and wondering if what he was doing was good enough, or if he was doing everything that was required of him because so much had been given to him.

And then it all had changed in one blindingly clear moment. As Will had worked to put the puzzle pieces of his life together, the still small voice had spoken. He now knew precisely what he had to do, and what that looked like.

He called Kiki Estrada back first. He already knew which direction the AF fight would go, so he might as well get the ball rolling on the Senate campaign.

"I'm in," he told her. "But hold off on announcing it or saying anything yet. I have a public fight I need to start first, and then we can get to an announcement about the Senate race."

"Great!" she said. "You've made my year. So you're definite?"

"I'm definite."

"I'll get one of our attorneys working on filing papers, and some staff to help with signatures," Kiki promised. "Just remember. There isn't much time before the primary."

"I'll be ready. And we both know that I don't need to worry about raising money. I'll loan my campaign what I need for the primary."

Next he called Drew and asked him to start pulling together all of the information on the Worthington Shares holdings in AF—just in case.

"Do you need to talk to your father about any of this first?" Drew asked.

"Maybe. But he'll support this. He's actually gotten more progressive, not less so, as he's gotten older. He'll think of it like our own personal divestment campaign in fossil fuel industries. I have no doubt he'll think this is a good idea."

"And what about you? Are you absolutely sure this is what you want?" Drew pressed. "I mean, this could blow up in our faces. The financial press will see this as a power struggle. It'll be a donnybrook."

"Good," Will said firmly. "It needs to be. We should never have drilled in deep water in the Arctic. It was a colossally stupid thing to do, and I should have fought much, much harder against it at the board level. I can't believe it's taken me all this time to see it so clearly. Now the whole thing is a huge mess. If Worthington can't use its shares as leverage to force the right decision—to get out until we have more answers about the risks involved—then we walk. No matter the consequences. We don't need to hold on to American Frontier stock because it's made us money. There are plenty of other ways to make money in New York."

"And the CEO job?" Drew asked, his concern clear.

"It will take care of itself," Will answered with more conviction than he'd felt in some time. "Eric Sandstrom was never going to walk away without a fight. So now he'll get it, and the board will decide whatever it's going to decide."

"Understood," Drew said simply. Will could hear the relief.

Finally, Will called his little sister. "I'm heading over to your office right now, if you're around. I want to talk about the shareholder lawsuit—and the criminal negligence case, if you're able."

"I'm here, Will," she said. "And let's talk. It's proceeding."

"Good. I intend to help. Worthington Shares will help."

Sarah had never seen her older brother like this. He had always been such a people pleaser, not a fighter. "So you want Worthington in the shareholder lawsuit? That will change the dynamics quite a bit. It will get the Street's attention, the financial press too. It will become an awfully public fight—you against Sandstrom."

Will's chin firmed in determination. She knew what that look meant.

"It will also get the board's attention," he said. "They'll be forced to make a decision one way or another. They sort of drifted onto this path because Sandstrom and the executive team kept pressing, and they didn't say no. Now they'll have to make a *firm* decision."

"And if it goes against you?"

"Actually, I assume that it will, but we still have to try. Sandstrom is in too deep on this, and he's dragged the White House into it as well. They have no choice but to defend this position, no matter the consequences. They'll do everything they can to stay the course. So I've already told Drew to get the paperwork ready in case we need to sell our shares in AF."

Sarah's heart ached for him. For all their differences, he'd always been there for her, backing her up. Now, for the first time ever, it was her turn to support him. "So then what—for you, I mean?"

Will paused. "You know how we've always talked about the Worthingtons getting into politics over the years, during those family vacations at Chautauqua?"

She nodded. "I remember them well. I've wondered when you'd get around to asking this question, honestly."

"Well, it's time. I'm getting into the Senate race against James Loughlin. And if you thought the fight with Sandstrom was bad, well, buckle up. This could be a whole lot more interesting and a lot more public."

37

"You safe, Sean?" Will asked. "Shouldn't you—"

"I'm fine," Sean said. "And no, I'm not leaving."

"But Mom and Sarah are a mess, worrying—"

"They'd worry no matter what. I've got a job to do."

Their phone call kept cutting in and out, due to the hurricane Sean said was blowing in. Each time it did, Will's heart rate sped up. Sean always took risks . . . too many risks. But a hurricane?

And that wasn't the only storm brewing. Everything was going to hit the fan at the next AF meeting. He'd know the results of that storm very fast, as soon as the meeting concluded.

But there was still another storm lurking in the background. If Will's suspicions were true about the bombing, then more about AF might eventually come to light. However, unless the Polar Bear Bomber crawled out from whatever rock he was under and got captured or turned himself in, there might never be proof one way or the other. Still, Will's gut told him he was on target.

But no reasoning changed the stark fact that Sean was doubly in harm's way. Will couldn't help one reason for that. The other, though . . .

It's because of me that Sean is directly in the line of fire.

If Sandstrom indeed had hired a bomber to dress up as an eco-crazy and to bomb his own office building—just to turn public support his direction—what kind of lengths would the man go to in order to cover up anything that happened in the Arctic?

Suddenly Will felt sick. He'd learned the hard way that desperate people would do desperate things. The rich ones would never get their own hands dirty, but hired guns like Jason Carson had no conscience.

Sean's irritated voice broke in. "Are you listening to me, Will?"

Will snapped his focus back to the phone call. "Sorry."

"This is a bad one, and the captain says it's almost certain to do some damage, if not cripple the oil platform on the surface."

The Arctic Ocean was notorious for unpredictable, fast-moving hurricanes whose course couldn't be charted as easily as those that swept through the Atlantic and Pacific regions. Hurricanes in the Arctic had never really been studied that much, largely because there weren't very many people impacted by them.

"I just got a text from Elizabeth. She's really worried," Sean continued. "Something about methane mixing with the water. She didn't fully explain. I could tell she was in a rush. Add that to the hurricane ripping through here and making the platform potentially shaky, and we might be in for a rough ride."

This type of one-two punch was precisely what Will had warned the company of in his early memos about the perils of trying to drill in deep water in the Arctic before they'd perfected things like movable domes or platforms that could withstand unusual weather, ice, or windy conditions. But in the end, the board had made a decision, and AF moved into action.

An AF team had created a modern miracle of engineering—a new kind of platform that could drill through rock and handle crippling winter conditions at the same time. The combined subsea structure linked by graphene pillars to the platform at the surface was the combined work of can-do ex-NASA types and field-tested oil engineers.

But Will had worried and argued—until there was no more time or room for argument—that the platform simply might not be able to handle the subsea fracture and then still keep itself upright if a level 4 hurricane hit it.

He'd then called in a favor with a respected crew chief he knew. Adam Blunt had seen it all in his 30 years in the business—from the same sort of wildcatting days that Sandstrom liked to brag about until now, the heady days when the great oil companies straddled the world, influenced the rise and fall of governments, and settled the fate of compassionate, democratic rulers and despots alike.

Blunt had made his seasoned opinion clear. He concurred with Will. And he'd said that there was even further danger—of methane leaks and subsequent blowouts, like what had happened with the BP spill. If American Frontier guessed wrong about how much methane actually mixed in with the oil once they'd tapped the reservoir in the Arctic Ocean . . .

And my own brother is right there in the midst of the worst scenario I'd worried about.

When the BP crisis hit, people had tended to focus on the death of thousands of birds with oily feathers, or oil balls washing up on white beaches. But 11 people had died in the BP platform explosion.

His heart rate sped up. American Frontier was also gambling with all the people's lives on the platform. But if pride won the coin toss and Sandstrom wouldn't allow his people to move out, they'd be trapped.

Will understood the oil business—and the Worthington fortunes—had been built on exploration and risk. But his brother's life wasn't a risk he wanted to take.

"Sean, you've got to get out of there."

"I know, but—"

The line went dead.

38

At least one thing had gone Sean's way in this whole mess.
The Russian ship, leased by Green Justice officially but funded
with Worthington money, would soon be accepting some
additional passengers.

Sean had been shocked when Dr. Shapiro had contacted
him, asking if the ship would be willing to take the scientists aboard. "We're getting kicked off the *Cantor*," he said
when he called from the *Cantor*'s sat phone. "I just ran into
the ensign, our babysitter. He said they were moving all of
us off the ship. The Navy doesn't want to keep track of us
anymore, now that our research mission is basically kaput.
And they need to stay in the area, he said, to be available to
help with the spill."

"They're not heading back to Alaska?"

"I don't know. But they're off-loading us."

"Off-loading you? Where?"

"They said we have our pick." Dr. Shapiro's tone was

sarcastic. "Then again, yours is the only other ship around. Care to take us aboard? I, for one, would rather not be floating around with the carcasses in the sea."

"How much time do you need to pack up?"

"We already did, as soon as we heard." Dr. Shapiro lowered his voice. "Elizabeth and the rest of the team transferred the files off the systems on board the *Cantor*, put the big data pools on my laptop, and saved the documents and research notes on a flash drive. And then, just to be safe, I backed everything up on a portable hard drive."

That was so Dr. Shapiro, Sean thought. Covering his bases and then double-covering them.

"So we're good. We can take all the data with us and write it up when we're on board your ship." He chuckled. "Elizabeth's pretty steamed."

There was a slight scuffle on the other end of the phone line, and then Sean heard a prickly female voice declare, "Just our luck. We finally get some answers back on methane hydrates in the Arctic from some of our colleagues, and we're starting to write up our observations with the infrared and our buoy system. Provided, of course, as the Navy says, that we limit it to facts only and don't draw any premature conclusions. And I was beginning to write up the findings for a research post. Now a hurricane chases us out of the area. Honestly!"

Sean grinned. Elizabeth was in full swing.

"I just want to see how it all turns out," she concluded.

"You want to see how a *hurricane* turns out? 'Not good' is the answer. It's never a good thing to be on something that can move when a hurricane hits."

"No, I mean the oil spill," she said. "We know that everyone thinks it's a small thing and that everything is mostly under control. But Dad and I have our doubts."

"Well, I guess we'll have to read about it in the papers like everyone else."

She huffed. "I am so *not* good with that."

Indeed, Elizabeth was at her finest, and Sean couldn't wait to see her.

NEW YORK CITY

He'd been living in abject fear and paranoia ever since the beginning of the massive manhunt to find the Polar Bear Bomber. He hadn't dared go back to his tiny flat in Brooklyn, for fear they were waiting for him there.

He'd spent the first night in the church on Madison, the second night in the furnace room of an apartment complex on the East Side, and the third night—at least he thought it was the third night—collapsed in a heap in a corner of the one train that ran between Harlem and lower Manhattan. His nights and days were all starting to run together.

He'd barely even noticed that he hadn't taken a shower for days on end, or that the entire end of the subway train emptied out to avoid the horrific smell while he slept at the end of the subway car. He was just glad to have the peace and quiet.

On the streets, he'd gotten into the habit of walking to the other side of the street whenever he saw some NYPD cop out walking his beat. He was sure that at any moment the police were going to descend on him, pick him up, and drop him in a deep, dark hole somewhere for his role in the American Frontier bombing.

He didn't want to be famous—not this way. His lifelong goal had been to make it on Broadway, in front of the stage lights. It was why he spent so much of his time in Times Square, wandering from one theater to the next, studying the marquees and the posters, discerning patterns and trends, and waiting for that one big break that would allow him to reach his goal.

But right now, he merely needed to avoid *them*. They were going to find him—he was certain of that. He needed to get his money and disappear. He'd come back to the city when it was safe again. Now wasn't the time. They were all searching for him, trying to find him. He needed to flee. But he needed the money first. That was the thing. And it was the only thing in the world that mattered.

39

"Will, did you do something to your mother? Say something to her?" Laura frowned, toe tapping, as she confronted him the instant he walked into the door at home.

Will had thought his wrestling with storms would be temporarily suspended, at least for an hour.

Evidently not.

"What makes you think I upset my mother?" he tried in a calm tone.

"She's called here four times today, said it's urgent. Said you haven't picked up her calls on your cell today." Laura crossed her arms. "And she said she needed to talk to you *alone*."

"Honestly, hon, I have no idea what it's about."

Laura narrowed her eyes. "And the last time she called, I could tell she'd been crying."

Crying? His mother? She was a bastion of strength. He couldn't remember the last time he'd seen his mother cry.

Then an image fluttered at the edges of his vision. His

mother, sitting alone in their backyard garden at Chautauqua. Will must have been very young at the time, but he distinctly remembered her looking sad.

Even now, all these years later, it was a startling memory. His mother was a powerhouse in their family and in society, known for encouraging everyone she knew. But that day her usual vibrant smile had been missing.

Will hadn't said a word. He'd simply climbed up into her lap and hugged her.

She had held him tightly. To this day he could taste the salt of her tears as they dripped onto his hair and then down his cheek. It had been the first inkling he had of what shared sorrow meant. And from that moment on, something had built in him to be her protector. He never wanted to see his mother sad again.

"I'm waiting," Laura cut in. She lifted a dubious brow.

"Seriously, I haven't done anything. I've barely talked to her, with everything going on."

"Well, it has to be something."

Will almost chuckled. *Women—they sure stick together.*

"Anyway, give her a call. Get it worked out," Laura directed.

"Yes, ma'am," he said in a contrite tone, even though he didn't know what he was being sorry for.

She pivoted toward the kitchen. "And be quick about it. Dinner's waiting."

Funny. He could walk fearlessly into the tightest situations in boardrooms without a flicker of anxiety. But when sparks were shooting from his wife's eyes, he was putty.

40

THE ARCTIC OCEAN

The Green Justice ship was riding the waves long before the sun came up. Chunks of ice had battered the hull of the ship all night, and no one had gotten much sleep. Though there would definitely be high winds, it was still an open question about when, or if, an actual hurricane would hit.

The Navy ship still hadn't budged. Sean continued to network but had yet to hear from the Russian ambassador. The director at AIA hadn't been able to convince any of their staff contacts yet to force action from either Finland or Sweden. They appeared to be at a standstill, unless something else intervened.

Is Drew right? Sean thought. *Am I putting myself and the entire Worthington family in danger, without accomplishing anything?*

Still, his conscience wouldn't let him give up. Sean's last gambit—an effort to extract a quid pro quo from some of his NOAA friends to intervene with the Navy—had been a spectacular failure. The Navy hadn't budged, and NOAA had zero clout with them. The net result of those efforts, oddly, was that the Navy realized they could off-load the science team to the Russian-flagged ship, and they had allowed Dr. Shapiro to call Sean when they found out the good doctor had a direct contact on the ship. Sean had agreed to that request, not only because he was glad to welcome the scientists on board—especially Elizabeth and her father—but also because he thought it might help with negotiations to sail past the American Frontier platform for at least one quick sighting before shipping out to the nearest coastline.

It didn't work. The Navy had refused on safety grounds and the fact that the Arctic Council still had not authorized anything other than US military or American Frontier rescue ships into the area.

The science team had been told to leave all of the gear and equipment aboard the USS *Cantor*. They'd received a promise that they could pick it up later, after the storm had passed or the ship had returned to port. Either way, the science team's mission was done. They would now simply play the role of passengers aboard the Green Justice ship.

"I'm sorry," Sean told Kirk and Jon as they waited for the Navy ship to send the crew of scientists over their way on smaller boats.

"For what?" Kirk asked.

"I failed." Sean sighed. "I couldn't get us clearance. I tried. I tugged every string or every thread I could find. It didn't work. NOAA has no pull with either the Pentagon or the White House. The Navy is calling the shots here, probably under orders from AF. Because the Russian ambassador hasn't called back again with news, we can assume we're dead in the water there as well."

"The Aleut NGO?" Jon asked.

Sean shook his head. "No progress. At least not yet. These things take time, through staff channels. But by the time we get some sort of clearance from another country that isn't the United States or Russia, we'll be long gone from this place, tucked away safely in some port."

"So we come back." Kirk narrowed his eyes fiercely. "I'm not giving up. We'll be back. We aren't out of this yet by any means. We may just turn around if the storm passes and head right back here before we ever get to port. We can be defeated today and tomorrow—but not forever. Remember the Sun Tzu philosophy: 'If you know the enemy and know yourself, you need not fear the results of a hundred battles.'"

Sean smiled wanly. He loved Kirk's courage and his pluck. He never gave up. He was always on the attack, ready to find any chink in the armor, and constantly quoted passages from *The Art of War*. It was one of Kirk's charms. He seemed to genuinely live his life as Sun Tzu might have instructed, albeit in the context of a civil society.

Whomp!

The ever-increasing waves ferociously tossed a massive ice chunk up against the side of the Green Justice ship. The skies darkened almost by the minute. The winds were already strong enough that the three of them had to hold on to something while they stood out on the deck.

Sean's smile turned wry. "I think even Sun Tzu would admit defeat right now in this particular battle. We'll need to leave the area as soon as the scientists arrive on board. The weather is clearly getting much worse, and quickly."

Kirk drew himself up taller. "Never admit defeat. You merely retreat. You're not defeated."

Jon jerked his head in the direction of the Navy ship. "I'll be curious to hear from them. We'll at least be able to get some firsthand observations. That'll give me something to report, assuming I can quote them in anything that I file from here."

The smaller boat pushed off from the side of the Navy cutter and struggled to make its way through the choppy waves. Even though there was a short distance between the two ships, it still took nearly 20 minutes.

The scientists all looked frazzled and more than a bit unhappy as they climbed up the ladder and onto the deck of the Russian ship.

Sean recognized Elizabeth as soon as she nimbly pulled herself over the edge of the railing and clambered on board the Green Justice ship. Her father followed. Sean hurried across the deck, trying not to stumble on the uncertain deck surface. He got there in the nick of time to smile at Elizabeth before he grabbed Dr. Shapiro and helped him finish the climb onto the deck.

At that moment, Jon stepped up.

"Jon Gillibrand!" Dr. Shapiro said brightly. "It's so great to see you. Elizabeth told me you also were here." He lowered his voice. "Uh, do the Green Justice folks know you're a reporter?"

"I've been quiet about it," Jon said swiftly, smiling at Elizabeth. "Haven't gone out of my way to let anyone know what I was up to. Green Justice's research director on board and a couple of others know, but I haven't been advertising it."

Dr. Shapiro peered over his shoulder at the Navy crew that

was helping his science team unload whatever gear they'd managed to bring with them. "They're not happy." He sighed. "We had to leave a lot of expensive equipment on board the *Cantor*."

"Doubt you were given a choice," Sean said.

"Now that's an understatement," Elizabeth fired back. She looked more steamed than he'd ever seen her.

"The Navy boys certainly weren't aware of the fact a reporter was so close to the scene," Dr. Shapiro continued in a quiet tone. "And I didn't tell them. Didn't think our chances would be very good to get on this boat if I did. I can guarantee it would freak out the AF executives on that platform. They're trying to keep an extraordinarily tight lid on who knows and sees what in the middle of all of this mess."

"I'll bet," Jon said.

Dr. Shapiro studied Jon as if trying to form an answer for a question in his mind. "I think there's an opportunity," he began slowly, "a rather unexpected one, in front of us. And we need to adapt to new data when it presents itself."

Elizabeth rolled her eyes. "Dad, in English, please. Not everyone here is a scientist."

"All right, all right." He waved a dismissive hand in her direction. "Having a *New York Times* reporter on board and on the scene is new, unexpected data we didn't have available on the *Cantor*. Two postdocs who've been with me from the beginning on this research mission were in the middle of writing up some firsthand observations. They've brought the data sets and graphs with them. They were about to post a few of those items on their research blog. But it occurs to me"—he wiggled his brows in emphasis—"you may be able to make better use of that data."

Sean grinned. *The wily ol' fox.*

Dr. Shapiro cocked a thumb toward the Navy ship. "It will blow our research mission sky-high and make the Navy quite mad at us." Glancing over his shoulder as the small Navy boat made its way back to the *Cantor*, he added, "Then again, our mission is over anyway. And I doubt they'd be inviting me back this way anytime soon."

"What do you have in hand?" Jon asked, his keen eyes focused on Dr. Shapiro.

"Some very interesting pictures with an infrared camera from near the ocean floor and the spill itself. And I must say, it doesn't show anything even remotely close to what has been reported publicly for a few days now. The oil is likely leaking at a vastly greater rate—and from multiple sources well below the surface drilling platform."

Jon stared dumbstruck at Dr. Shapiro. "This is from your research mission? Not from the Navy or from American Frontier? I can use this, with attribution?"

"It's our equipment. We dropped the camera. But it . . . it isn't exactly a central part of our research mission. We happened to have the camera with us for other purposes. Once we let this news out, though, you can guess at the reaction."

Sean could see the predicament Dr. Shapiro was in. He'd catch holy you-know-what when this was reported. The Navy or American Frontier—or both—would blow a gasket immediately once Jon had reported the story in the *New York Times*. And if it wasn't part of their defined research mission, which it almost certainly wasn't, Dr. Shapiro's job would be on the line.

But Sean caught the glint in Jon's eye. That reporter kind of drive where he knew he had an incredible story, and he wasn't about to let it go. And he'd be the only one who had the data.

Jon looked at Elizabeth. She nodded. "Dr. Shapiro, I need those pictures," he said. "To be more precise, people need to know about what your camera saw."

The scientist didn't hesitate. "Truth is, the postdocs and I already talked about that when they asked to post on it." He shrugged. "And I'm an old goat. I have tenure. Makes me tougher to get rid of."

Elizabeth rolled her eyes again. Sean laughed. The father-daughter scientist team made quite the pair.

"But there's one more thing you should know," Dr. Shapiro said. "We had nearly all of our buoys deployed and online with the Argo system when the accident occurred. We'd already started collecting data and feeding it back to the NCAR supercomputer in Wyoming. When the spill happened, we deployed one more buoy—directly beside the American Frontier platform."

Sean knew a bit about Argo and what it might be capable of because of Elizabeth. "So let me guess. You were able to ask it to monitor chemical reactions?"

"Sure did," Elizabeth announced triumphantly. "We jiggered it a bit to test for the presence of the sorts of chemical combinations that look like crude oil. And then we nudged it a bit more to see if we couldn't extrapolate for both volume and direction."

Dr. Shapiro jumped in. "Then we correlated all of that initial data with known migration patterns for critical species as well as ocean currents that move out of the Arctic from the top of the world to the Pacific and the Atlantic."

"After that, we asked the NCAR team to run the simulation

from conservative to speculative at high volumes," Elizabeth added. "But still within the range of what we think could be leaking at the ocean floor, based on both the infrared and the buoy chemical reaction monitoring."

"So what did you find?" Jon asked.

The older scientist hesitated a minute, then looked at Elizabeth, as if silently pleading for her to summarize.

She reported, "The oil is leaking at a massive rate, well beyond the rate of the BP spill, and it isn't going to stay put. It's moving away from the spill site rapidly, straight toward the two exits at either end into the Pacific and Atlantic. And it's already heading into the huge ice patterns along all of the coastlines that ring the Arctic. Everyone is going to be affected, and not only in the Arctic Circle. This is moving out beyond—to the rest of the world—whether AF likes it or not."

41

Will had always liked the straightforward, no-nonsense writing style of Jon Gillibrand. The guy seemed to find and tell the facts as they were, instead of putting a political spin on them. And when Sean had introduced Jon to Will, he'd liked the solidness of Jon's handshake and the steady intelligence in his eyes. Since then Will had kept a keen eye on any stories Jon wrote. This time the veteran reporter had caught American Frontier in the midst of a big lie—with the facts to boot.

This certainly will stir the pot, Will thought, smiling at the reporter's tenacity in telling what was really happening in the Arctic Ocean. *Nothing like catching Sandstrom and the White House with their pants around their ankles.*

Then he sobered. *But who knows which way it'll go . . . or how Sandstrom will spin it?* That remained to be seen. With the facts presented, somebody had to figure out very soon that a Worthington had been the one who leased the ship for Green Justice . . . and brought a big-time reporter on board to boot.

Things were about to get even more interesting at the next board meeting—and potentially dangerous.

Who knew what Sandstrom would do when he took his boxing gloves off?

Will was barely out of the shower when his phone rang early in the morning.

"The A section of the *New York Times* sure rattled the president this morning," Drew told Will. "In fact, the entire section landed in a heap on the floor of the Oval Office. All the senior aides who'd gathered for the 6:00 natural security briefing froze." He laughed.

Will wasn't surprised. Those who were in the inner circles with President Thomas Spencer Rich III knew he was prone to such outbursts. His father, Thomas Spencer Rich II, a former president of the United States whose friends called him Thomas, had learned to control his Irish temper when he was caught by the press in the midst of one. Some said he'd pushed his son into the limelight, perhaps before he was ready, and that Spencer was merely riding his father's coattails.

"I don't have to ask. You've seen it, right?" Drew continued.

Indeed, Will had. You couldn't miss the picture of the leaking oil that dominated the front page of the paper. The headline was blunt and to the point: "Scientists report Arctic oil spilling at much higher rate than White House or oil company claims." And the subhead was equally as condemning:

"Despite efforts, American Frontier unable to locate source of the massive leaks or keep oil from migrating to Pacific and Atlantic waters."

"The president demanded to know who would take credit—or blame—for this," Drew said. "As soon as he started yelling about the fact Gillibrand basically told the American public the White House had lied to them, the aides found reasons to leave the room. Chalmers tried to calm him down, but the president called him a moron."

Will lifted a brow at that. The president had to be really off-kilter to lay into his chief of staff, Mark Chalmers. Chalmers had been an administrative assistant to three egocentric senators, as well as senior staff in several presidential campaigns. He knew American Frontier quite well, because he'd been paid handsomely to run the American Petroleum Institute before agreeing to help run Rich's presidential campaign. He was also a confidential background source to most of the reporters and correspondents who covered the White House and knew how the media worked and reported on issues like this.

Will jumped to the most obvious conclusion. "So Chalmers passed the buck to AF, saying that the White House press has been relying on what AF gave them for the Fact Sheets. So if any of the information is inaccurate, wrong, or even misleading, it's AF's fault. Right?"

Drew chuckled. "Right as usual. The president called it a bunch of bull bleep, but Chalmers stuck to his guns. He said AF remained firm about their information. They were standing by it." Drew paused. "Then President Rich switched gears."

"How so?" Nothing about the conversation thus far had surprised Will. But now Drew's tone had changed.

"The president got a call from Frank Stapleton." Not only was Stapleton on AF's board of directors, he was one of the Rich campaign's biggest donors. "Stapleton told the president a massive shareholder lawsuit was being filed this very morning in Manhattan, and you're joining it. He says you called an emergency meeting of the company's board of directors, and you're officially requesting Sandstrom's presence at the board meeting, whether in person or by remote video. He believes you're going to demand that American Frontier get out of the Arctic altogether, or else you'll sell your stock."

"What I requested in writing," Will clarified, "is that American Frontier cease drilling operations in the Arctic for the foreseeable future until a comprehensive risk and damage assessment study has been completed by a series of outside engineering and oil industry consulting firms. I didn't include that Worthington Shares would sell its share if the board vote goes against me."

"Well, I'm sure Sandstrom's own regulatory lawyers advised him that was a safe assumption. That makes you even more the bad guy, standing in Sandstrom's way. The president called it extortion. Said you'd stepped out on a limb and it would crack under you."

At that moment Will's phenomenal clarity again kicked in. American Frontier, like any other company in the oil industry, had taken risks, seen failure or blowouts, learned from them, and come back even stronger. They had not become the largest, most dominant industry the world had ever seen by avoiding risk. No, they'd conquered failure time and again. He was sure Eric Sandstrom believed they'd do so again in the Arctic.

There were only two people standing in his way: Will and Sean Worthington.

The board simply couldn't afford the public relations disaster that would ensue if it appeared that a major shareholder had engineered a coup d'état in the midst of a crisis. So Sandstrom would do everything in his power to see that Will wouldn't get his way, even if it meant that Will would take his toys with him as he left the sandbox. Sandstrom also couldn't afford a Worthington as an eyewitness to what was really going on with the spill.

"Rich insisted this was AF's problem and he wasn't going to get tagged with it," Drew continued. "So Chalmers suggested they put out some new Fact Sheets, saying they'd received some updated information from the company. But it would be a big problem if AF stuck by their earlier story."

Of course it would. That would put the White House directly at odds with American Frontier. And only AF had direct access to what was really going on in the Arctic.

"Rich should have been an actor," Drew added with a chuckle. "With the national security advisor, the ODNI director, the deputy Secretary of State, and several others in the room, he walked slowly around his desk, picked up the copy of the *New York Times* off the rug, and held it out. And then he said . . ." There was a pause, then Drew quoted from his notes: "'This is now the new truth. Every news organization in every developed country in the world is going to take what the *Times* has reported this morning and expand on it. This spill may have been about to disappear from the public's mind. It isn't now, and we can't ignore or get away from that immutable fact. There will be a loser here, and it had better not be the White House. Have I made myself clear?'"

Crystal, Will thought. His disgust and dislike for the Rich administration grew. The boy who'd been a bully had grown up to be a man who still insisted on getting his own way, even if it damaged an entire nation or the whole world.

"And Will," Drew said, "the rumors you're going to jump into the Senate race in New York put the president completely over the edge."

Will could just hear President Rich's tirade: "The last thing we need is another one of those privileged, progressive, wealthy twits over in the Senate . . ."

"Word also is that Sandstrom has already begun to conspire with James Loughlin to derail your rumored entry into the Senate race, in case you make progress toward his job."

Will wasn't surprised. Indeed, the boxing gloves had come off, and Sandstrom was ready to fight with everything he had. "What's their plan?" he asked.

"Nobody seems quite clear on that. But they were all clear that the two were teaming up. If you sail in a new direction—assuming the board vote goes against you—Sandstrom wins. And he's more than pleased to assist a senator who has been so helpful and generous with his time over the years. So Sandstrom will gladly play out his part to short-circuit your effort to enter politics."

42

The category 4 hurricane hit the American Frontier platform with a force usually reserved for quiet, undisturbed atolls in the middle of the Pacific Ocean that didn't much care whether the winds were 150 miles an hour or 15. With the delay to pick up the scientists from the USS *Cantor*, the captain of the Russian ship had decided it would be safer to batten down the hatches where they were rather than trying to make the run to land.

Sean, Jon, Elizabeth, and Dr. Shapiro hunkered below deck on the Russian ship, peering out of the portholes toward the American Frontier platform. It swayed and bowed under the pressure of the icy, bitter-cold hurricane winds that descended on it. The water churned so deeply and thoroughly around the platform that enormous chunks of ice lodged at the very top of the platform.

"It's starting to crack!" Elizabeth cried.

The winds were finishing what the ocean had begun. At

that very minute the platform, already weakened at its subsea structural base, lost its foundation on the side straining most against the raging wind. The platform tilted. Finally, with a mighty screech of metal on metal that could even be heard over the hurricane, the platform's base cracked. It began to collapse on one side. Within minutes, the platform had toppled over. What was left in the wake of the hurricane was a crippled platform, partially submerged.

The four on the Russian ship watched in horror.

Dr. Shapiro shook his head. "And that is the end of that," he said in a solemn tone.

There was silence for several minutes as they all grappled with the weight and long-term consequences of what had just happened.

Then Elizabeth spoke. "This isn't even a particularly severe hurricane for the Arctic Circle. Usually they're only witnessed by a few polar bears or the occasional beluga whale coming up for some air."

Elizabeth had told Sean that hurricanes in the Arctic hadn't been charted often because there wasn't much of a reason to do so. When anyone thought of the North Pole or the Arctic Circle, they did so in terms of Santa Claus and barren, windswept stretches of white ice as far as the eye could see—not oceans and water.

"So AF puts an oil platform in a place that's known for its hurricanes, without adequate research about what would happen if the platform got hit," Sean reasoned. "No wonder my normally sedate brother was so hot under the collar about the drilling. He argued against it so much and continued arguing. But he didn't win out on the board vote."

"If the board had listened," Elizabeth said, her usual

sassiness now returning, "we wouldn't be here watching this mess."

"Will said Sandstrom assured everybody on the board that his engineers had taken it upon themselves—as many of them had done when they worked for NASA and had built rockets that could carry men and women to the moon—to do everything in their power to build something that could survive the Arctic's worst."

"So they did their best. Clearly it wasn't good enough," Elizabeth concluded in disgust.

"Right before we were kicked off the ship, there was a big flurry in and out of the communications room," Dr. Shapiro reported. "You can bet some of those same engineers were watching when the hurricane ripped through that platform structure."

"Yeah," Jon added, "like an invisible villain in a silent horror film. Only it affects a lot more people."

"You can bet that AF's CEO was watching too," Sean said. "And now he's trying to figure out how to spin it in his favor."

NEW YORK CITY

Will was pacing. He'd received two calls. The first was from Sean.

He'd never heard such a somber tone in his brother's voice. Once Sean told him the news, he knew why.

So the mess has become even messier.

Even in their short conversation, he could hear the hurricane winds.

Within half an hour, Drew returned his call. It always

amazed Will how many sources Drew could quickly pull from to get almost any information they wanted.

Will zeroed in on the target. "So, the plan?"

"To make a good show of sending in any ship AF has available to pick up oil and display it to the world, so they look like they're serious about cleaning up and recovering the oil," Drew said. "Sandstrom's confident that will shift public opinion their way and the heat will be off."

"They only have to pursue that course for a month," Will reasoned, "because then the ice will really set in for the winter."

Sandstrom's plan was simple. Make the world believe you're doing something, then let Mother Nature and the ocean take care of the rest.

And most likely, it would work.

43

Will was strangely calm. It had been years since he'd paid attention to the still small voice that had guided him when he was younger. He was glad to follow it now, regardless of the outcome of the emergency board meeting.

He hadn't even felt the need to hold his usual pre-meeting breakfast with Drew. This time there was no need for a pep talk or moral support. Will was more than ready for this challenge.

Soon afterward he would make another concerted effort to connect with his mother. He'd only been able to leave a message after Laura had insisted he contact her. There had been too much on his mind.

Strangely, it was Sarah, who had always in childhood plunged into anything with little forethought of consequences, who'd tried to caution him to slow down a bit. She'd called him right as he was getting in a cab on the way to the American Frontier offices. She'd wanted to check in on him, make sure he still wanted Worthington Shares to be included in the lawsuit, and generally just encourage him to make sure he was okay with any possible outcome.

"Don't worry. It'll be fine," Will said to his little sister. "Isn't that what Dad always told us whenever we'd get overly worried about a test or an event like a lacrosse championship?"

"It's certainly what he told you." Sarah laughed. "You were always the one who got stressed out about everything, no matter what it was. I never cared all that much either way. But you're a perfectionist, and you get a bit freaked out when things aren't all neat and tidy."

"Well, they're not all neat and tidy right now. This is a mess, and I need to do everything in my power to get it straightened out as much as I can."

She chuckled again. "That sounds like my older brother." A slight pause, then, "You know the shareholder lawsuit will be filed while you're in the board meeting?"

"I know. Hang on for a sec, have to pay the cab fare," he said. The cab pulled into an open space in front of the offices. Will pulled out a 20-dollar bill and handed it to the driver. He didn't ask for change as he left the cab curbside. "Okay, I'm back."

"You're at their offices?"

"I am."

"So are there protests today? What's happened there since the bombing?"

Will stopped and perused the plaza in front of the American Frontier offices. He hadn't been by the offices since the Polar Bear Bomber had struck.

"There's no one here," he said. "A bunch of NYPD milling around the plaza. But no protesters. The place is quiet, almost peaceful."

"What I figured, and probably the way they hoped it would go," Sarah murmured.

"Huh? What?" Will was a bit distracted. He was so focused on the board meeting and what he was walking into that he hadn't quite been paying attention to his sister.

"Oh, nothing," she answered. "It's just some speculation we've heard here in the office. We've been deposing some of the investigators as part of the case, and one of them is convinced that the bombing isn't nearly what it seems. But for now, it's all talk."

"Really, so . . ."

"Will!" Sarah barked. "You need to focus. I know you. If you rush into this meeting thinking about other things, you'll get all tangled up. So stop dillydallying and get inside. Focus. Prepare. And then give it to them."

"Yes, ma'am," he said, smiling. People underestimated his carefree, charming, social butterfly sister who always seemed to duck the hard work of life. But Will knew better. His little sister was tougher than anyone knew—and a whole lot smarter and focused.

"Call me soon," she said.

"I will," he answered, and hurried inside. He ran into the head of City Cap, Frank Stapleton, almost the instant he stepped off the elevator.

"I'm glad I saw you before the meeting." Stapleton took Will's arm and drew him off to one side, out of earshot of several other board members who had started to gather.

"Good to see you too, Frank."

"Look, we only have a few minutes," Stapleton said. "You need to know something before the meeting starts. I talked to the president at the White House not more than 30 minutes ago. He's furious at American Frontier right now. He feels like we deceived him and his administration."

Will cocked his head. "I'm no fan of this president, as you know, but he may very well have a point."

"Regardless of what you may think of him or his party, you need to know this," Stapleton said. "He's not a happy camper right now. He's got his headhunters out en masse, and they're going to make someone pay for this disaster. He made it abundantly clear that he's changing course on the oil spill. He has no choice. He can't have the public turning on him over this so early in his first term."

"Fine," Will declared. "Then he'll like my plan, which is to force American Frontier to get out of the Arctic. He may not like the rest of what I'll have to say very publicly, which is that this White House should never have authorized any oil company, including AF, to start drilling in the Arctic. I do put that decision firmly at his doorstep. But if he wants a scalp, he should start with Sandstrom's. The two of them engineered this disaster together."

"But that's precisely my point, which is what I wanted to make sure you understood," Stapleton said. "Sandstrom is like a caged animal that's been let loose in a crowded room and is now backed into a corner. Now that the president is likely to walk away from him rather publicly, Sandstrom is going to come out fighting. You're his target, Will. He'll come after you with everything he has. You need to know that and be prepared."

Will squared his chin. "I'm ready. And I'm a big boy. Let him come after me with guns blazing. I can handle him and whatever he wants to dish out. Now let's go see about this board vote."

Sandstrom hadn't been able to make the board meeting in person, for obvious reasons. But his IT staff had rigged a satellite uplink from aboard the USS *Cantor*, so his unsmiling face greeted the board members from a huge video monitor as they made their way into the ornate American Frontier boardroom.

Will noticed immediately that the executive staff had assigned board members to seats around the table. There was a stenographer sitting quietly by herself in one corner, prepared to take notes and minutes. Usually the sessions were merely recorded by audio and transcribed later as minutes. *An interesting tactic*, Will thought. Sandstrom was putting everyone on notice that he was paying close attention to what each board member said—and did.

Will hadn't taken even a quick pulse check of his fellow board members. While he knew that most were not entirely comfortable with the decision to drill in deep waters in the Arctic, very few had spoken up during their previous board discussions. Sandstrom had dominated all of those discussions and would likely do so here. This was his initiative, for good or ill. The board had largely acquiesced.

Once the board members were settled, Sandstrom didn't waste any time. "Before we get started, I want to tell you a quick story about my heritage. As some of you know, my family came to the United States from Sweden, and we trace our family roots back centuries throughout Scandinavia. One of those tree branches intersects squarely with the Vikings."

A family heritage story at a board meeting? Will's thoughts buzzed. *Where is Sandstrom going with this?*

"Over the years the Vikings have gotten a bad rap from writers and the film industry. The popular depictions of them as noble but vicious savages make for awfully good stories, and good stories are hard to resist, even when they aren't true. But what most people have forgotten is that the Vikings were probably the first true explorers of an uncharted planet. Long before Christopher Columbus 'sailed the ocean blue in 1492,' the Vikings engineered wooden longships with unique, wide hulls that could sail on deeper waters and handle rough seas but also operate nearly as well in shallow waters or even rivers. They were marvels, allowing the Vikings to raid, explore, and ultimately trade goods all across Europe and beyond. Thanks to these extraordinary ships, the Vikings became fearless, courageous explorers, taking enormous risks and traveling widely into dangerous, uncertain parts of the planet. As a result, that era is rightly called the Viking Age."

Sandstrom paused dramatically. "I believe that American Frontier and our brethren at the other extraction companies that provide cheap energy for the billions of people on this planet are the modern equivalent of the Vikings—though without the savagery, of course. That's one reason I'm so passionate about the essential, necessary risks we must take in the name of discovery."

At that moment Will instinctively knew that what Sandstrom would say next would chart a far different path for the meeting than the one most of the people in the room expected.

"The truth is," Sandstrom continued, "like the Vikings, companies in the twenty-first century such as American Frontier have no choice but to take risks, innovate, and search out new sources of energy in dangerous, uncharted waters like the Arctic. We explore—or we die. We explore for new, abundant sources of cheap energy while others walk comfortably in their warm, heated homes in the winter and turn on light switches without a thought about where that energy might originate. We spend billions on exploration in places that had previously been unimagined—much less mined or drilled—while most people merely turn the key in their cars to drive to work. We don't ask them to think about where their energy comes from. And they don't ask us the lengths to which we must go to find and deliver those sources of energy. That is the bargain nearly every country of the world has struck with American Frontier and others in the oil, gas, coal, and natural gas industries."

Sandstrom leaned in closer to the camera. "'To those who are given much, much is required,' someone once said. We've been given a lot at American Frontier, and it is our duty to take that extraordinary gift and make certain we are striving for new worlds.

"I know you may feel we have failed in our efforts to explore the Arctic, as you see the images of that collapsed platform in the icy waters. I share that immense pain. But like the Vikings before us, we fail sometimes as we explore brave, new worlds. Yet in that failure, we learn, and then we conquer. American Frontier is an exploration company, the same way the Vikings were in their age. If we end our efforts in the Arctic, we will have given up that heritage and that mission, and history will ultimately judge us badly for that decision. I implore all of you to recognize that—and the true greatness American Frontier stands for in the time-honored traditions of exploration and discovery."

As Sandstrom ended his opening remarks, Will was a bit

in shock. The passage "much is required" had defined his life and ambitions. To hear Sandstrom take it, twist it, and crown American Frontier's mission with it had shaken Will to his core. He had no immediate, steady response.

And that was a new experience for William Jennings Worthington VI.

Will gazed around the boardroom at the approving smiles and warm sympathy on the faces of so many of the other CEOs and titans of industry. All those gathered here in the boardroom of the modern era were the equivalent of the Vikings, as Sandstrom had so accurately described. At that instant Will realized precisely what he was up against. He knew that he'd lost, and he had not yet even begun to fight.

There was, in fact, no path forward to victory here.

American Frontier was an exploration company, risking failure in the name of discovery and innovation. It took risks and failed at times. But when it succeeded, it reaped great rewards. Sandstrom was correct. When AF stopped taking risks, it would die. There was an elegant, awful truth in that concept.

Truly, American Frontier was the modern equivalent of the Vikings. AF and the other companies built around the same principles could never be expected to stop exploring at the edge of the universe. They could never be expected to stop their efforts to exploit and harvest every drop of oil from even the most remote places on the planet, no matter if it altered Earth's systems, brought the world to the edge of the abyss, and threatened the livability of human civilization. Others who'd been appointed and elected by the people would have to keep watch. American Frontier would marshal its armies, and others would marshal theirs.

After Sandstrom spoke, the engineering team chief gave the board an update on the platform collapse and the imminent recovery and cleanup efforts. The chief was upbeat and optimistic that they would be able to have new ships in the area with skimmers and booms within days. He also expressed some level of confidence in their ability to find an innovative way to seal the leaks at the ocean floor and learn from the stress failure of the subsea structure. No one questioned his assessment or his optimism on the recovery efforts.

Attorney Jason Carson then delivered a brief report on the successful efforts and negotiations with the members of the Arctic Council, the US Congress, and various senior regulatory officials at the major federal science agencies. All were supportive of AF's recovery plan, he reported, and of its plans to reimburse any and all harmed communities through both monetary and restorative efforts.

When the board members finally took up the discussion of AF's actions in the Arctic, Will did not counter Sandstrom with an impassioned speech about why the company needed to cease its operations in the Arctic. It would be futile to do so now. There was another obvious, clear path forward for him, and he was a bit surprised that it had taken him so long to see it.

Laura's words rang in his head and his heart: "Honey, the only way you can fail is by not taking the risk to do what you know is right. Nothing is a failure if you learn from it and come back even stronger."

So Will did speak up. He repeated arguments he'd once made to this board about the risks in the Arctic, which were now self-evident. But even as he spoke, he could see the truth in the eyes of his fellow board members. They, like the Vikings before them, were clearly willing to take necessary risks and build their longships to explore new, uncharted territories.

The board vote on Arctic policy, in the end, wasn't even a roll call. When Sandstrom moved to a motion on whether AF would continue its efforts to explore and drill in the Arctic—knowing full well there were great risks and possible failures—he'd asked for a simple show of hands for those who opposed the current policy. Will raised his hand, along with several others. But the vast majority did not. The company's Arctic policy remained intact.

The question of Eric Sandstrom's leadership of the company was not taken up. It simply wasn't raised, not even by Will. *Drew was right*, he thought. *This situation will shape my destiny.*

As the meeting ended, Will did not wait around to speak with his fellow board members. He'd already made his decision, and it was time to move on.

He phoned Drew first on his way out of the building. "Sell our shares in American Frontier," he ordered. "Find somewhere else to invest Worthington Share funds."

There was no sound of surprise on the other end of the line. Only a simple, "I'll take care of it immediately."

Will phoned Sarah next. "The board maintained the Arctic policy," he told her. "It wasn't even close."

"I'm sorry," she said. "But perhaps the criminal negligence case combined with the shareholder lawsuit will change their minds. I know for certain that they're worried about the criminal negligence case."

"We'll see—but I doubt it. But you need to do what you believe is right, regardless. It's time for others to take up this fight."

His next text was to Paul: *Walked away from AF. Senate, here I come.*

Paul's response came seconds later: *Out of the frying pan, into the fire. Go get 'em. Change the world.*

And finally, Will phoned his longtime acquaintance, the senior editor at the *Wall Street Journal*, to see if he was available to meet for a cup of coffee in Midtown. Will had two important exclusives to discuss with him. One of them—the American Frontier board vote to maintain the Arctic policy and keep Eric Sandstrom in place as the company CEO—might not surprise the editor. But the second story—that Will was going to challenge New York's senior senator—just might.

44

Darcy was on a rant. "I may not be the smartest dog in any fight, but I certainly know what a bone looks like. And when I find one, I don't let go."

And right now, she told Sarah as they sat together in Darcy's office at DHS, she had a bone. American Frontier was either covering up what it knew of the Polar Bear Bomber, or they were flat-out lying. She couldn't tell yet which it might be, but she was certain it was one of the two. How she got to the bottom of that question was something else entirely.

As Darcy mouthed off about the executive vice president for this, that, and the other thing at American Frontier, Sarah grinned. Darcy had a thing about titles. She hated them. The longer and fancier they were, the more disgusted she was. It was why she only called herself an investigator when people asked her what she did. Not a senior investigator for domestic terrorism, which is what her actual government title was. *Investigator* was good enough for her.

"That guy all but lied to me on the phone, and I know

it," Darcy said. "I tried to get the chief to let me fly to Barrow, Alaska, to find that press aide who'd pointed out the polar bear suit guy to Catherine Englewood, the CNN field producer."

"I'll bet that sailed like a lead balloon," Sarah said.

"He said I could take my vacation in Alaska if I wanted, but that was the only way I was getting there anytime soon. So I booked a flight to Barrow."

"What!" Sarah was rarely shocked by anything her friend did, but this one stopped her.

"Yeah, I got the ticket, called that guy at AF who'd stonewalled me, waved the ticket around, and asked him to arrange for a face-to-face meeting with his press aide when I landed in Alaska. I asked him for very specific instructions about *precisely* where I would be able to find the aide so I could interview him." Darcy smirked. "He was shocked."

"I'll bet." Sarah grinned.

"I don't think he believed me," Darcy said. "So I scanned in the ticket and emailed it over to him. We went back and forth about the address where I could find the guy. Mr. Executive VP was coughing and hacking and backpedaling the entire time. But by the end of the day, he'd miraculously located the guy and put him on the phone with me. I think he figured it was a whole lot safer to have the guy talk to me remotely than to risk what I'd learn by grilling him physically out in Alaska with no corporate suits around."

Sarah started laughing. "So let me guess. The guy had a lawyer present for the phone conversation?"

"Two of them." Darcy wiggled her eyebrows.

"And you never actually intended to fly to Alaska on your vacation?"

"Well, I *have* always wondered what it was like there . . ."

"The plane ticket you were waving around?"

"In the round file." Darcy smiled victoriously as she thumbed toward the ticket she'd recently shredded and tossed away. "The airline has already sent the refund back to my credit card account."

"So I'm dying to know, what did the press guy have to say about the Polar Bear Bomber?"

Darcy leaned forward in her chair. "That's where it gets interesting, my friend. I asked him about the Polar Bear Bomber, what had caught his eye. He started rambling about how goofy the guy looked, how he'd been wandering around the plaza in the middle of the protesters for at least a couple of hours. Well, I stopped him there and asked him how he knew the bomber had been out in the plaza for two hours. The guy didn't even take a breath. He said one of his buddies from the CEO's suite had stopped by his office and pointed him out from the window. They'd apparently had quite a laugh. Then, for good measure, that same guy stopped by two hours later and suggested that it might be a good idea for him to meander down to the plaza and see if Catherine had the guy in the suit on video."

"No way," Sarah said. "Someone from the CEO's office basically told the press aide about the Polar Bear Bomber? He'd been keeping his eye on the bomber for a couple of hours, and then suggested the aide make sure they had the guy on video?"

"It would seem so. At that point, one of the AF lawyers ended the interview. Right on the spot."

"Just ended it?"

"Yep." Darcy smiled. "Right then and there."

"So . . ." Sarah's mind kicked into high gear, connecting the dots. "AF knew something about the Polar Bear Bomber before that backpack was ever planted, or suspected something about him, or possibly put him up to it in the first place as a diversion."

"Yep." Darcy gave a single nod.

"So American Frontier staged that whole thing? Planted their own bomber in the plaza to draw attention away from the incident that was threatening to bring their company down?"

This would certainly impact her case against American Frontier. With public opinion turned more empathetic toward AF with the bombing of their building, Sarah and the Justice Department would have a tough go of it. But if this really was true, and the media got ahold of it . . .

"There's a lot of money at stake, I've been told," Darcy said. "Like billions and billions. People have done far crazier things for a whole lot less money."

"True, but blowing something up outside your own building?" Sarah argued for the sake of arguing. But her gut told her the truth.

Darcy shrugged. "Think about it. Would it be any different than the storefront owner who realizes that he'd make more money and save his business by burning down his building for the insurance money than by continuing to hang on? A diversion, in this case, proved to be an extraordinary stroke of good fortune for AF. It dried up the protests and diverted the media attention. It made them victims instead of villains almost overnight. A good day's work, if you ask me."

"One big problem. You'll have a tough time proving that. Unless, of course, the Polar Bear Bomber shows up and confesses."

Darcy smiled like the Cheshire cat. "I may not have to. If you just hold on to a bone long enough, eventually everyone else either loses their grip or gives up. Sometimes you merely do nothing and wait to see what happens next."

"So you wait."

"Yep." She crossed her arms in her best I-mean-business pose. "But first, you and I and a number of other investigators are going to shake the trees a bit, see what falls out. We're going to spread the word that we suspect American Frontier may have had knowledge about this bombing beforehand, that we're looking into questions about whether they put somebody up to it as a diversion. Then we'll see who shows up to try to defuse the information."

Sarah leaned forward. "That's the girl I know. Force AF to make a decision."

"Exactly. I'm sure AF hoped I wouldn't keep pursuing this line of inquiry. They were betting it would all go away quietly. But when they realize I'm not letting go, they'll have to do something about it."

"And the truth will be revealed."

It was so classic Darcy. Now they had to wait to see if the gutsy move would work. But Sarah was betting it would. With Sandstrom's ego and the AF board's push toward making the public happy, how could it not?

45

Will sat at his kitchen table, skimming the *Wall Street Journal* over a cup of black coffee. He'd already received a call from his father.

"So you stepped out. Took a risk. Good for you, son." After those few words, William Jennings Worthington V hung up.

But it was enough for Will. He smiled. He could see his father, pipe in hand, sitting in his favorite rocker on the porch of their summer home, telling him, "If you dream big, do the right thing, set your direction, take your compass, and never stray from the path, you can accomplish anything you decide to do."

Bill Worthington had spent a lifetime fulfilling his own words. Now he'd passed the baton of leadership for the empire he'd built to his son. That trust meant more than Will could ever say.

That was why he didn't waver now and why walking away from American Frontier was an easy decision. William

Jennings Worthington VI was sailing in a new direction, and the world would soon know it.

Will gazed back down at the paper spread out on the table. To most people, the two exclusive stories in the *Journal* would have very little in common. One was about a shareholder lawsuit filed the day before. This story was full of fight, emotion, and financial implications. It warranted a front-page, down-the-right-side spot because the fate of the lawsuit was entangled with American Frontier's efforts to deal with an oil spill in the Arctic that was beginning to dominate global news coverage.

The second, much briefer story was about a wealthy billionaire and director of Worthington Shares who intended to run against the senior senator from New York. This story, relegated to a spot deep inside the newspaper's second section, was neither uncommon nor special. Wealthy people ran for high political office all the time. Billionaire Michael Bloomberg, for instance, had become the mayor of New York City while simultaneously running Bloomberg Philanthropies and a smattering of business interests, such as national news magazines.

To those who understood such things—like the White House chief of staff, Mark Chalmers, or Frank Stapleton—the two stories were both inextricably linked and a sad, woeful commentary on their collective failure to bring Will Worthington into the welcoming arms of the Grand Old Party.

Will had already made his Senate run official. In fact, he had a team out in the field right now, gathering signatures, and would have those wrapped up and the papers filed in less than 24 hours. He'd already hired campaign staff and a media firm. An advertising agency had made inquiries about space and cost in every major media market in the state.

"So," Laura said as she slid into a kitchen chair next to him, "you stepped away from one fight and began another."

He laughed.

"And you're wondering what's next?" Her liquid brown eyes probed his. "Since you're not really a Republican and not really a Democrat?"

They'd had this discussion tons of times since the day they'd walked down the aisle. Drew, Laura, and Paul were the only ones who understood the pull between his conservative morals, which aligned him with the values of the Republican Party, and his passion for federal or national goals that encouraged innovation and entrepreneurs, which aligned him with the Democratic Party. But now, as far as the public was concerned, he was clearly choosing a side.

He sighed. "I was so close to becoming the CEO of American Frontier. I had my heart and mind set on that. It seemed like the type of job I was born for. But when the game changed . . ."

"Something changed inside you," Laura said softly.

At that moment, his cell phone buzzed. It was Drew.

Laura simply smiled and got up to leave.

"You stirred up a hornet's nest already," Drew reported. "Senator Loughlin is clearly worried. New York is always a tough crowd for a Republican. As you know, he's survived for years on his ability to deliver for Wall Street, your industry, and others. But that only goes so far. Word is, if you turn into some sort of a populist with a virtually unlimited campaign checking account, that doesn't bode well for Loughlin."

Will laughed. "I can only imagine what the guy is thinking, and it can't be good."

Drew sobered. "Remember that discussion we had when I called all of you Worthington siblings to my home?"

"Of course I remember it. It's been on my mind ever since."

"Well, all three of you are really now in the midst of the fray. And it's about to get much, much worse. Loughlin may attempt to take you out at the start before you can get any traction."

Opposition research—a polite way of describing efforts to demonize, tear down, and ultimately destroy a political opponent by exposing hidden or secret things at important moments in campaigns—was a well-known tactic in any campaign. The bigger, well-funded campaigns had operatives who were highly skilled at opposition research on opponents. They knew precisely where to dig and probe—and what made sense once exposed. They didn't let facts necessarily get in the way. A good lie, well told, was nearly as good as a harmful truth.

"Will, you're new in the political scene. Untried." Drew hesitated. "And a little naïve. Your father was too in some of his ventures. He couldn't understand why people, when given a chance to do right, sometimes chose not to. He had a strong sense of justice, just as you do. But the political arena isn't about justice, and the fight can get vicious. Word has spread that you sold your American Frontier shares yesterday evening, or at least announced your intention to do so. And that you only put up a token fight at the board meeting on the Arctic policy. So they're assuming you're gone from AF, even though you haven't said so."

"So now they assume I'll throw Worthington wealth and

connections toward the political fight next," Will said. "And they're worried."

"Sure. You remind them a lot of Jack Kennedy, and you're just as well connected. Not to mention you have a track record of being a fast learner." There was a weighty silence before Drew went on. "There's something else you need to know. Chalmers and Stapleton are in bed together to take you down. Make sure you don't get far in the Senate race."

"What?" Will felt a twist in his gut. He was no fan of the White House staff, but Frank Stapleton had been a friendly mentor to Will since the beginning of his career.

"Yes, Stapleton. I have a feeling it's why he's always worked so hard to bring you in, take you under his wing. Will, you can be a dangerous opponent, and Stapleton knows that. Even as a first-term senator, you'd be someone to reckon with if you decide to run for national office . . . maybe even in three years. If you develop a national platform around the economy, a following, and the populist touch to go along with the Worthington wealth and connections, then they'll have a fight on their hands."

"You know that doesn't scare me," Will said. His determination hardened. He had never backed down from a fight, and he wasn't about to now. Even when Stapleton's betrayal stung.

"I know, but it should, a little," Drew replied. "You're the real deal, and they're smart enough to know it. With your wealth and a family history of getting what you want, you have an instant Senate campaign." He laughed. "Just add water and watch it grow. But that's the problem. Reports are that Chalmers and Stapleton are teaming up to take you out before you get to the playing field."

Will narrowed his eyes. He really hated bullies. Especially those who pretended to be your friend first before they socked you in the eye. "Well then, those reports are going to be wrong. I'm going to figure this out, and quickly. Once I strap on my helmet, I'm going to start knocking some heads around myself."

46

Will was perturbed by his mother's phone call.

"Your father told me. And then I read it in the paper. You decided to do it—run for the Senate."

They were simple statements, so why did they bother Will so much? Was it because he sensed a quiver in her voice? Or a hidden reprimand? Or was it . . . fear?

His mom had never once stepped into the Worthington Shares business. She had seemed happy to create her own society network and then step into her husband's world when he needed her by his side.

"Yes, Mom, I decided to do it. It's what makes sense for me now."

Why was he, for the first time in his life, explaining himself to his mother?

"But William, are you sure? Absolutely sure you want to do this? It affects not only you but all of us. As soon as you step into this race, all of us are going to be under a microscope."

He laughed. "Seriously? As if we're not now? As if we

haven't been for six generations? What makes now so different?"

"Because now it's about politics," she fired back, sounding a bit more like the mom he knew. "And too many people play it dirty."

"Ah, I see. So you're worried I'm going to get in over my head and your boy will get hurt?"

There was a long pause, then she said haltingly, "You stepping out of American Frontier may make it easier on Sean at the Arctic Circle—that remains to be seen. It probably will make it easier on your sister. At least she won't be suing a company where her brother is CEO. But you stepping out of one fire and into another even hotter fire? Where people will start digging for any dirt they can get on any Worthington?"

"Mom, you're worrying too much about this. It's just part of the game. I'm pretty good at taking on trouble when it comes up, and knowing when to back off when I know it's not a fight that can be won."

There was another pause, as if his mother was thinking.

"What? Are you worried about some skeletons in the family closet from way back somewhere? That they'll be revealed? Like in the Civil War?" He laughed. "There have always been rumors about the Worthingtons gathering some of their wealth from unscrupulous deals in the Civil War. That gossip has swirled for years. It's not going to go away, but it's not going to hurt us either."

"Yes, but there are some things that can," his mother insisted.

"Like what?"

"Son, I have to run or I'll be late for an appointment. We'll talk more soon."

Just like that, the conversation terminated. And his mom had never answered his question.

But Will wasn't one to let any moss grow on his rolling stone. His real estate broker had already found him a sublease in the city for the Senate campaign, a one-room office in a triple-digit building near 50th and Madison. Worthington Shares owned several companies that leased space in the building, and it hadn't been difficult for the broker to shake loose a room in one of those spaces.

Will was on his way there now.

Sarah headed to Will's campaign office after filing an amendment to her own case. The building had facial recognition cameras upon entry, so she didn't need to sign in as a visitor. Presumably, if she was a known terrorist or person of interest in a federal investigation, the software would kick her profile out immediately and trigger an alarm. Sarah smiled at the camera above the monitor and waggled her fingers in a wave as she walked by on her way to the elevators.

She made her way to the 37th floor and wandered down the hall until she'd found the suite number her brother had texted her. There was no sign on the door yet. Sarah thought about knocking but figured that would look silly. So she turned the knob and walked in.

Will was sitting in a metal folding chair behind a portable card table. Two other tables and chairs stood off to the side, both still folded up. No one else was in the office.

"Well, don't you look all official and everything," she said.

Will looked up, smiled broadly, and spread his arms wide. "Welcome to Will Worthington for Senate!"

Sarah stared at her older brother. He looked genuinely happy—happier than she had seen him in a long time. His ever-present suit was missing. He wore simple khakis and a shirt with the sleeves rolled up. There were no worry lines on his face. He didn't seem to care that he was sitting in a mostly empty room with card tables and folding chairs for office furniture. He also didn't seem all that bothered by the events of the past few days with American Frontier.

She leaned against the doorjamb. "You're really doing this, aren't you?"

"I am. I mean, why not? We've talked about this, you and I, for as long as we can remember. Dad has talked about this. *His* dad used to talk about politics with us when we were little, and I still remember some of those stories about our great-great-granddad's days running around with Teddy Roosevelt at the start of the last century."

She smiled. It made her glad to see her brother happy and productive. She'd been worried about him. He'd always been intense and hard on himself. She knew how badly he'd wanted the American Frontier job, and how committed he'd been to turning that particular ship around. Now that fight was left to her. Ironic.

"Well, can I be the first to say it's about time?" Sarah waved an arm around the room. "You're right. We've been talking about politics for as long as I can remember. I've never understood why no Worthington ever jumped in before now, at least since . . . well, you know, so long ago. I'm glad it's you, Will. But"—she hesitated—"are you sure this is what you want?"

He scowled. "What? Have you and Mom been talking or something? I spoke to her earlier, and it sounded like she was trying to talk me out of it."

"I know she's worried, but it's a mom's job to worry. Or so my friends who are moms have said. I think that's even more true right now because Sean is way out of her mama-bear reach, and you know he's not good about calling home when he's traveling the globe." She tilted her head and shot him a comic expression.

Will laughed. "Like he's ever good about keeping in touch when he's in New York City." He scanned the office and the piles of papers spread out across the card table. "But to answer your question, yes!" He flung his arms heavenward in uncharacteristic excitement. "I'll tell you what, though—this is hard work. I've been plugging away at a whole slew of research papers on everything that you can possibly imagine. I thought corporate finance was hard. This is a whole level tougher than that."

"So what is all that stuff?" Sarah leaned forward to peer at the stash.

Will looked down at the pile. "I didn't know exactly where to start, so I basically searched for everything James Loughlin has ever commented on or been involved in and then for background research on those topics. I figured it was as good a place to start as any."

"Logical." She winked. "It always pays to know your opponents."

"Problem is, he's been a senator for such a long time, there are probably a couple dozen big issues he's been involved in. It's a lot to get through and master."

"You'll manage, I'm sure." Sarah grinned. "You always do. So who's going to be your campaign manager? Have you thought about that at all?"

"I have a bit. I've made a couple of calls. The smart thing

to do, everyone tells me, is to line up one of the hired guns who's done this before. Time is short, and we need to assemble a professional team quickly. I've already asked the Worthington Shares senior executives to task a media and ad team. They're making some calls. I don't have to worry about fund-raising. I decided I'll loan the money to the campaign myself and worry about fund-raising later. So I don't need a finance chair."

"What you need is someone who can manage your network, who has massive social skills, who has your best interests at heart, who you trust completely and will have your back no matter what, and who is able to say no to you when you're about to do something monumentally stupid."

He opened his mouth, but she shushed him with one hand up.

"Let me finish, big brother. You can hire everything else, but you can't hire that kind of loyalty to run your campaign." Sarah smirked, waiting for the none-too-subtle suggestion to sink in.

"I see," he said finally. "So when did you get interested in politics, kid?"

"No, silly. I meant Sean. I have no interest whatsoever in politics. Never have, and almost certainly never will."

"Don't say never. Life's short and things change." He laughed. "I of all people ought to know that, based on recent events."

"You're right. But still, Sean's your guy. He'd love to do it as well."

Will tilted his head to one side and squinted his left eye. It was an old habit, and a dead giveaway that he was confronting unexpected information.

"You've talked to him about it?" he asked.

"Sure have. Thirty minutes ago, in fact. The Green Justice ship made it to the Alaska shoreline safely. They're going to go back to the spill site when they can. But not Sean. He's flying back to the States. He knows what's going on, and he wants to help you."

"Well, I'll be." Will sank back into his chair. "I never would have figured. He complains all the time about how I get the glory and he gets the dregs. So he'd really do this—stay behind the scenes while I'm out there running around in the spotlight? And it wouldn't drive him crazy?"

"He'd do it in a nanosecond," Sarah said firmly. "And to answer your second question, of course it'll drive him crazy. But Sean will always be a bit crazy." She grinned. Propping her hands on his table, she said with intensity, "You know, Will, it's what he's good at. I don't know anyone with a greater network and who sees all sides of an issue more clearly than Sean. He's perfect for this. And you'll need someone you can trust. There isn't anyone you can trust more than him."

"Unless it's you." He waggled his eyebrows at her like he used to when they were kids. It had always made her giggle.

She couldn't help it—she giggled. Old habits died hard, for both of them. Then she sobered. "But I'm not available, willing, or interested in the job. Sean is. So call him, talk it through. You'll see. It makes sense." Sarah folded her arms and waited for her brother's answer.

Will thought about trying to stare down his extraordinarily self-confident little sister, realized how futile that would be in the end, and threw up his hands in resignation. "All right, you win," he declared. "Sean is my new campaign manager. I'll talk to him, and I'll have the media team put it in a campaign announcement we're making on a speaking tour in the morning."

"Good." Sarah made a big show of wiping her hands. "Now that we got that out of the way, let me tell you the other reason I stopped by."

"Wait a minute. You mean, you planned this? You came by here to convince me to bring Sean on as my campaign manager?"

"You're a bit slow, aren't you?" she teased. "Oh well, that's all right. I get the beauty, Sean gets the brains, which leaves you with—"

"So what's the other reason you stopped by?" he asked before she could continue.

"To tell you about our case in confidence. We're not only going after AF on the financial stuff, we're going after them for fraud and criminal negligence. Eric Sandstrom is named repeatedly in the documents we've filed. I just thought you'd want to know. But more importantly, I wanted to pass on some other information. It's confidential and speculative, and I'm not sure what you would do with it, or even if you'd want to do anything. I know you've moved on. But I thought you should know. It has to do with American Frontier and the bombing."

It was true—in his mind, he'd already moved on. But that didn't mean he didn't want to know about something that might have a bearing on what they were doing.

"What is it?" Will asked.

"I think I told you that we've been working quite closely with a team of investigators who are looking into allegations of criminal negligence," Sarah said. "We've cast a pretty wide net. But my best source, confidentially, is my friend Darcy. She's been asking some hard questions about the purported bomber."

"The guy in the polar bear suit?"

"Yes. And she's been quietly looping me in wherever she can. Though it's just speculation at this point, DHS is now taking a really hard look at what American Frontier knew about that bombing beforehand."

So my suspicions might be true. Sandstrom and maybe some others at American Frontier might have arranged the bombing of their own building.

He gripped the seat of the folding chair. "What do you mean, beforehand? How's that possible? And do they have proof?"

"It's possible if they put the guy up to it."

Will opened his mouth, closed it, then opened it again. He'd already landed on the same conclusion himself, but he still argued the point to see if his prior reasoning had been solid. "That's insane. There's just no way. Who would do something like that?"

"Someone with an awful lot on the line, that's who."

"I guess." His mind was already spinning with a thousand questions, trying to link what his gut told him with the information he'd just received. "But I'm not sure it makes a great deal of sense. That's a big roll of the dice."

"It is," Sarah agreed. "But remember who we're talking about, who we're dealing with. I know you've sweated blood for American Frontier. You wanted to be its CEO because you wanted to blaze the company ahead on a new trail. But Will, you're all about integrity and doing the right thing. Sadly, others aren't. This is the same company that tried—and failed—to lie about or cover up the facts about perhaps the biggest oil spill in history. We still don't know the extent of the cover-up, but I can tell you that we intend to keep driving at the truth in the criminal negligence case. We both know what the stakes are in this."

"Yeah. What's that saying: 'Desperate times call for desperate measures'?"

"Something like that." She pursed her lips.

"So maybe you're right, and maybe it is possible," Will said. "But it still seems more than a bit crazy."

But in his heart, he knew the speculation was true.

47

Sean picked up as soon as Will called. He was still in a small port city on the coast of Alaska but was working on getting a plane ride out of there as soon as possible.

Will heard the disgust in Sean's voice as he reported on the situation. "Once the storms subsided, a fleet of American Frontier ships with enough skimmers and booms to clean up half of the free oil in the oceans set sail from this little port. To the public, AF must now look pretty good, seemingly sparing no expense in the cleanup. It's a zoo around here. The company's press office has made certain that dozens of television news crews are on hand to film the event. I'm sure it's by far the biggest photo op ever in Alaska's history."

"So they're doing the big dog and pony show, huh?" Will asked.

"Yeah. They even just walked the media, including Jon, through a new concept to cap the leaking well. It has only been modeled so far, but the engineers say they're confident based on past successes. Talk about a bunch of bull."

"So with the ice moving in, American Frontier has the next six months under control," Will reasoned. "And the media will only report on the expected progress, complete with pictures, because they won't be able to get close enough to report on anything else anyway."

"And by the time the ice clears, all the reporters will have moved on."

So Sandstrom has won nearly every battle, Will thought. American Frontier had fought off a coup d'état at the board level. They'd dodged a massive public relations nightmare, despite the platform getting hit with a hurricane. And in spite of initial flurries around Jon Gillibrand's *New York Times* article and some follow-up coverage, the media had seemed to lose interest, as they tended to do these days. American Frontier's stock price had even rebounded since the accident in the Arctic. And the board had reinforced and supported the Arctic policy.

"They're not home free," Will told his brother.

"Oh yeah?"

"Let's just say I heard from a very good source that Sandstrom is fit to be tied and has been taking it out on Jason Carson. Sandstrom's getting hit with a fresh round of attacks from the White House, Wall Street, and the Department of Justice's Criminal Division—thanks to Sarah. And remember her friend Darcy Wiggins at DHS? Seems even the domestic terrorism investigators there are lobbing some shots American Frontier's way. It's a real mess. As much as I can't stand Jason Carson, or anybody else of his ilk, I wouldn't want to be him right now."

"Well, it's justly deserved."

"Speaking of justly deserved, brother," Will said, "a little bird told me you might be interested in adding something more to your already overwhelming plate."

There was a slight pause, then, "Sarah? You mean that little bird?"

"Indeed."

"So come right on out and ask me, and quit stalling."

Will grinned. With everybody else on the planet, Sean was Mr. Negotiator, smoothing over any ruffles between parties. But with his brother, Sean tended to go head to head. Still, Sarah was right. There was no one else Will trusted more than Sean to do what was right. Even if his brother did color outside the lines every once in a while, he'd never stepped over a moral or ethical line, at least not that Will knew about.

Both brothers were cut from the same cloth. Their father had raised them to always tell the truth because the truth would always win out. You never had to fear any hidden consequences that could bite you in the keister. So as a Worthington, Sean was trustworthy and honest. He simply liked to do things very differently than his brother. And Sean had developed enough pull in his social network to accomplish just about anything he set out to do.

Now Will was counting on that skill to help them streamline the Senate race. "Okay, brother, I want you to become my campaign manager for the Senate race." He paused, then added, "Please."

A chuckle resounded on the other end of the line. "When you say it that way—done."

Drew swept in the door looking impeccably groomed, as usual, in a Giorgio Armani suit. But his expression was grim.

"The game's just ramped up," he reported. "And Worthington Shares is the target. Sandstrom knows he'll be in trouble when you complete the sell-off of your shares. It'll kill the stock price. Sandstrom's worried you're going to use every opportunity during the Senate race to beat up on American Frontier. Loughlin seems certain of it and is demanding that Sandstrom do something about it. He doesn't want you in the Senate race and now blames Sandstrom for forcing your hand." He raised a brow. "They're not happy bedfellows at the moment."

Will wasn't worried. He could take the heat. He was used to it in the boardroom—surely politics couldn't be any worse.

But Drew wasn't done. "Sandstrom says you three Worthington kids are the key to all this mess. That your sister is calling the shots on the criminal negligence case at Justice and has investigators digging every which way but Sunday. It doesn't help that Sean's little ecological biodiversity NGO is talking about billions in damages if they can prove a lot of oil is spilling out."

Will narrowed his eyes. He understood that he was in the spotlight. After all, he'd been in it every day since he could remember. But thus far, Sean and Sarah had only been highlighted here or there in the media and could go about their business quietly most of the time. Now they too were being targeted. And not just by the media. By some power-hungry people who might be willing to do anything to ensure they got what they wanted—William Jennings Worthington VI out of the Senate race.

"And Sarah's DHS investigator friend is starting to come to certain conclusions that could blow American Frontier sky-high as a company." Drew raked his fingers through his hair and rubbed the base of his neck.

"So?"

"Word is that Sandstrom has decided to take out the Worthington family—that it's time to play that card. And he told Jason Carson he wants to tie up loose ends for good. That it's the only way to get you Worthingtons out of the way. He wants to kill three birds with one stone."

"Do you know how?" Will couldn't help the little shiver of fear that coursed through his body. Sandstrom indeed had to be desperate and the situation dire to be thinking of taking out a family like the Worthingtons.

Drew shook his head. "All I know is that his plan is to cripple the criminal negligence, shareholder lawsuit, and NGO center cases all at once. And he's sending Jason Carson back to New York to do it on the QT."

48

When Will decided the best place to announce his Senate race was in Chautauqua, the siblings did something highly unusual for three busy Worthingtons. They decided to pile into Will's Land Rover and make the long drive through the Catskills and Western New York to arrive at the quiet family summer estate together.

Laura and the kids were coming too, but would drive separately and arrive in time for the Senate announcement. "Are you sure?" he'd asked her. "Want me to wait and drive with you and the kids?"

She'd tilted her head and studied him. "I couldn't be more sure. Will, you need this time with your family. With all of them together. It's important, for more than the usual reasons. I don't know why, but a still small voice is telling me that." She sighed. "And you need to find out what's wrong with your mother. She really hasn't been herself ever since you announced your Senate race. Even when she talks to me on the phone, she's distracted. Promise me you'll find out what's up? For her sake and yours?"

He smiled into her eyes. "I promise." Then he'd given her a lingering kiss before packing his one bag into the Land Rover.

As Will drove toward Chautauqua, Sarah, who sat in the front passenger seat, was her usual chatty self. Sean, slumped in the backseat, pretended he was sleeping. But Will knew all the signs, including the tension in Sean's forearms as they rested in his lap, that his brother was awake and alert to every nuance of the conversation in the front seat. Clearly Sarah had wangled the agreement for this trip out of Sean, and he wasn't crazy about it. Just as he wasn't crazy about any family event where their father would be present.

I doubt anything will ever change that, Will thought. *And there's nothing I can do about it, as much as I want to try.*

He'd given up trying a long time ago. Some things just were what they were. But the disconnect between their father and Sean still made Will sad.

As the miles passed, Sean sat up and seemed to exhale away the tension. The three siblings shed the stress of their jobs and started to joke, with Sarah as usual taking the edge off between the two brothers.

As they shared memories of their times in Chautauqua, Will realized how magical the place really was to all of them. Though the three siblings were poles apart in looks and personalities, Chautauqua was the one common bond they could always return to.

As Worthingtons, they'd had experiences at early ages that most could only dream about. They'd been helicopter skiing on six glaciers. They'd been scuba diving in the most amazing places on the planet. They'd fished in Lake Malawi and traveled the Amazon with the world's leading native tribe expert. They'd set foot on three of the tallest peaks in the world.

But their favorite vacation spot was still their wood-framed and stone circa-1885 home on Chautauqua Lake. The house had seen six generations of Worthingtons and still stood proudly, welcoming the next generation. Time and again, their father had threatened to tear the old thing down and build a mansion that was more in keeping with the Worthington lifestyle in New York, but Ava and the siblings would have none of it. They loved the feel of the aged house, its history, and the memories of their times in it.

Since Will had grown up hearing so many inspirational lectures in the outdoor amphitheater at Chautauqua, it had seemed logical to him to formally launch his Senate campaign from that amphitheater. Will would hold a more proper media launch event in the city later. New York City and the media would still be there when he returned. He had no doubt of that.

Will loved the fact that Chautauqua Institution existed as a forum where great ideas could be discussed and shared. That was, after all, what political discourse was supposed to be about. It was also the one place on the planet where the Worthingtons could walk around in the village largely unnoticed or unobserved, and just listen to the steady hum of ideas that made the world seem like a place to support, nurture, and protect. It was the place that would center Will's thoughts before he plunged into the Senate race.

Things were already heating up. Sean had been announced as his campaign manager. The Democratic Party primary was right around the corner. But Will wasn't concerned about the primary. He was already focused on the general election against James Loughlin. Will's name recognition alone virtually assured that he would win the primary handily, his new campaign aides said, so he could afford to focus on the general election now.

Will had yet to settle on his campaign themes. But he was certain of one thing. He would not be shy about criticizing Loughlin's ties to large companies such as American Frontier that had kept him in office for two decades. It could get ugly, but Will felt like he was ready for that fight.

It wasn't long before he stopped the Land Rover as close as possible to the Worthington vacation home, which sat at the northern edge of the small village. Bill Worthington sat reading in an ancient rocking chair at one corner of the enormous porch that overlooked the lake. Will detected the distinctive aroma of his father's pipe as they walked up the stone path.

Their father briefly looked up from his book, waved at his sons, blew a kiss to his daughter, and then returned to his book. Will laughed. All three kids knew better than to take it personally. Their father would finish his chapter and then join the family discussion. He had a favorite theory that multitasking was a myth.

"You can only do one thing at a time," he'd always said when they were growing up. "You do that one thing very well, then you close the chapter in your mind and move on to the next thing." The three siblings called it their dad's "chapter theory" of life. It was, he always maintained, the only way in which you could get a great many things accomplished roughly all at once. Clearly it had worked for Bill Worthington. He had accomplished a great many things in his career, and as he said often, "I'm not dead yet."

Whether Sarah and Sean realized it, Will knew all three of the Worthington children had adopted their dad's chapter theory in the way they lived their lives. Will especially was following precisely that path right now. He had closed the CEO chapter of his life and was now ready to forge ahead with his politics chapter.

Their mom burst through the screen door, practically ran across the porch and down the steps, and hugged her three kids one at a time. She lingered for an especially long time with Will.

"You're all right, William? Everything is good? You are sure this is what you want?" Her questions were simple, but her intense green eyes seemed to be saying more, asking more.

Their recent conversations flitted back into his mind. His mom had never much cared what Will, Sean, and Sarah pursued in their lives. She just wanted them to be happy in doing it. She didn't care if Will was the CEO of the most powerful company on the planet, or whether he was starting to chart a new path toward the most powerful political office on Earth. She'd never cared whether Sarah went to Harvard Law School, or whether Sean started the next Google or Facebook that fundamentally altered the way in which the world received its daily information. She only wanted to know that they were happy, that they were pursuing their dreams, and that they were at peace with all of their many daily decisions.

"I'm good, Mom," Will said. "I'm happy. This is what I want to do. It's the right next chapter in my life."

His mom didn't reply, merely swiveled toward the screen door to lead them into the house.

As Will stepped onto the porch, he smiled, inhaling the aroma of slight mustiness with a hint of oak from the aged wood.

It was at that precise minute their father closed his book, set it on the table beside the chair, and stood to join his kids. He looked as fit and clear-eyed as always.

"What took you so long?" he asked Will without preamble. This too was another of their father's quirks that all three of the kids had grown accustomed to since babyhood. He would ignore two of the kids and drive straight at a third without any warning. It was a bit like a predator cutting prey from the herd—only with a well-meaning intention behind it.

The siblings exchanged glances. Sarah, the only one not directly in her father's vision, rolled her eyes. Will almost laughed at the predictability of the scene.

"I presume you mean the Senate campaign?" Will answered. "My decision to get into politics?"

"Yes, of course," their dad said. "You all have been talking about it for years. I can still remember some fairly intense political conversations on this very porch. But none of you ever took it up as a profession. So why now?"

"Other than the fact you insisted it was a good next step the last time I was here?" Will grinned. "And that it was about time I jump into the political arena? Honestly, it didn't seem right until now. Until the CEO possibility was laid to rest. You know, your chapter theory."

At this, Sean hid his smile, and Sarah outwardly snickered.

Their father scowled at Sarah, then continued. "I have to say, it doesn't surprise me that you're the one to take the leap. Out of the three of you, I'd always assumed you'd be the one to try this. It isn't that Sean and Sarah aren't capable of it. But you've always been a natural leader."

Will glanced over at his brother and sister, but neither reacted to the statement. It wasn't like they hadn't heard it before. And it was also typical of their dad—he merely called it like he saw it and didn't worry all that much if feelings got hurt in the truth telling. He genuinely believed that Will was the natural leader, almost by birthright. The others could argue with it all they wanted, but they'd get nowhere. It was a belief entrenched too deeply in their father, just as it had been in Bill Worthington's own father.

"You know, Dad," Will said, "I might fail at this. I hope that's all right with you." He turned and faced his two siblings and his mother. "In fact, I hope it's all right with all of you. I don't ever want to do anything that harms us or the Worthington family name. If I don't succeed in this—if I fail—it will reflect on all of you. I just wanted to say that. It's been weighing on me."

His father reached out and put a hand on Will's shoulder. Unlike their mom, their father had never been one for hugs or affection. When he did show affection, it always came as something of a shock to the three kids.

"William, we can only do our best," his dad said. "When that isn't enough, it's perfectly fine. Trying, and failing, is part of life. It's the failure to try that's the unforgivable sin. But there's one unalterable truth that should govern everything you do. It takes as much energy to think big as it does small, so you might as well think big. So give it everything you have. It doesn't matter to us, to our family, if you fail. It only matters if you don't try."

Will smiled. Sounded a lot like what Laura had told him.

"And," their dad added, "always . . ."

"Do the right thing," all three siblings chimed in.

"Enough," their mom said. "You four can settle the world's problems later. It's time for dinner. And I worked too hard for it to get cold."

49

CHAUTAUQUA INSTITUTION

The campaign announcement at Chautauqua Institution had gone exactly as planned. Will heaved a sigh of relief since another step in the process was now over.

Laura and the kids had been there, beaming, watching Will make the announcement. When people in the crowd started cheering, Davy had jumped out of his seat and fist-punched the air with a "Yaaaaah!" Patricia hugged her mother. Andrew merely straightened in his seat, but Will could see the pride that radiated from his eyes.

Yes, Will thought, *Andrew is a natural to lead the next generation of Worthingtons.*

At that moment he realized that what his father had said and thought about him was the same thing he was thinking about his son. No matter how much Will tried not to put pressure on Andrew, the boy would always feel it. Just as Will had. As he was feeling it now.

As he left the platform, he saw tears of joy in Laura's eyes and saw her mouth the words, "I love you."

"I love you too," he mouthed back before he was swallowed by the crowd.

That night after dinner, Will grabbed a small blanket and made his way alone from the family home toward the lake. He wanted a long dose of peace and quiet and hoped to drink in the colors of the sunset—something he'd missed on his last visit when the conversation with his father had turned intense.

He and his mom were the only ones home. His father, though semiretired, still kept a busy schedule, even from Chautauqua. Right after dinner, he'd excused himself for a meeting in the village.

Sarah had declared her intention to stroll through the village, enjoying the cobblestone streets under the lights and the ambiance that only Chautauqua had. Their mother claimed tiredness. But Sean and the kids immediately took Sarah up on the invitation.

"Guess I'll have to go along to keep you all out of trouble," Laura had said in a mock grudging tone.

"Ice cream, Mom! We gotta get ice cream!" Davy exclaimed.

Laura nodded, then turned toward Will. All she did was jiggle her head toward his mom. The message was clear: "Find out now what's up with your mom, and quit stalling. And you better have a report for me by the time we're back."

Will sighed. His hoped-for peace and quiet would be shorter than he'd planned. Still, he was on his way now, determined to enjoy the slight slapping of the water in the lake before he faced the next whatever-it-was.

He'd only been there for five or so minutes when he heard footsteps behind him.

"Beautiful, isn't it?" a soft voice said. "And peaceful."

His mother stood behind him. He patted the blanket as an invitation, but she didn't join him.

Instead she murmured from behind his back, "Son, what happens next is going to be anything but peaceful for you . . . and for us. Desperate people will do desperate things. And sometimes even good people can get desperate."

Sandstrom, good? Loughlin, good? Was that what she meant? His mind grappled in confusion. *But who else can she mean? What am I missing?*

"In the long run, the truth will always win out," she continued. "Things that are hidden will be revealed."

Why was she quoting what his father normally said?

"Mom . . . ," he began.

"Wait, son, I need you to hear what I'm going to say."

There was enough of a mother's reprimand in her tone that he kept his silence.

"All of us—the entire family—will now be in the spotlight because you're in the Senate race. There are things you don't know, that even your father does not know."

"But what—"

She put a hand on his shoulder, shushing him. "There was a time"—she took a deep breath—"when you were very young that I felt incredibly lonely. Your father often traveled. If it wasn't for the friendships I'd developed from my days at Harvard, I would have felt lost in the middle of the Worthingtons. The power, the prestige was so much pressure."

Will was even more confused now. Where was his mother going with all this?

"One summer, Thomas invited us as a family to Camp David."

Thomas Spencer Rich II. At that time the president of the United States. Will's memories of that time flitted into his consciousness.

"That was back when we were doing a lot together as families. I was hopeful it would draw us—your father and I—closer together again to have a little vacation." Her voice quivered now. "But Bill was only there a few hours before he was called away. And then Victoria decided she'd already had enough of 'camping,' as she called it, and whisked herself and Spencer back to the White House."

And Will had been glad of it. He remembered being happy when Spencer left, and he could explore the woods to his heart's delight.

"Thomas and I had a wonderful time catching up on our lives. That night"—she took another breath—"I rediscovered a part of myself I had forgotten about. The passionate Irish spirit that I thought had been locked away forever in the pressure of becoming a Worthington."

Will's heart skipped a beat. His mind struggled to put together the disparate pieces of what he was hearing.

"Nine months later, your brother was born."

In that moment Will's world stopped. He gasped for breath. He started to shake.

She squeezed his shoulder and moved in front of him. Sinking to her knees, she looked at him, her usually vibrant green eyes muddied now with sorrow, with regret.

"Will . . ." She wrapped her arms around him and held

him as they both cried. Then she whispered into his hair, "Now you know what no one else does. I never told Thomas. But at times I think he has guessed. I saw the flicker in his eyes the first time he saw Sean, years later, and learned that Sean's middle name is Thomas."

Will had no idea when his mother finally left his side. He hadn't even heard her footsteps as she made her way back to the house. He simply sat on the blanket, staring blankly into the sky. He didn't see the vibrant sunset, nor the sky darken to night. His world was forever altered, spinning on a different axis.

At last a gentle voice called, "Will?"

It was Laura. And oh, how he needed her.

NEW YORK CITY

It seemed like an unusual place to receive payment for his street-acting job, but he didn't care. He just wanted to be paid, to be done with all of it. As soon as he had the money, he'd get on a train or a bus and leave the city.

He had no plan. He didn't know where he'd go next. But he knew that he had to leave New York. First, though, he had to get his money. If it meant that he had to meet his contact on the roof of a 30-story building at the edge of Times Square, then that was what he'd do.

He'd planned to take the elevator up to the top floor when he got to the building, but he was fairly certain the guy at the desk was connected to *them*. The desk guard stared directly at him when he walked inside, and he feared the man would do something, call someone. So he panicked and bolted into the stairwell. He started walking up the stairs, listening for footsteps behind him, and sped up with every new sound.

He almost collapsed from the effort of climbing all the stairs, but at last he made it to the top. He wasn't sure what time it was or whether his contact was there with his money. But it would all work out now. He'd made it to the top. He'd survived the trip. They hadn't found him. In a short while he'd have his money, and he could leave.

At the top of the stairwell, he found the last door. He ignored the signs about the emergency exit and didn't pay any attention to the buzzing as he went through the door, out onto the roof. The burst of bright sunshine startled him. He shielded his eyes and scanned the rooftop.

As he stumbled toward the center of the barren rooftop, he took a quick peek over the horizon. He could see Times Square from here. Even in the glare of the midday sun, the dazzling lights of the displays in Times Square were stunning.

He could also make out famous people and well-known brands on the advertisements from here. It really was a magical city, from almost any vantage point. And now he was here, at the highest point of this particular part of the city. The tops of other buildings, including two of the most famous theaters in the district, were directly below him.

He was halfway across the rooftop before he spotted the person in an NYPD uniform. Pivoting swiftly, he prepared to run back to the door. But a second person in an NYPD uniform emerged from the shadows.

As the officers approached him, he froze. There was nowhere

to go. Panicking, he scanned every corner of the roof for a way to escape.

"It's over," one of the officers said soothingly.

Neither officer made any sudden moves. They just kept coming at him as a pair, step by deliberate step.

He was trapped. He really had nowhere to go any longer . . . not here and not now.

As the two officers closed in on him, he felt sure he could see guns in holsters on their belts. They probably had Tasers and chains and handcuffs too.

The haze of darkness descended over his vision once again. He shook in fear. They would bind him, lock him up, and throw away the key forever.

His heart was pounding. He had one chance to escape. This was it. He'd already forgotten about the money.

Only one thought remained. He had to get away.

They were only feet from him now. As they took a step closer, suddenly he knew what he had to do. It seemed clear. The path forward made sense.

He didn't hesitate. He could do this . . . could make this. The lights of the city beckoned to him. They lit the way. He could make it to the stage on the other side. Finally. Wouldn't his mama be proud?

He turned and half stumbled, half ran toward the edge of the roof. He didn't stop at the edge. Running off, he leaped as far and as high as he possibly could. He grasped for the heavens and the lights off in the distance with every ounce of his resolve and conviction, striving with his last will to reach the rooftop of the theater building on the other side.

He heard the screams from the onlookers and theatergoers as he plummeted to the pavement below.

50

EN ROUTE TO NEW YORK CITY

Laura drove the Land Rover back to New York City to give Will the time he needed to think. He feigned sleep so the kids wouldn't ask any questions.

He and Laura had talked over nearly every aspect of his mother's revelation that they could think of. They hadn't even made it to bed until 6:00 a.m., just in time to be roused by their kids less than two hours later.

Things now made sense. Sean had always been different from Will, from Sarah, in more ways than one. Will had chalked it up to all the birth order theory he'd read—that the secondborn would go in the opposite direction of the firstborn. But Sean's red hair was brighter than their mother's light auburn, his complexion ruddy while his mother's was pale with freckles. But no one had thought anything of it. His mother, after all, was of pureblood Irish stock.

So was Thomas. Now it was crystal clear. The red hair and ruddy complexion had been from Thomas.

Did Will's father guess? Is that why he'd been so hard on Sean all these years? Because he had an inkling that Sean was not his true son?

If the truth is revealed, how will Dad handle it? How will Sean? Sarah?

Will's thoughts were in a muddle. *What is the right thing to do here? Or should I be doing anything? What if the truth is never discovered? Then again, if it is, how betrayed will the rest of the family feel if they don't know?*

There were too many questions and no answers.

And the anxiety in his mother's eyes haunted him most.

NEW YORK CITY

Will listened to the odd voice mail on his cell phone at least three times. It didn't make a great deal of sense. He'd closed that chapter and moved on. Eric Sandstrom had won. So why was Sandstrom's sycophant calling to ask for a meeting as soon as possible?

Their New York campaign launch event was in four hours. A fair amount of media would be there, which didn't surprise him. They loved a fight, and the Loughlin-Worthington fight could be one for the ages. The Worthingtons had the resources to make it a race. The campaign's initial polling, which had already been leaked to the press, showed that the race was competitive because of the family's name recognition in New York.

Will checked his watch and decided that he had time for the meeting. He had his talking points for the launch event. He didn't need any more preparation.

The location of their meeting was nearly as curious to Will as the voice mail had been. They were meeting outside, at Washington Square Park in the village. The park had changed over the years and was now mostly a place where families hung out. It wasn't typical for a business meeting. But perhaps that was what Jason Carson was looking for.

Will had never liked Carson much, and not only because he was Sandstrom's lackey. There was something else about the guy that turned his stomach—a feeling that there was little Carson wasn't willing to do to get what he wanted. Much of corporate America or Wall Street exuded that, but Carson seemed to take it to another level.

Will spotted Carson shortly after he'd paid for the cab fare. He was sitting by himself in one corner of the park, away from the clumps of kids who played in the center of the square. He was dressed casually, without a suit coat or even a tie, and held only a file folder in one hand. As Will approached the bench, Carson rose. "Mr. Worthington," he said as they shook hands. "Thank you for meeting on such short notice. I know it's a busy day. You have a lot going on later this afternoon."

Will decided not to take time with idle talk. "So why am I here, Jason? What's on your mind?"

Carson glanced down at the file in his hands. He sat on the bench and invited Will to join him. "I want you to look at something. But before I do, I have some news. It hasn't been reported to the media yet and won't be for a bit. It is highly relevant to our discussion, however. It's a helpful back-story, and its importance will become clear in a moment. The American Frontier bomber in the polar bear suit committed suicide earlier today. He jumped to his death from a building near Times Square. The police and DHS investigators found his signed suicide note explaining his actions in an apartment in Brooklyn, once they'd positively identified the body."

Will's skepticism kicked in. "Are they sure it's the guy?"

Carson waved a hand. "No question about it. They have DNA matches from his body, the apartment, and the traces of the bomb's remnants at headquarters. This is our guy. DHS knows it. I'm quite sure they'll announce the conclusion of their investigation shortly, once they've tied up loose ends. They have a bit more to go to solidify what the guy talked about in his note, why he did it. But that won't take long."

Will's laser-like focus zeroed in further. "So who is it, and why did he do it?"

Carson was quick with his answer. "The guy, it turns out, was an activist connected to Green Justice. He was one of those ecoterrorists. He hated American Frontier and everything it stands for. When the Arctic spill happened, that set him off and pushed him over the edge, so to speak. The domestic terrorism experts say this sort of thing is common. People become activists for all kinds of reasons, and then someone goes to an extreme every so often after a trigger event. The Arctic spill was such a trigger event in this guy's mind."

Nothing revelatory there, Will couldn't help but think.

"The investigators said the note is self-explanatory. I have a scanned copy of it here in this file, in fact. You're welcome to look at it. He spews all sorts of hateful venom at American Frontier and big oil companies in general in his note. None of it would surprise you. It isn't anything we haven't seen before. Clearly the guy was a bit of a wack job who had been contemplating such an act and only needed a trigger to activate him. It didn't surprise anyone that he went to this extreme as an activist, did something he probably later regretted, and then took his own life. It's all somewhat mundane. A story we've heard before. American Frontier is glad to put this sad, sorry episode in the rearview mirror. And I'm sure the police and DHS are happy to have all of this wrapped up in a tidy package."

Carson stopped. He leaned forward a bit, as if wanting to make absolutely certain Will was paying close attention. "But there is one aspect of this that hasn't made its way into the police files. It's a happy circumstance, actually, and I wanted to share it with you. There's no reason at all to share this with investigators, now that the case is closed. But it is available. And I wanted to discuss it with you briefly."

He handed the file to Will, who flipped it open. Someone had snapped a series of pictures of two guys sitting at a bar. Will couldn't tell how the pictures might have been taken, but that didn't matter. The pictures were clear. He knew exactly what they meant.

As he stared at them, it took every aspect of his upbringing and moral composure to sit still and say nothing. Even more, not to pound Jason Carson to a bloody pulp for being a bully. He desperately needed that still small voice. He wanted someone to tell him what to do next, because he could feel the bottom of his world dropping out from under him—for the second time in 24 hours.

One of the guys in the picture was Sean, his little brother. And Will felt fairly certain that this slug of a human being sitting on the bench beside him would soon tell him who the second man was.

"You know the gentleman on the right in these pictures,

of course," Carson said. "But it may surprise you to learn that the man on the left is our Polar Bear Bomber, recently deceased. As I said, it's all just a happy circumstance, and one that may or may not be relevant to the investigations. It depends, I guess, on the nature of this conversation we're having, and how quickly they close the books on this rather sad, unfortunate life and the bombing."

While it was nearly impossible to tell with any degree of certainty about such things, any reasonable person would look at these photos and assume that the two men were sharing drinks and a discreet conversation at a bar somewhere in midtown Manhattan. Rage churned now in Will's gut, along with fear.

Carson continued in a calm tone. "At the present time, I would have to say that we don't see a need to bring any of this new information forward to the investigators, now that it seems they're all but certain to wrap up their investigation and close the books. But then again, perhaps not. We all know what an activist your brother is and what causes he donates to and works for. We all know that Green Justice is one of his favorites, that he recently confronted a US Navy cutter in the Arctic while aboard a Green Justice ship, that he has given a great deal of Worthington money to various Green Justice causes, and that the two of you were very actively opposed to our Arctic operations. I can't say whether any of that would be relevant or pertinent. I'm not a Harvard Law School graduate like your sister, running the Department of Justice's corporate fraud office in the Criminal Division—and who now has a criminal negligence case against my company. I'm not a billionaire investor from a wealthy family who tried and failed to seize a company for personal glory. And

I haven't given millions to activist environmental causes that some might construe as misguided at best or beyond the pale at worst. That's all a bit above my pay grade."

But I'm sure you're being paid well for all the dirty work you do, Will seethed inwardly.

Carson settled back casually against the bench. "But what I *do* know is that even a hint of this sort of a connection between your brother—the activist donor—and an ecoterrorist bomber who took his own life because of his avowed hatred of big oil companies would make for an awfully scandalous media story. I can only imagine what they'd do with these pictures, and the sort of lasting damage it would do to your family."

Especially to Sean and Mom, Will thought. And leave it to slimeballs like Carson to uncover his mother's moment of weakness.

"And I must say, if you choose to become a public figure and run for the Senate, I believe that these pictures will become relevant. I have to believe that they will make their way out of this file and into the light of day. I can almost assure you of that, in fact." Carson's shrug was falsely apologetic. "The only reason that something like that would *not* happen is if you choose to just get out. If you run for the Senate, if you and your family continue your foolish and misguided efforts to bring down American Frontier, then I think you can assume that these pictures will become highly relevant."

Despite the sunshine and the happy, playful voices of the children gathered at the park, Will could feel a certain darkness enshrouding the place. "Why are you doing this?" he asked, desperately trying to keep his emotions in check.

"I'm not sure that matters," Carson stated bluntly. "But

I will tell you this. For your own good—for your family's good—I believe it's best for you to just walk away, Mr. Worthington. Walk away from the Senate race while there is still time. Walk away from your fight with American Frontier. Your family has a great deal of wealth and connections, and there are lots of sandboxes in the world. You don't need to play in this one any longer. The Worthington family has vastly overstayed its welcome. It's time to exit the stage."

Carson reached out and took the folder back from Will. "I'm sure you'll do what's right for your family."

51

After Jason Carson left, Will sat on the bench in Washington Square Park for some time, his thoughts wildly fluctuating.

So Sandstrom has played his trump card and thinks he has me trapped.

But William Jennings Worthington VI wasn't the type of man to go down without fighting hard first.

He heard his mother's voice: "Family first. Promise me."

He heard his father: "Always do the right thing. But always know when it's time to fight and when it's time to back away. Listen to that still small voice."

But was it time to fight? Or time to back away—and make certain the secret about his brother would never see the light of day? The still small voice wasn't talking.

How Will wished he could talk with his dad, get his wisdom. Or talk to Drew. But no, neither knew why this was such a difficult decision for Will. Only his mother and Laura knew part of his quandary.

Will hailed a cab. By the time he arrived at the campaign launch, he had to have the answer.

It was one of the larger political media events New York had seen. The campaign staff had to build two risers to accommodate all of the camera crews. That was simply the nature of media in New York. They loved a heavyweight fight and a good story. It didn't take much to bring out the klieg lights, and they'd been waiting for the Worthingtons to enter the political arena for years.

Sean knew his older brother was prepared for this—both for today and for whatever a potentially brutal, ugly campaign might throw at him. Will was tough and resilient. Sean was convinced Will wasn't in awe of a soul on the planet and there was very little he feared. Will had already mastered many of the issues that could trip up a new candidate. He was a very quick study. He was also prepared to answer questions today about the latest developments on American Frontier and his role in it.

Worthington Shares had indeed sold its position in the company. The stock market had wobbled a bit, then moved on.

The White House had begun a concerted effort to walk away from its earlier rosy assessments of the Arctic spill and its consequences. But it was also taking a cautious, diplomatic approach and was being careful not to trigger additional stories that pitted the president against a company and its executives who had been consistent allies. Various White House aides had made the rounds of the Sunday talk show circuit to walk back the president's position on Arctic drilling, but they were all careful not to overtly criticize American

Frontier's handling of it. They were also not willing to commit to any future course of action in the Arctic.

Despite repeated efforts by Green Justice and the NGO community to get access to the oil spill site, the eight nations of the Arctic Council had continued to allow the United States to manage the recovery operations. That meant American Frontier continued to have a clear, unfettered, unrestricted hand in controlling what the world knew about the spill.

Will was fully prepared to take all of this on and also to challenge the president and tie both Senator Loughlin and the White House to the disastrous Arctic drilling policy. Now that he was clear of the board and Worthington Shares had divested itself, Will was free to speak his mind about American Frontier and its efforts to corrupt the political process for its own purposes.

Sean was confident virtually nothing would take Will Worthington by surprise.

Will arrived at the campaign launch and media briefing with only a minute left before the scheduled start. He didn't stop to speak to Sean, Sarah, or any of his campaign staff, but instead strode briskly past them and took his place at the podium. The room grew quiet and waited. The rows of television cameras lit up.

Before he spoke, though, Will looked off to the side, directly at his younger brother and sister. His parents had made the trip from Chautauqua and were sitting with them. Laura was sitting next to his mother. Will knew his next words would greatly impact their lives, but in ways none of them were anticipating.

At last the still small voice spoke. It whispered, "To those who are given much, much is required."

In that flicker of an instant Will realized, *No one ever said that the "much required" would be easy.* Drew had been right all along when he'd invited the siblings over for dinner and said, "What happens next will change each of your life paths. It will define each of you personally."

And Drew didn't know two-thirds of it. At least not yet.

At that moment Will spied Jason Carson in the darkened left wing of the stage. *So he's here to make sure they get what they want*, Will thought. *But I have to do the right thing . . . for my family. For Sean, and my mother.*

Gripping the podium, he began his speech. "I know that all of you came here today to hear about an announcement and a campaign launch," he said slowly and deliberately. "I know that's what all of you were expecting and anticipating. But I'm sorry to tell you, I've decided not to run for the United States Senate seat in New York. I've made this decision for personal reasons. I don't intend to discuss those reasons now or in the future. Thank you."

Will turned away from the podium as dozens of questions were shouted and made his way toward Jason Carson, standing in the shadows. His eyes locked with Carson's.

"You got what you want . . . for now," Will said, his chin lifted. "My brother comes first. My family comes first. I made the decision to protect them."

Carson's expression was gloating, condescending. "You did the right thing."

"No," Will said, "I did the necessary thing. You won this round, but I'm coming after you. So get ready."

He paused a split second longer, just enough to see fear

flicker across Jason Carson's face. Then he exited the stage and pushed his way through the door that opened onto the crowded sidewalks of New York.

Will started walking then and didn't look back.

He had plans to make. And they would be plans greater than any he'd ever made before.

Of that he was utterly confident.

Birth Order Secrets

Have you ever felt compelled to act a certain way, as if you've been programmed?

The Worthington siblings—Will, Sean, and Sarah—grew up side by side in the same family, yet each sees life through a completely different lens. As a result, they respond to events differently.

Have you wondered why your sister or your brother is so polar opposite of you in lifestyle, behavior, and everything else? Why you're a neat freak and your sibling is a messy? Why you're a procrastinator and your sibling is a finisher? Why you pick the friends you do? Why you're driven to succeed? Why you're less comfortable around your peers and more at ease around people older than you? Why you're attracted to a certain type of person, or to a specific occupation? Why you struggle day to day with never being good enough? Why you're always the one mediating between warring family members or co-workers?

The answers to these questions have everything to do with birth order secrets. Your place in the family has a lot to say about why you do what you do. It gives you important clues about your personality, your relationships, the kind of job you seek, and how you handle problem solving.

This Birth Order Secrets bonus feature highlights key traits of firstborns, onlyborns, middleborns, and lastborns. You don't have to meet all the criteria in a certain list to be a specific birth order. In fact, if you don't, there are reasons for that too. (For more intrigue, read *The Birth Order Book*.)

Discovering and understanding the secrets of birth order can powerfully change your life and revolutionize your relationships at home and at work.

Millions of people have already seen the results. You can too.

I guarantee it.

Dr. Kevin Leman

FIRSTBORN

First on the scene.
Held to a higher standard.
Star of the show.

If you're a firstborn:

- You are a natural-born leader. People look up to you.
- You have a strong sense of what is right and just.
- You love details and facts.
- You like to know what's expected of you and have high expectations for yourself and everyone else.
- You love rules . . . well, you call them "guidelines." In fact, you may have a few too many.
- You always feel under pressure to perform.
- You don't like surprises because you're a planner and organizer.
- Books are some of your best friends.

Onlyborn

Goal-oriented.
Self-motivated.
High-flying achiever.

If you're an onlyborn:

- You are a planner and an organizer and work well independently.
- You have high expectations for yourself and others. The word *failure* is not in your vocabulary.
- You were your parents' first and only guinea pig in child rearing.
- You were a little adult by age seven, comfortable with those older than you but not always at ease with your peers.
- You find yourself saying *always* and *never* a lot.
- Add *very* or *really* in front of any firstborn trait, and that describes you.
- You are extremely conscientious and reliable.
- Books are your best friends.

MIDDLEBORN

Navigator.
Negotiator.
Relational genius.

If you're a middleborn:

- You're determined to choose your own path.
- You're pretty good at avoiding conflict.
- You're even-keeled, the mediator, the peacekeeper. You see all sides of an argument.
- You sail through life with calm and a sense of balance.
- You thrive on relationships.
- Friends are your lifeline.
- No one in the family ever asked you, "What do you think we should do?"
- You navigate life's seas in your own subtle way—although you may be the only one who realizes you're the peanut butter and jelly of the family sandwich.

LASTBORN

Winsome.
Natural entertainer.
Rule breaker.

If you're a lastborn:

- You're great at reading people.
- You've never met a stranger.
- You can be very persuasive.
- Admit it—you like to be the center of attention.
- You're good at getting other people to do what you want them to.
- You're a natural salesperson.
- Many people still call you by your pet name, even if you're an adult.
- You love surprises!
- Although you don't like to admit it, you were just a little bit spoiled.

Acknowledgments

Grateful thanks to:

- All who read our books, enjoy the journey, and find their own "aha moments." You make writing worthwhile.
- Our family members, who each relentlessly pursue making a difference in the world in their own unique ways.
- The Revell team, especially Lonnie Hull DuPont and Jessica English, for their enthusiastic support of this publishing dream.
- Our longtime editor Ramona Cramer Tucker, who is the peanut butter and jelly of our sandwich.

About Dr. Kevin Leman

An internationally known psychologist, radio and television personality, speaker, educator, and humorist, **Dr. Kevin Leman** has taught and entertained audiences worldwide with his wit and commonsense psychology.

The *New York Times* bestselling and award-winning author of *Have a New Kid by Friday*, *Have a New Husband by Friday*, *Have a New You by Friday*, *Sheet Music*, *The Birth Order Book*, and *Have a Happy Family by Friday* has made thousands of house calls through radio and television programs, including *Fox & Friends*, *The View*, Fox's *The Morning Show*, *Today*, Dr. Bill Bennett's *Morning in America*, *The 700 Club*, CBS's *The Early Show*, James Robison's *Life Today*, *Janet Parshall*, CNN, and *Focus on the Family*. Dr. Leman has served as a contributing family psychologist to *Good Morning America*.

Dr. Leman's professional affiliations include the American Psychological Association, the American Federation of

Television and Radio Artists, and the North American Society of Adlerian Psychology.

North Park University in Chicago awarded Dr. Leman the Distinguished Alumnus Award in 1993 and an honorary Doctor of Humane Letters degree in 2010. In 2003, he received from the University of Arizona the highest award that a university can extend to its own: the Alumni Achievement Award.

Dr. Leman received his bachelor's degree in psychology from the University of Arizona, where he later earned his master's and doctorate degrees. Originally from Williamsville, New York, he and his wife, Sande, live in Arizona and have five children and two grandchildren.

For information regarding speaking availability, business consultations, seminars, webinars, or the annual Love, Laugh and Learn cruise, please contact:

Dr. Kevin Leman
P.O. Box 35370
Tucson, AZ 85740
Phone: (520) 797-3830
Fax: (520) 797-3809
www.birthorderguy.com
www.drleman.com

Follow Dr. Kevin Leman on Facebook (facebook.com /DrKevinLeman) and on Twitter (@DrKevinLeman). Check out the free podcasts at birthorderguy.com/podcast.

About Jeff Nesbit

Formerly Vice President Dan Quayle's communications director at the White House, **Jeff Nesbit** was a national journalist with Knight-Ridder, ABC News' Satellite News Channels, and others, and the director of public affairs for two prominent federal science agencies: the National Science Foundation and the Food and Drug Administration.

For nearly 15 years, Jeff managed Shiloh Media Group, a successful strategic communications business whose projects represented more than 100 national clients, such as the Discovery Channel networks, Yale University, the American Heart Association, the Robert Wood Johnson Foundation, and the American Red Cross. Shiloh Media Group helped create and launch three unique television networks for Discovery Communications, Encyclopedia Britannica, and Lockheed Martin. They also developed programming and a new cable television network concept for the Britannica Channel; global programming partnerships for the successful launch of the Discovery Health Channel, including a novel CME

programming initiative and the Medical Honors live broadcast from Constitution Hall; and programming strategies
for the creation of the first-ever IPTV network developed
by Lockheed Martin.

Jeff was the cocreator of the *Science of the Olympic Winter Games* and the *Science of NFL Football* video series
with NBC Sports, which won the 2010 Sports Emmy for
best original sports programming, as well as *The Science of
Speed*, a novel video series partnership with the NASCAR
Media Group.

Believing in the power of the written word to change
hearts, minds, and lives, Jeff has written over 20 inspirational and commercially successful novels—including his
latest blockbusters, *Jude*, *Peace*, and *Oil*—for publishing
houses such as David C. Cook, Tyndale, Zondervan/Thomas
Nelson/HarperCollins, WaterBrook/Random House, Victor
Books, Hodder & Stoughton, Guideposts, and others.

Jeff is executive director for Climate Nexus, strategic advisor and cofounder of Thrive Sports/Thrive Entertainment
Network, and managing director of OakTara (www.oaktara.
com). He writes a weekly science column for *U.S. News &
World Report* called At the Edge (www.usnews.com/news
/blogs/at-the-edge) and comanages the *Faith Matters* blog
(www.usnews.com/opinion/blogs/faith-matters).

Resources by Dr. Kevin Leman

Books for Adults

The Birth Order Book
Have a New Kid by Friday
Have a New Husband by Friday
Have a New Teenager by Friday
Have a New You by Friday
Have a Happy Family by Friday
Surviving Planet Middle School
The Way of the Wise
Be the Dad She Needs You to Be
What a Difference a Mom Makes
Parenting the Powerful Child
Under the Sheets
Sheet Music
Making Children Mind without Losing Yours

It's Your Kid, Not a Gerbil!

Born to Win

Sex Begins in the Kitchen

7 Things He'll Never Tell You . . . But You Need to Know

What Your Childhood Memories Say about You

Running the Rapids

The Way of the Shepherd (written with William Pentak)

Becoming the Parent God Wants You to Be

Becoming a Couple of Promise

A Chicken's Guide to Talking Turkey with Your Kids about Sex (written with Kathy Flores Bell)

First-Time Mom

Step-parenting 101

Living in a Stepfamily without Getting Stepped On

The Perfect Match

Be Your Own Shrink

Stopping Stress before It Stops You

Single Parenting That Works

Why Your Best Is Good Enough

Smart Women Know When to Say No

Books for Children, with Kevin Leman II

My Firstborn, There's No One Like You

My Middle Child, There's No One Like You

My Youngest, There's No One Like You

My Only Child, There's No One Like You

My Adopted Child, There's No One Like You
My Grandchild, There's No One Like You

DVD/Video Series for Group Use

Have a New Kid by Friday
Making Children Mind without Losing Yours (Christian—parenting edition)
Making Children Mind without Losing Yours (Mainstream—public school teacher edition)
Value-Packed Parenting
Making the Most of Marriage
Running the Rapids
Single Parenting That Works
Bringing Peace and Harmony to the Blended Family

DVDs for Home Use

Straight Talk on Parenting
Why You Are the Way You Are
Have a New Husband by Friday
Have a New You by Friday
Have a New Kid by Friday

Available at 1-800-770-3830 • www.birthorderguy.com • www.drleman.com

Connect with the Authors

DR. KEVIN LEMAN
DrLeman.com

Follow Dr. Leman on
 Dr Kevin Leman | drleman

• • •

JEFF NESBIT
JeffNesbit.net

Follow Jeff on
 jeffnesbit

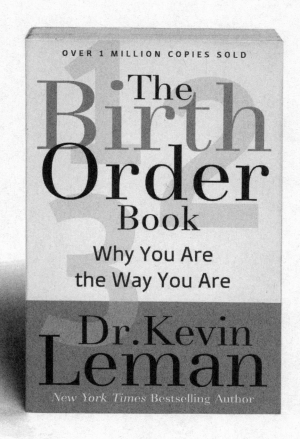

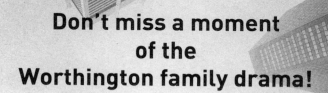

Don't miss a moment
of the
Worthington family drama!

A Powerful Secret

Book 2 in
THE WORTHINGTON DESTINY
series

COMING SPRING 2016